BURIED TREASURES
OF THE AMERICAN SOUTHWEST

*"I know of nobody who knows the stories and
folklore of the old lost mines and their caches in
more detail than Jamesonor who tells stories better, the late
J. Frank Dobie notwithstanding."*
—DALE WALKER, ROCKY MOUNTAIN NEWS

*"Rarely has such a book been written with such sensitivity...
It conveys the irresistible siren's call and captures
the spirit of the search."*
—TREASURE SEARCH

Buried Treasures
Of The American Southwest:

Legends of Lost Mines, Hidden
Payrolls and Spanish Gold

W. C. Jameson

ILLUSTRATIONS BY WENDELL E. HALL

August House / *Little Rock*
P U B L I S H E R S

Printed in the United States of America

10 9 8 7 6 5 4 3 2

LIBRARY OF CONGRESS CATALOGING-IN-PUBLICATION
DATA

Jameson, W.C., 1942-
Buried treasures of the American Southwest: legends of lost
mines, hidden payrolls, and Spanish gold/W.C. Jameson.—1st ed.
p.   cm.
Bibliography: p.
ISBN 0-87483-082-6 : $8.95 (alk. paper)
1. Southwest, New—History—Miscellanea. 2. Treasure—trove—
Southwest, New—History—Miscellanea. 3. Spaniards—Southwest,
New—History—Miscellanea. 4. Gold mines and
mining—Southwest,
New—History—Miscellanea. 5. Legends—Southwest, New. I. Title.
F799.J36 1989
976—dc19
88-38149
CIP

First Edition, 1989

Cover and text illustration by Wendell E. Hall
Production artwork by Ira Hocut
Typography by Lettergraphics, Little Rock, Arkansas
Design direction by Ted Parkhurst
Project direction by Hope Norman Coulter

This book is printed on archival-quality paper which meets the
guidelines for performance and durability of the Committee on
Production Guidelines for Book Longevity of the Council on
Library Resources.

AUGUST HOUSE, INC.   PUBLISHERS   LITTLE ROCK

For Michael

Though you are gone,
your spirit of adventure will always be with us

Contents

Introduction

For centuries people have been captivated by and infatuated with tales of lost mines and buried treasure. The attraction has not dimmed through the ages; if anything it is stronger than ever. We continue to be enchanted by the stories of King Solomon's mines; the lost gold mines of the pharoahs; the forgotton emerald mines of Cleopatra; the land of Ophir and its documented fortunes in precious metals; the legendary wealth of Nebuchadnezzar of Babylon; and the Lost Dutchman Mine. Indeed, people the world over are still searching for these famous lost hoards.

In North America, legends of lost mines and buried treasure begin with the early explorations of the Spanish in the sixteenth century. The conquistadors, under instructions from their king, were to explore the New World, determine its suitability for colonization, and search for and retrieve wealth in the form of gold and silver to be used to further the expansion of the Spanish Empire. Almost from the moment of their arrival in South America and on the shores of Florida, the Spaniards were regaled with stories of El Dorado, a fabulous city which supposedly contained great wealth and abundance. From South America they traveled north, eventually crossing the Rio Grande into the American Southwest. From Florida they journeyed westward, crossed the Mississippi River, and entered the Ozark and Ouachita Mountains. The Spanish moved with a large mounted military contingent and hundreds of Indian slaves, herding swine and sheep along with them for food. Thus armed and fortified, they traveled throughout much of what is now Arkansas, Texas, Oklahoma, New Mexico, and Arizona.

On a regular basis, men were dispatched from the main party

to scout mountains and valleys for precious ores. They searched, they prospected, they excavated, and they extracted untold millions in native ore, most of which was smelted, shaped into ingots, and shipped back to Spain. But as they mined throughout the American Southwest, they never lost sight of their original goal— El Dorado. All the gold and silver they were finding was insignificant compared to what they believed awaited them at the city of great wealth.

In their all-consuming search for the gilded city, the conquistadors rode roughshod over the native American tribes they encountered. Often they forced local Indians to reveal the locations of their mines, under threat of death or enslavement. But soon the Indians began to fight back against the Spaniards, and many bitter battles were waged. Years passed, and with the constant wars with native Americans, the loss of men through disease and starvation, and the continued disappointment of failing to locate El Dorado, the Spanish determination to colonize this part of the New World began to crumble. Many missions and settlements had to be abandoned due to the constant threat of Indian attack. As the Spaniards were gradually driven out of the country, they sealed up and covered over many of the mines, intending to return when the hostilities subsided. Maps were drawn up showing the locations of many of the richest sites, and accounts of the locations of the mines and caches were collected and stored in church archives both in Mexico and Spain, but the Spanish never returned to reopen the mines or renew their search for El Dorado.

The early part of the nineteenth century witnessed an influx of settlers to the American Southwest. Thousands crossed the Mississippi coming from the East, while hundreds of others coming from Europe arrived at ports along the Gulf Coast, attracted by the new colonies being established in Texas. Many came in response to the promise of free land and the opportunity to farm and ranch; some were running from the law; some came seeking adventure; but in some way all simply desired a new way of life.

As this new country opened up, many settlers encountered evidence of previous occupation by the Spanish and heard tales of lost mines and hidden caches. Friendly Indians told of their ancestors' having been enslaved by the conquistadors and forced to dig gold and silver. Several ancient mining sites, and more than once caches of gold or silver ingots, were discovered. Into the developing Southwest rode strangers carrying old and faded Spanish maps and documents purporting to show the way to a lost mine or a buried treasure. The passion for wealth began anew when, in their own way, a new generation of searchers took up the pursuit of El Dorado.

The treasure hunters came in all shapes, sizes, and nationalities, but they had one thing in common—their dreams and hopes. They maintained and nourished dreams of wealth, and they never lost hope as they dug into the ground. Despite the hazards of continuous drought and hostile Indians they pursued their quest. The attraction of fabulous wealth exerts a strange magic and generates a fanaticism and zeal unlike anything else in the world. Many dreamers perished in their search for riches. Many simply gave up and walked away. A few achieved success and lived long fulfilled lives, while others found wealth only to lose it. But all of them were obsessed by the search, and all clung to the hope that their fortune lay just another turn of the soil, a moment or two, away.

Today the search continues. Modern-day counterparts of the Spanish conquistadors and the early nineteenth-century settlers still cling to the figurative image of El Dorado. The folklore of the land still exerts the magical pull it had over four centuries ago. Today the pickup truck has replaced the horse and mule, but searchers still arrive with little more than their dreams and hopes. They can be found even now in the mountains and the valleys of the American Southwest, still hunting for the elusive riches they believe await them.

Arizona

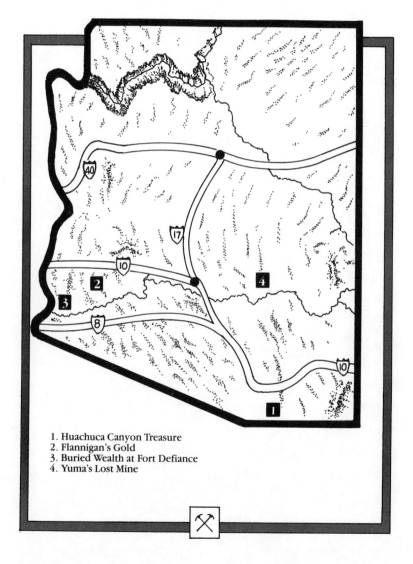

1. Huachuca Canyon Treasure
2. Flannigan's Gold
3. Buried Wealth at Fort Defiance
4. Yuma's Lost Mine

Huachuca Canyon Treasure

The month of June in southern Arizona is always hot, but in 1941 the temperature soared far above normal several days in a row, forcing residents to seek relief. Robert Jones, an enlisted man at Fort Huachuca, decided to spend a Saturday in the cool, shaded canyons of the nearby Huachuca Mountains. Jones invited a friend to accompany him. Both men were assigned to a communications division at the military post and both were eager for the weekend diversion from their normal duties.

The men drove into Huachuca Canyon along an old dirt road. They parked the vehicle where the road was washed out and elected to walk in the shadow of tall pines and oak trees. Blue jays darted and twittered among the branches and squirrels played throughout the forest canopy. As the two men walked up the canyon, Jones noted a subtle change in the color of some rock rubble near the base of a canyon wall. Curious, he climbed the adjacent slope to investigate. As he walked among the jumble of rock the ground suddenly gave way and Jones plummeted thirty-two feet underground.

Shaken but only slightly injured, he called out to his companion. By the time the friend arrived, Jones discovered he had fallen into a steeply slanted shaft. From where he stood he noted that the shaft leveled off and continued laterally into the solid rock of the canyon wall. Using a flashlight dropped by his friend, Jones followed the passageway until he came to a large room carved into the granite rock of the mountain and reinforced with hand-laid stones and mortar. Jones, who stood five feet seven inches, claimed he could just barely stand upright in the chamber.

As Jones circled the stone room he saw that it was partially filled with bars of gold and silver stacked like cordwood along the walls. The gold bars were twenty inches in length and each weighed about fifty pounds. Jones said there were at least a hundred bars of each metal. He also claimed he discovered one large wooden box as big as three washtubs which was filled with gold nuggets, and another one half-filled with gold dust. While Jones was exploring the room he noticed a large glass bottle on the floor and picked it up. There was something inside. Carefully, he withdrew what he said was a rolled-up sheepskin containing Spanish writing. Not able to read the parchment, he rolled it up and replaced it in the bottle.

After spending nearly an hour inside the chamber, Jones made his way out and back to the top of the shaft with the aid of his friend. The two men then hurried back to the military post and told their story to their company commander. The captain did not believe the tale, and neither did two other officers in whom Jones confided. Matt Venable, Jones's first sergeant at the time, later recalled the story. Venable said that Jones was an excellent soldier and that buried treasure stories were common in the area at the time. Venable recommended to military authorities that they investigate the claim, but no action was taken. Discouraged, Jones and his friend decided to bide their time and wait for an opportunity to retrieve the ingots. They returned to the shaft, which was within the boundaries of the military reservation, and covered it over with logs, branches, rocks, and forest debris. Satisfied they had camouflaged it properly, Jones blazed two slashes in a nearby tree and carved his initials with a rock hammer into a granite boulder located about thirty feet from the concealed shaft.

The two friends intended to return to the site soon with digging equipment and remove the fortune stored deep underground. They talked often of what they would do with their wealth and shared their nightly dreams, dreams filled with visions of fortune.

But events did not work out as planned. A few months later war was declared, and Jones and his partner were transferred out of southern Arizona—Jones to the Pacific and his friend to the African-European theater. The friend was killed almost immediately after arriving in Europe, and Jones was severely wounded in a firefight on Wake Island. Jones spent the next several years recovering from his wounds. The continuing medical treatment and subsequent financial difficulties combined to keep him from returning to Huachuca Canyon. He eventually received a small disability from the army which, along with the income of his wife, a nurse at the Dallas Medical Center, afforded the Joneses a modest living.

During the eleven-year period of his rehabilitation, Jones returned to Fort Huachuca several times. Because of his slightly crippled condition he was unable to dig for the treasure himself, so he sought help from the U.S. Army. Time and again he was informed he would not be granted permission to dig for the treasure on the military reservation.

Finally, in 1959, Jones met Major General F.W. Moorman, the Post Commander, who believed his story. Moorman examined Jones's military record and found that he was always considered reliable and regarded as an excellent soldier. Moorman arranged for two army psychiatrists to interview and examine Jones and they both reported that he was competent and was probably telling the truth about the treasure. With these and other materials testifying to Jones's credibility, Moorman granted permission for him to excavate the shaft in Huachuca Canyon. A two-week period was allowed for the project.

Jones formed a company to undertake the excavation, with each member to share in the wealth upon its retrieval. They entered the canyon early on the morning of the first day allotted for the excavation and followed Jones's halting limp to the large boulder where he had carved his initials some eighteen years earlier. He also pointed out the two slash marks on a nearby tree. In a moment, Jones stood atop a pile of rubble he said covered the ancient shaft. Smiling, he told the men to begin digging.

After removing the cover of trees, rocks, and debris, the diggers exposed a man-made shaft that led downward at a steep angle oriented slightly toward the canyon wall. One side of the shaft had collapsed during the intervening years, filling the entrance with tons of rock. The excavators were now faced with the difficult task of removing large pieces of rock from the vertical opening. Finding that their picks and shovels were useless in breaking up the large rocks, Jones asked the army for permission to bring in some heavy equipment at his own expense. Instead, Major General Moorman allowed the use of an army bulldozer to help elongate the opening of the shaft and excavate it to a depth of ten feet. At this point considerable underground water was encountered, making further excavation impractical. The operation was halted. Jones was informed by the military that the time granted for the excavation had expired and he would have to discontinue his treasure hunt.

In September of the same year, Jones and his excavation company returned to Fort Huachuca and were once again successful in gaining permission to excavate further. Jones brought a drilling rig onto the site in order to punch a hole straight down into the chamber. If water was encountered it would be pumped out while the material filling the shaft was removed. The drill had reached about twenty feet into the rock when it suddenly plummeted into the chamber. The men became excited, eagerly anticipating the removal of the gold and silver ingots. This time two army bulldozers attacked the shaft, deepening it and widening it even more, but after they had cleared the shaft of another six feet of rock, water again began to seep in. More pumps were brought in and work continued throughout the night.

After three days of pumping out water, the bulldozers attained a depth of about twenty feet into the shaft. The work was often made hazardous by water seeping into the excavation, caving in the sides and threatening the workers.

During a break, a geologist who had been brought in from Colorado examined the shaft and stated that it was obviously man-made and very ancient. He also said evidence indicated that the shaft was dry when Jones stumbled into it eighteen years before.

Soon newspaper and television journalists entered the canyon to record the progress of the search. Because of the large numbers of outsiders, the military had to enact security measures and informed Jones that unless the work was completed soon the digging would have to be terminated for safety reasons. A Treasury Department operative arrived to monitor the progress. He announced that he was empowered to take charge of any and all treasure that might be encountered during the excavation. He informed Jones that, should treasure be discovered, the federal government would receive sixty percent of it and Jones would get forty percent, with his share being taxable.

Two weeks later a large clam shovel crane was brought onto the site. The crane was able to penetrate to twenty-five feet but at that point it hit resistant rock. A hole was drilled into the rock and stuffed with an explosive. The resulting blast created more problems by dislodging several tons of rock which collapsed into the shaft and refilled it. The geologist suggested that the chamber in which the ingots were stored may also have collapsed. For several more days the men and equipment labored to remove the rock, but all traces of the shaft had been obliterated. Reluctantly, Jones decided to call off the search. He thanked the military authorities and suggested that he would attempt to acquire some private backing to facilitate another search. At that point, however, the army officials stated flatly that no further digging would be allowed in Huachuca Canyon.

Jones continued to solicit investors and seek permission from the army to dig for the treasure he knew lay under tons of rock. Colonel Elbridge Bacon, post inspector general and project officer for the digging operation, said he believed there was an excellent chance that a treasure existed as Jones had claimed, but he was unable to persuade the military authorities to grant permission for another search.

Two years later Robert Jones died in his sleep at his home in Dallas, Texas.

The search for the Huachuca Canyon treasure did not end with Jones's death. In 1975, the army granted permission to Quest Exploration, a California-based treasure-hunting company, to search for the lost cache. Quest used state-of-the-art computer sensing equipment to determine the location of the chamber in which Jones said the ingots were located. If they could retrieve the treasure, the army said it would be placed in escrow until all claims on it were settled.

Although they spent a week at the site trying to locate the chamber, the searchers finally gave up, stating that whatever passageways or chambers may have existed had undoubtedly caved in as a result of previous excavation work. The late Captain William S. Jameson, who commanded the military police unit in charge of security during the second and final excavation, said he had spoken often with Jones and believed his story of the treasure cache. Following the abandonment of the search, Jameson was ordered to close off Huachuca Canyon to inhibit any more digging by treasure hunters. During this process, one of the military policemen discovered a small man-made shaft in which were found several digging tools, a pair of Spanish spurs, some ancient glassware, and several Spanish coins. Jameson believed this discovery lent credence to Jones's story, but when he reported it to his superiors, the items were confiscated and he was ordered to keep the find confidential.

The official position of the U.S. Army is that the treasure cache described by Jones does not exist. Unofficially, however, they are apparently still searching for it. In 1979, a squirrel hunter who has frequented Huachuca Canyon for forty years observed two army bulldozers excavating the debris-filled shaft that Robert Jones had fallen into thirty-eight years earlier.

Flannigan's Gold

In the first days of summer in 1869, the area of Gila Bend, Arizona, had been blessed with a better than average rainfall. The few settlers living in the region were grateful for the gift from the skies as they nursed their normally thirsty crops and gardens. One settler, Abner McKeever, along with his wife, son, and daughter, rode from his cabin out to the nearby floodplain of the Gila River to see how the latest rain had affected their corn crop. McKeever raised horses and was concerned about being able to provide enough corn for the animals this year. As they walked among the rows of chest-high cornstalks, a dozen Apaches galloped over a low rise and charged straight for the McKeever family. Armed with only a six-shooter, McKeever gathered his wife and children behind him and made a valiant attempt to repulse the attacking Indians. In a matter of few moments, however, his son lay dead, he and his wife were both seriously wounded, and their eight-year-old daughter, Belle, had been taken captive.

McKeever rode to the ranch of his closest neighbors, some three miles away, and they in turn alerted a company of United States Cavalry encamped nearby. The cavalry, along with several residents of Gila Bend, took up pursuit of the fleeing Apaches in hopes of rescuing the little girl.

The Apaches, using a typical escape strategy, split up into several small groups and rode away in different directions. Not knowing which of the groups carried Belle McKeever, the military detachment likewise divided into small groups, each following trails left by the Indians.

One detachment of soldiers followed the tracks of a group of Apaches northward into the Gila Bend Mountains but soon lost the trail where it crossed a stretch of bare rock. The small patrol consisted of Sergeant Crossthwaite and Privates Joe Wormley and Eugene Flannigan. All three men were newcomers to the arid Southwest and were poorly prepared for chasing warring Apaches across the sparse and forbidding desert. As the sun was beginning to set, the soldiers found themselves hopelessly lost and out of water. Night came and the three rode in a northwesterly direction in search of a spring or stream. As dawn approached both the men and the horses were tired, thirsty, and suffering from exhaustion. Suddenly Wormley called out and pointed to a cluster of cottonwood trees in the depression of a wash located in some low hills just ahead. In the center of the shade of the trees they found a pool of water formed by a gurgling spring.

The three soldiers abandoned any hope of catching up to the fleeing Apaches and were now more concerned with saving their own lives. They decided to rest at the spring for a full day before making an attempt to return to their company. Wormley had become delirious and began raving and screaming as the men prepared camp for the night.

Late in the afternoon, as Flannigan was filling canteens, he spied some color at the bottom of the little pool of water. Scooping up a handful of rocks and pebbles, he was surprised to find nuggets of gold among them. Several more handfuls yielded more nuggets. Flannigan stuffed the gold into his pockets and began to explore the area around the pond. He soon found two veins of gold-laden quartz in a rock outcrop located several feet above the spring. Flannigan later described one of the veins as being five inches wide and the other as sixteen inches wide. He returned to camp and informed Sergeant Crossthwaite of his discovery. The two men returned to the rock outcrop and dug the exposed gold out of the quartz with the points of their knives, eventually collecting about fifty pounds of the precious metal.

The next morning they packed the gold into their saddlebags, tied the still delirious Wormley onto his mount, and struck out in a southeasterly direction, harboring hopes of encountering the Gila River within two days. On the morning of the third day they were still lost and decided to split up. Crossthwaite took Wormley and rode toward the east while Flannigan rode south. During the night Crossthwaite and Wormley became separated.

The next morning another detachment of cavalry found Wormley, still sick and raving, lying on a bank of the Gila River. Neither his companions nor his horse could be found nearby and

Wormley was unable to tell the soldiers anything. He was eventually returned to his company, but he never recovered his sanity.

Around midmorning the cavalry found Flannigan's horse dead on the trail, with footprints leading away from it. Following the footprints the soldiers found Flannigan a few hours later, face down on the desert floor clutching a saddlebag filled with gold nuggets.

The next day as Flannigan was recovering from his ordeal on a cot inside a medical tent, he was informed that Crossthwaite had been found dead the previous evening. The soldiers who found him had come back with his body along with his gold-filled saddlebag.

Flannigan informed his superiors of the ordeal in the desert and tried to describe the location of the spring where they had found the gold, but none of the men who heard his story was familiar with that part of the country and none could relate to the location or any of the landmarks.

Several months later Flannigan was discharged from the army and undertook to outfit himself for a search for the spring and the gold-veined quartz. Braving the threat of warring Apaches and the waterless, trackless desert, Flannigan rode into the general area where he had become lost with Crossthwaite and Wormley nearly a year before. He led two mules loaded with enough provisions to last several weeks.

Flannigan searched until he ran out of food but was unable to locate any site that remotely resembled the low hills or the wash where he had found the spring. Many times he entered the desolate hills and valleys that comprise much of southwestern Arizona, and each time he returned empty-handed. Flannigan and his story became well known in the Southwest, and other prospectors joined the search for the lost spring and its gold.

One April morning in 1881 Flannigan was purchasing supplies at a Gila Bend trading post and readying himself for another search in the mountains to the northwest. He was a cheerful sort, and his suntanned face was etched with lines radiating out from perpetually smiling eyes. On this day he talked with several of the townsfolk and two other prospectors as he loaded his mules. Around midmorning he bade them all farewell and rode out of town. It was the last time anyone saw Eugene Flannigan alive. Two months later his body was discovered by some travelers in the desert in the northwestern part of Yuma County. He had apparently walked a great distance, as the soles of his boots were worn nearly paper-thin. Both his canteens were empty, and clutched in his arms was a saddlebag. When the travelers opened it up they found it was filled with gold nuggets! Flannigan's horse and mules were never found. It was impossible to tell from which direction he had walked when his body was discovered.

For ten years Eugene Flannigan had searched the desert for his lost spring and its gold. Each time he ventured into the waterless environment he wondered if he would ever come out of it alive, but the lure of the wealth that he knew awaited him kept him returning. Apparently he did relocate the spring and the gold in the nearby rock outcrops, but that time he was not lucky enough to escape the desert.

Buried Wealth at Fort Defiance

In his lifetime John J. Glanton acquired a reputation as a ruthless and cunning bandit and scalp-hunter in Mexico and the American Southwest during the 1840s. Unlike most badmen, he possessed a remarkable ability to hold onto his wealth, carefully saving it and carrying it with him everywhere he traveled. After ten years of banditry and questionable business practices, Glanton had amassed a large fortune which he hastily buried only a few hours before his death. For over a hundred years people have searched for his wealth, but the cache has never been found.

John Joel Glanton was born in 1819 in Edgefield County, South Carolina. As a young boy he left home and wandered to central and west Texas where, at seventeen years of age, he was hired as an army scout for Lieutenant Fannin. Glanton soon left this job, took a Lipan Apache bride, and settled on a small farm near the Guadalupe River in Gonzales County, Texas. After being married for only a few months, Glanton returned from a hunting trip to find his wife murdered and scalped, presumably by Comanches.

A short time later Glanton is believed to have moved to San Antonio, where he married a young girl from a well-to-do Mexican family. In the winter of 1847, however, he abandoned her and enlisted as a private in the U.S. Army. Records show that Glanton participated in the Snively Expedition, spent time under the command of General Zachary Taylor, and served with Captain Jack Hayes in the war with Mexico. As a soldier he gained a reputation of being boisterous and ready to fight at a moment's notice. In 1948, while on duty in Mexico, he was arrested for shooting a native during a barroom brawl. A week later he broke out, deserted the army, and fled deep into Chihuahua.

Several months later Glanton reappeared as a member of a band of scalp-hunters who worked for the Mexican government. Because of repeated difficulties between the Mexicans and Apaches, Glanton and his fellows were promised fifty dollars in gold for each Apache scalp they brought in. Fearless and ferocious, this small army attacked dozens of Apache encampments, killing men, women, and children in their grisly quest. When they were unable to find Indians, they sometimes lifted the scalps of Mexicans and passed them off as Apache. When government officials in Chihuahua learned of this they chased the band northward across the Rio Grande and back into the United States. During the flight, Glanton and the leader of the group, Santiago Kirker, had a violent argument. During an ensuing knife fight, Glanton killed Kirker and assumed the leadership of the group of scalp-hunters. Glanton went to Sonora, the Mexican state just west of Chihuahua, and made arrangements with military leaders there to bring in Apache scalps. The scalp-hunters ranged far and wide in their search for Indians, killing and scalping hundreds. Their journeys sometimes took them into New Mexico where, in addition to hunting the Apache, they raided and looted small villages and robbed stagecoaches and freight wagons.

As they accumulated booty, the always frugal Glanton began to pack his share onto mules he brought along to transport his wealth. It was said that he no longer slept at night but preferred to stand guard over his gold. It was also during this time that Glanton began to change. He now became obsessed with killing and seemed to take great pleasure in it. He would shoot or knife anyone who even mildly disagreed with him and often shot travelers encountered along the trail just for the sport of it. He also began to drink wildly and gamble frequently. Meanwhile, he continued to amass great wealth and now required several mules in order to transport it all.

Glanton's depredations took him and his band westward, and they settled into a camp south of Tucson. This group of cutthroats now numbered fourteen, half of whom were Mexican. The men made frequent raids on nearby gold-mining camps and often attacked freight wagons, collecting thousands of dollars' worth of gold nuggets. When a group of vigilantes attacked their camp, Glanton led his men north and east to Phoenix in search of more opportunities for raiding. They had not been in the area long when they discovered and attacked a Pima Indian village for the purpose of taking scalps. The Indians were well-armed, however, and during the ensuing battle half of Glanton's forces were killed or wounded. While retreating from the Indians, Glanton reportedly shot and killed the wounded members of his band so they would not slow down the escape.

The group continued to roam westward and in a few weeks arrived at the small town of Yuma on the Colorado River. In a short time Glanton and his men took over the town and seized the two ferryboats which transported goods and travelers across the river to and from California. Glanton believed he could become even more wealthy in Yuma, so he ordered the construction of an adobe-walled fortress on a hill in the town overlooking the Colorado River. He and his men took mistresses from the Mexican population of the town, and all moved into the fortress which he named Fort Defiance. From here Glanton managed the ferryboat operation as well as a saloon and several other businesses in town.

Men returning from the gold fields in California were systematically robbed and killed on the ferry and their bodies tossed into the current. In this manner Glanton piled up more gold and currency until he became what many believed to be the wealthiest man in the Southwest. As he grew richer he also grew more insane. His men, desperadoes of the first order, became fearful of his wild and unpredictable manner and one by one deserted him.

Eventually Glanton had nothing left but his money and gold. He stayed locked up within the walls of Fort Defiance for weeks at a time. When he did appear in the town he bore the look of a depraved maniac, with long, stringy, unkempt hair, filthy, ragged clothes, and a frightening look in his eyes. In one hand he carried a pistol and in the other a large Bowie knife.

One day Glanton learned from the townspeople that a large band of Yuma Indians was approaching and intent on attacking the town. Glanton believed the Indians were after his wealth, and he was determined to hide it. During the rest of the day and throughout the night Glanton worked feverishly at hiding his fortune in Mexican and American gold coins, gold nuggets, and currency. Some claim that Glanton never left the safety of Fort Defiance and buried his wealth somewhere within the confines of the adobe fortress. Others say that Glanton made several trips into the sandhills just outside of Yuma and buried his fortune there. In any case, the Indians attacked at dawn of the next day, burning much of the town and killing several of the citizens. Encountering no resistance, they stormed Fort Defiance and set fire to the structures within. After the Indians departed, several Yuma citizens entered the fortress and found Glanton's body, horribly mutilated and scalped. A preliminary search for his wealth turned up nothing.

As the news of Glanton's death spread throughout the territory, dozens of men arrived to search for the treasure they knew had to be buried somewhere within the fort or close by in the desert. Hundreds of holes were dug inside the fort, pitting virtually every square foot of ground, but nothing was ever found. Holes were likewise dug for miles out in the desert in all directions from the town, but no one ever found Glanton's cache.

An old-timer who subsequently took over the operation of the ferry befriended an aged Yuma Indian several years after the raid. He learned that the old Yuma had participated in the attack on the town. When he asked the old man if he knew anything about Glanton's buried fortune, the Indian related a curious story. He said that he and several other Yuma warriors observed Glanton make several trips from the fort with his mules laden with gold and watched as he dug several holes in the sand dunes south of town where he buried his wealth. When Glanton had returned to the fort for the last time, the Indians advanced on the site, dug up the gold and the money, and threw it all into the swirling waters of the Colorado River.

Yuma's Lost Mine

Somewhere in the Galiuro Mountains of southeastern Arizona is a shallow, scooped-out pit at the bottom of which lies a thick circular vein of almost pure gold that continues straight down into the surrounding rock. The Aravaipa Apaches conservatively dug the ore out of this "chimney" formation and used it to fashion ornaments to adorn themselves. For generations no whites had ever seen this mine, as its location was closely guarded and held secret by the Indians. But one day a man known only as Yuma arrived at the Aravaipa encampment and, after bribing one of the tribe's elders, was taken to the mine and allowed to extract a large amount of the gold. Within months, Yuma and another man with whom he shared the secret of the location were dead, and since that time thousands have searched for what might possibly be the richest vein of gold in North America.

No historical records remain which provide information on the real name of the man known only as Yuma. He did graduate from West Point Military Academy and served admirably with the United States Army along the Texas-Mexican border. Soon after his tour of duty there he was transferred to Fort Yuma on the Colorado River and was appointed quartermaster for the post. The quartermaster's duties included overseeing supplies that came to the fort overland and upriver on steamboats from the Gulf of California, and thousands of dollars' worth of supplies and equipment passed through his hands each day. Seeing an opportunity to make some money far above his meager army pay, the quartermaster began to hold out some of the supplies and sell them to unscrupulous traders who would in turn transport them to California and resell them at a huge profit. This scheme went well for several months, but eventually the quartermaster's thefts were discovered and he was subsequently court-martialed and discharged from the army.

As he rode away from the fort, the quartermaster had no inkling of what he would do. His life had been the army and his mistake meant he would never be able to return to it. With a deep discouragement and hurt pride, he rode northward. In a day he came to a Yuma Indian camp and discovered the band was led by Chief Pascual, whom he had known well for years. Pascual invited the ex-soldier to remain in camp until he was prepared to continue his journey.

The white man had long been fascinated by the Yuma Indians. They were tall, as Indians go, well-built, and muscular. Though the Yumas were relatively few in number, they were respected as brave and fierce warriors and were feared even by the mighty Apache who ruled most of Arizona. The women of the tribe were likewise tall and very beautiful. Weeks passed and the white man remained in the Yuma camp, participating in the hunting and breaking of horses. Soon he took a wife, the comely young daughter of Chief Pascual, and was adopted into the tribe. Thereafter he was known by other whites only as Yuma.

During times of relative peace, the Yumas often traded with the Apaches to the east. The Apaches needed rifles and ammunition and always paid for the goods with pure gold. Because of his familiarity with traders and merchants in the area, Yuma was able to procure guns and ammunition and maintained a lively trade with the Aravaipa Apaches. Many times he asked the Apaches where they obtained their gold, but their response was a stony silence. During one trip the Apache chief told Yuma it was not good to ask such questions because the source of the gold was a dear secret to the Indians and any who violated its trust would be put to death. Yuma replied that he had great respect for the ways of the Apache and inquired only out of curiosity, not out of a desire to be shown the location. Pacified with this answer, the chief went away.

The next day, however, Yuma found himself in conversation with another Apache, an older Indian no longer permitted to accompany the warriors on raids. He entertained Yuma with stories of his bravery in battle and his skill at stealing horses, describing the many things he would do if only they would permit him to go out with the raiders. But alas, he said, they had taken his weapons and his horse, thus effectively keeping him in camp. Yuma took the old brave aside and showed him a brand-new rifle. He told the Indian that the rifle and much ammunition could be his if he would reveal the secret location of the Apache gold. The old Indian told Yuma it was forbidden to speak of such things, but as he spoke his eyes never left the gleaming new gun. After more discussion, Yuma agreed to give the old Indian one of his best horses as well. Casting glances about the camp to ensure no one was listening, the old man agreed to show Yuma the mine.

The next morning the two men walked out of the Indian camp on the pretense of going hunting. They walked north for about two hours and, cresting a low mountain range, observed the San Pedro Valley to the west. They continued for another hour, mostly downhill, and eventually found themselves walking the edge of a deep arroyo. Following the arroyo for several hundred yards, they soon came to a small crater-like depression that measured about five feet deep and about six feet wide at the bottom. The old Indian said this was the source of the Aravaipa gold. On seeing the hole in the ground, Yuma was at first skeptical, but he jumped into the depression and with his bare hands began to dig through the accumulation of loose shale. In a matter of minutes he dug through several inches of the shale and reached the bottom of the hole. He immediately spied a thick vein of the purest gold he had ever seen. Using his knife, he dug several large pieces from the vein and filled his pockets. When he was finished, he and the old Indian covered the hole with the loose shale, leaving it as they had found it. Yuma took notice of the ridges and other landmarks so he could find his way back to the site. The place was rocky, desolate, and barren, and no one lived within dozens of miles of it. The old Indian reminded Yuma that to be caught at the mine meant certain death.

Returning to the Apache camp, the two men shot and killed several birds and rabbits to allay any suspicions about their hunting trip. Yuma remained in the camp to conclude his trading.

On the fifth day, he loaded up his wagon and left for Tucson, where he looked up an old acquaintance, a freighter named Crittendon. The two had met at Fort Yuma when Crittendon was hauling goods from Tucson to the military post. Yuma regarded him as a friend and told him about the gold mine. The two formed a partnership and began to make plans to journey to the site. Together they rode to Camp Grant, where they stayed for two nights. They left the outpost and headed toward the San Pedro River. Darkness fell just before they reached the mine and they made a camp. The next morning they rode straight to the crater and dug out enough gold to fill two saddlebags. They recovered the hole, cached their tools nearby, and returned to Tucson.

When they sold their gold for a total of twelve thousand dollars, word spread throughout the town and the two men attracted a following. Every time they tried to return to the mine they were followed and were forced to abandon the trip. After this happened several times, Yuma and Crittendon decided it was best to let the interest in the mine subside before trying another journey. Crittendon went back to his freighting business and Yuma and his wife rode west to conduct some trading with the Pima and Papago tribes. After a successful trading venture with the Pimas, Yuma and his wife rode toward a Papago encampment. She begged her husband not to trade with the Papagos, as they had been lifelong enemies of the Yuma Indians. Ignoring her pleas, Yuma rode into the Indian camp. The two were received warily by the tribe. Once within the confines of the camp, both were killed and their bodies dragged out into the desert for coyotes to eat.

Crittendon waited three months for Yuma to return. By that time he decided the trader wasn't coming back, so he left once again for the mine, this time alone. He stopped again at Camp Grant and told all who would listen to him that he intended to file a claim for the site of the gold mine. The morning he left the camp, he said he expected to return that same evening. After three days passed and Crittendon did not return, a cavalry unit was sent out to search for him. With the aid of Indian trackers, they picked up his trail easily enough and soon came upon his horse picketed at the place he and Yuma had camped three months earlier. The saddle and supplies were lying nearby, untouched, but there was no sign of Crittendon. For three days the soldiers searched. They found where he had left the camp on foot, and on a nearby crest found his boot prints paralleling a deep arroyo for several hundred yards, but they never found any sign of Crittendon. Eventually they had to call off the search and return to camp.

Three weeks later, a band of nearly one hundred Papago Indians attacked the camp of the Aravaipa Apaches and slaughtered everyone they found. This is recorded in history books as the Camp Grant Massacre of 1871. Those who have hunted for the Lost Yuma Mine believe that with the death of Yuma, Crittendon, and the Aravaipa Apaches, all who would have known the location of the small crater of gold are gone.

Arkansas

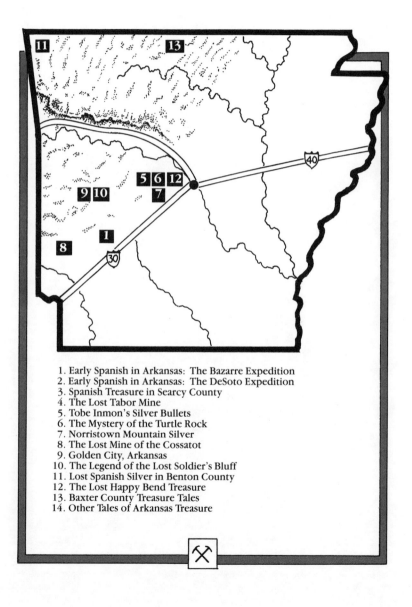

Early Spanish in Arkansas: The Bazarre Expedition

Any inquiry into tales of lost mines and buried treasures in Arkansas must begin with the Spanish explorers of the sixteenth century. The Spanish, in their zeal to establish new colonies and secure wealth, committed a great deal of energy as well as human and financial resources to exploring and prospecting for ore in the New World. Hundreds of Spaniards were assigned to the Americas, and under the leadership of men like Juan Ponce de Léon, Valisco Bazarre, and Hernando De Soto, they scoured the countryside in search of the gold and silver they believed existed. Undoubtedly there were many failures, but the evidence is overwhelming that they also experienced many successes, and it is these successes that have led to the evolution of dozens of tales of lost Spanish gold and silver mines in the New World. Records exist indicating that millions of dollars' worth of ore was shipped back to the Spanish homeland—gold and silver that came from the mountains of Arkansas.

The Spanish were also quite adept at disguising their mining operations so they would not be detected by explorers, hostile Indians, and adventurers from other countries. They would often seal the mine entrances with rocks, remove all of the mine tailings and other debris, replace the topsoil, and plant brush and grass over the concealed area so that in a year or two it looked exactly the same as the surrounding environment. This great attention to detail has made relocation of many ancient mines very difficult.

In the early part of the sixteenth century, the New World held a keen fascination for many European rulers. Many of them believed the potential of the Americas was in a great abundance of natural resources and fantastic wealth, and the King of Spain was particularly excited by the idea of sending batallions of soldiers across the Atlantic Ocean to realize some of this potential.

The king selected Juan Ponce de Léon to voyage to the New World and establish a colony in what is now Florida. Ponce de Léon had by this time achieved great status as an explorer and soldier and was the logical candidate for this mission. Besides fighting against the Moors in the conquest of Granada, he had accompanied Christopher Columbus on his second voyage to America in 1493. In 1508 he conquered Puerto Rico for Spain and was named the governor of that island from 1510 to 1512. He was responsible for naming Florida.

In 1521 Ponce de Léon landed on the coast of Florida with two ships, two hundred men, and a supply of livestock. His objective was to establish a Spanish colony to serve as a base from which to explore the New World. Luck was not with the group, however, because they were continually besieged by hostile Indians. Ponce de Léon himself was severely wounded during one of the attacks and, unable to withstand the continual onslaught of the natives, he ordered his men to the boats and left for Cuba. Unfortunately, Ponce de Léon never recovered from his wounds and he died on that island.

Valisco Bazarre, one of Ponce de Léon's officers, commandeered the second boat during the escape from Florida. Caught in a storm, he became separated from Ponce de Léon and sailed in the opposite direction, following the coastline of Florida and entering the Gulf of Mexico. Bazarre, along with about fifty-five men, continued to sail until they reached the Mississippi delta, and with considerable navigational difficulties finally managed to pole, sail, and row their craft up this river to the confluence of the Red River. During a prolonged encampment at this point, Bazarre and his men encountered more Indians. These Indians, however, were friendly and posed no threat to the Spaniards. In fact they appeared to fear the newcomers, perceiving them to be supernatural beings, and brought them offerings of fresh meat. The Spaniards, seeing the advantage of fostering this belief, did nothing to dispel the notion that they were anything but gods.

During one encounter with the Indians, Bazarre noticed that the leader of the small tribe was wearing an armlet that was obviously hand-crafted from silver. On inspecting it, he was surprised and pleased to discover that it was the purest form of the metal he had ever seen. When he inquired as to the origin of the piece of jewelry, the Indians brought forth others like it as well as many other kinds of amulets and ornaments.

The chief told Bazarre that far toward the north near the source of the Ouachita River there existed a broad valley shrouded in mist for most of the year. The floor of the flat plain beside the river fairly sparkled with the metal from which the chief's amulet was made. Often, he said, he and several members of his tribe would journey to the valley near the headwaters of the river and pick the metal from the ground at their feet. He added, however, that it was very dangerous because this valley was haunted and those who tarried too long never returned. He claimed the tribe had lost several good men who had disappeared into the mist as they sought more and more of the precious metal.

Bazarre, sensing wealth for himself as well as for his men and the motherland, ignored the warnings of the chief and made immediate plans to depart for the upper reaches of the Ouachita River. For many days they traveled until they finally arrived at a low point overlooking the mist-shrouded valley. They set up a camp on the floodplain adjacent to the river across from which lay the field of silver.

Bazarre summoned his priest and ordered him to cross the shallow river, enter the haunted plain, and command the evil spirits to depart. Reluctantly, the priest gathered his robe above his knees and waded the river to the other side. Climbing to the opposite bank, he clutched his rosary and prayed. As he came upon the plain he dropped to his knees and continued to perform the rosary, occasionally calling out in a loud voice for the spirits to vacate. For many hours he knelt and prayed while Bazarre and his soldiers watched from the opposite shore. After a long while the mist finally lifted and the priest beckoned to Bazarre that it was safe to cross.

True to the word of the Indian, the Spaniards found silver lying atop the flat rocky outcrops that protruded slightly above the silt deposits laid down by the river during flood periods. They filled their pockets and sacks until they could carry no more and then returned to camp.

Bazarre had his men construct a more permanent camp. Half of them were put to work building crude log cabins while the others, including the priest, were assigned to harvest silver from the opposite side of the river. Following several weeks of effort, most of the surface ore was removed, and the Spaniards undertook to sink shafts into the rocky outcrops where seams of silver had been discovered. Three shafts were dug, with one of them eventually reaching a depth of over one hundred feet. Several more promising veins of ore were discovered in this shaft, and more of the metal was collected.

During the mining activity, Bazarre had his craftsmen build several flatboats with which to transport the ore back down the river and thence to the Gulf of Mexico.

Bazarre and his men spent nearly eighteen months in the mysterious valley working the silver mines before hostile Indians came. Initially, only a few at a time were observed from far away, but as the days passed they became bolder and approached to within just a few yards of the Spaniards.

Soon the hostiles began to launch minor raids into the camp of the Spaniards, killing one or two of them with each foray. The Indians became more and more aggressive until Bazarre began to fear for the survival of his company.

Another version of this story relates that for a while Bazarre and his men lived peacefully with the local Indians and even married several of the women. To this day it is claimed that many people now living near the headwaters of the Ouachita River in the area that includes Polk and Montgomery Counties are descendants of those early Spanish-Indian unions. Over time the Indians came to believe they were being used by the Spaniards only to get the silver, and relations became strained. Eventually, full-fledged battles took place, causing the Spaniards to consider departing the country.

In any event, one evening a young Indian girl walked into Bazarre's camp and told him that her father, the chief, planned to attack at sunrise and slay all of the intruders. Immediately, Bazarre ordered his men to fill the shafts and start loading the ore onto flatboats. They worked all night long while Bazarre made maps of the area showing the locations of the mine shafts. Just before dawn the men abandoned camp and stole down the river, out to the Mississippi, and on to the Gulf of Mexico. Ancient documents reveal that Bazarre and his men at last reached Cuba where they shipped the silver to Spain.

In 1836, the year Arkansas became a state, an old man was seen walking along the banks of the upper reaches of the Ouachita River. He was described as being dark, probably of Mediterranean origin, and he carried an old weathered parchment map with locations marked in Spanish. From time to time he would stop at residences in the area and ask, in broken English, about locations of certain landmarks. He always politely thanked the people he spoke with. After spending several weeks in the vicinity, the stranger disappeared and was never seen again.

Was he a descendant of Bazarre or one of his men? Was he seeking the lost field of silver? If so, history has not recorded whether he found it.

In the upper reaches of the Ouachita River, there are several areas where the river valley flattens out to accept flood waters after unusually heavy rains. On cool mornings it is not uncommon to see mist gather in the low areas between the folded sandstone ridges of the Ouachita Mountains. Any one of these flat valleys could be the famed field of silver that Bazarre found. In one of them several artifacts have been discovered that have been identified as being of Spanish origin, and many of these artifacts are mining tools.

A weather-sculpted old gentleman who lives near Pine Ridge in Montgomery County has several of the ancient mining tools left behind by the Spaniards. He will not reveal exactly where he found them but says he is very close to locating the mine shafts that the Spaniards opened up. The old man says he has been searching for Bazarre's lost mines for well over thirty years. He refuses to take visitors to where he suspects the shafts are located, but his belief in their existence is unshakable. Though he is aged, his enthusiasm remains youthful and is apparent as he speaks of the great store of wealth he believes lies hidden deep underground. He is convinced Bazarre and his men were unable to carry away all of the silver they extracted from the mines, and he feels certain they buried most of it in one of the shafts. He claims that is why the Spaniards went to such great lengths to seal the mine entrances. He also believes that the Spanish man who appeared in the valley in 1836 was searching for the silver hidden in one of the deep shafts.

This old man with the darkened skin and the deep creases in his face smiles as he claims he has one big advantage over Bazarre: he doesn't have hostile Indians to cope with. But he also acknowledges he has a huge disadvantage: he knows he will live only a few more years and he wants badly to locate the silver while he still has time.

The promise of silver first lured the Indians and then Bazarre to the rugged country of the Ouachitas. Today, hundreds of years later, that promise continues to lure the same kind of adventurers in search of wealth. We have changed so little.

Early Spanish in Arkansas: The De Soto Expedition

While Bazarre's entry into Arkansas and subsequent exploration was accidental, following his separation from Juan Ponce de Léon, Hernando De Soto can claim credit for the first formal exploration of the state.

Like Ponce de Léon, De Soto was commissioned by the king of Spain to claim land to be settled by the Spanish and to execute a systematic search for gold and silver. Also like Ponce de Léon, De Soto brought with him excellent credentials for his new position. He served under Pizarro in Central and South America and participated with the force of the Spanish army that conquered Peru.

De Soto had always been fascinated by the possibility of wealth in North America, so after his duty with Pizarro he sought for and received permission from the king to explore the region, establish permanent settlements, and search for and retrieve as much wealth as possible. Because of De Soto's enterprise, the king appointed him governor of Cuba and Florida and authorized him to venture into the continent and inventory the resources.

In 1539 De Soto, along with six hundred soldiers, landed near what is now Tampa Bay, Florida, and there established a colony. While involved in the activity, he encountered a man named Juan Ortiz who had come to Florida in 1528 on a minor expedition led by Captain Narvaez. The puny expedition force had been captured by Indians and tortured horribly, killed and eaten one by one until only Ortiz remained. The wife of the tribal chief pleaded for the life of Ortiz because he was only a boy. Eventually the chief acceded to his wife's pleas and spared the Spaniard's life. He lived with the tribe for ten years until finally he found an opportunity to escape. He wandered aimlessly through the Florida wilderness for nearly a year before stumbling into the De Soto encampment. When found, he could barely remember his native language.

Having made certain that Ortiz was well rested and recovered, De Soto offered him an opportunity to serve as guide and interpreter accompanying his expedition into the interior of the continent.

For two years, De Soto and his forces explored the regions now known as Florida, Georgia, Alabama, and Mississippi. The journey was fraught with hardship as dozens of men succumbed to disease and starvation and were felled by Indian attacks. Because Narvaez had treated the Indians so cruelly during the previous expedition in this area, those De Soto's party encountered were very defensive and hostile. In a battle with Indians during the month of October 1540, near where Mobile, Alabama, is now located, De Soto lost eight men and forty-two horses. As the numbers of Spaniards decreased, De Soto began to raid local villages and capture Indians whom he enslaved and used as porters.

It is believed De Soto reached the broad Mississippi River in 1541. The local Indian name for the river, from which the current name Mississippi is derived, was *Meschacebe*—"Father of Waters." De Soto remained encamped on the bluff overlooking the river near where the city of Memphis now stands while barges were built to facilitate the crossing. With his men, livestock, and baggage he floated downriver until, in August, they landed near what is now Helena. Their arrival represents the first recorded instance of Europeans on Arkansas soil.

De Soto and his now diminished forces traveled up the St. Francis River and explored much of northeastern Arkansas. It is reported that he engaged a local Indian tribe in a large battle near present-day Osceola and was badly defeated. He turned back toward the southwest, eventually encountering the Arkansas River. He and his dedicated soldiers followed the river upstream to a point where Little Rock is now located and established a camp. For the next few years, De Soto sent his men out in various directions into and throughout the Ozark Mountains in search of gold and silver. That the Spaniards explored the Ozarks is certain: there have been so many Spanish artifacts found in northern and western Arkansas that the evidence is hard to dispute.

In time, several of these search parties returned with stories of riches in gold and silver which lay in the mountains. Many of the search parties never returned and it is assumed they met their fate at the hands of hostile Indians who lived in the mountains. It is also presumed that many of the Spaniards, on discovering ore, elected to remain in the area to mine the wealth for themselves rather than return to their leader. In any event, it is known that De Soto shipped several mule loads of silver back to Spain from his camp near Little Rock.

De Soto eventually broke camp and moved his force up the Arkansas River until he reached present-day Dardanelle. He crossed the river and continued into the Ouachita Mountains, which he called "Land of the Cayas." Here De Soto became seriously ill and had to be carried. While his men scoured the near-by mountains in search of gold and silver, he lay near death in camp. After a while he was taken by a friendly Indian to "the land of hot water," where his illness temporarily abated. Historians believe this was Hot Springs, Arkansas. From here De Soto traveled westward for some distance in the Ouachitas until he met resistance from a particularly ferocious tribe of Indians, which forced him to change direction.

His ragged company made their way to what is now Camden, where they established a poor camp in order to rest the men and the livestock. There they engaged in trade with the friendly local Indians who, they discovered, possessed a wealth of crudely fashioned ornaments of silver. The Indians refused to reveal the locations of their silver mines, but they freely continued to barter the precious metal for goods carried by the Europeans.

De Soto ordered his men to search for the Indians' mines. They made many trips up the Ouachita River and its tributaries, acting on leads obtained from Indians they kidnapped and tortured. The Spaniards sank several exploratory shafts near the river and some of its tributaries, and even today the sharp-eyed searcher can find evidence of this mining activity along the riverbanks in remote areas. In the four centuries that have elapsed since De Soto vacated this region, treasure hunters have used Camden as a starting point for expeditions searching for what is now known as the Lost Indian Mine.

The first settlers at Arkansas Post around 1696 heard stories from local Indians about the existence of a silver mine far back in the Ouachitas. Over the years several of the original Spanish diggings have been reopened but so far none has yielded any ore. The Indian silver is apparently still there.

De Soto's health continued to fail and eventually he thought it prudent to continue his journey toward the Gulf of Mexico and thence, he hoped, home to Spain. He ordered his men to load up their gear and proceed down the river. Once again they ran into hostile Indians who forced them to stay on the move constantly. The soldiers continued to travel southeastward until they reached a point near the Arkansas-Louisiana line where they spent the winter.

When spring arrived, De Soto ordered his men to continue once more to follow the river until they reached the Mississippi. De Soto died just before his party arrived at the junction of the Ouachita and Mississippi Rivers. At this point, his body was consigned to the Mississippi so that the Indians could not reach it. His men proceeded down the river, carrying with them the dozens of mule loads of silver they had extracted from the mountains of Arkansas.

What has happened to the many mines excavated by the Spaniards during this period of exploration? Ever since the Spanish explorers passed through Arkansas, evidence of their presence and mining activity has been plentiful. Many people believe fabulous deposits of gold and silver still exist in the Ozark and Ouachita Mountains, deposits that have gone undiscovered by contemporary seekers. One must remember that many of these stories have entered the realm of legend as they have been passed down over the many generations since the Spanish visited. But the fact remains that the Spanish did indeed participate in extensive exploration and mining activity throughout Arkansas's mountains. By the many accounts of great wealth being shipped out of the mountains and back to the Spanish homeland, one must believe that they were successful at retrieving hundreds of pounds of ore.

In addition, the Spanish invested a considerable amount of time and energy in extensive excavation of mine shafts in the solid rock of the mountains. Surely they must have had a serious motive in leaving behind the numerous symbols carved in stone reputed to mark locations of the long hidden mines. One must also wonder why they went to such great lengths to conceal shaft openings if they did not intend to return someday to reopen the mines.

It is safe to assume that, during the many years that have elapsed since the Spanish abandoned the area, much of the wealth they discovered has gone unclaimed—unclaimed and still lying underground, awaiting the fortunate treasure hunter.

Spanish Treasure
in Searcy County

During the early part of this century a man named Herndon was occupied with some exploratory mining near Silver Hill in Searcy County. Here and there throughout the mountains where he prospected he would find traces of silver ore, but never enough to justify any serious excavation activity. One day, however, he located a vein of silver that held some promise. He filed a claim and immediately employed a surveyor to locate and mark some property lines for him. The surveyor was a local man knowledgeable about the history of the area. As he and Herndon were walking around the claim, he said that not too far from where they stood was evidence of some ancient Spanish mining activity. Intrigued, Herndon asked the surveyor to lead him to the location so they could investigate it. Eventually they came to an area of bare bedrock in the center of which was a crater-like excavation ringed by several large mounds of rock debris that apparently came out of it.

The surveyor related an interesting story about the site. Many years earlier, he said, a Mexican who identified himself as a priest had arrived in the area. He claimed he was an emissary from a church in Mexico in which was discovered an aged Spanish map purporting to show the location of a fabulous wealth of silver. The priest produced the map from a well-made leather case and showed it to several residents of the area. It was of heavy parchment and showed many landmarks that matched the Silver Hill environment. The priest said his information suggested the map had been drawn by one of de Soto's soldiers and it designated the site of a very rich deposit of silver that had been extensively mined centuries earlier. The map gave the location of the mine in precise degrees of latitude and longitude and was dated 1580. The story accompanying the map told of how great quantities of silver had been taken from a deep shaft carved into the rock of the mountain and smelted down into ingots for ease of transportation. The Spanish miners were forced to cut short their activities, however, because of continued threats from hostile Indians. The shaft was filled and the area abandoned as quickly as possible and, for reasons unknown, the Spaniards never returned to work the mine. The surveyor told Herndon that the priest had offered a resident half of the silver remaining in the shaft if he would organize the excavation of the fill material. An agreement was made and several local residents labored to remove the debris from the shaft.

As they began to dig, it became quite obvious that they were excavating an old mine which had been filled in. In several days they removed about twelve feet of rock from the wide shaft. Then they encountered a huge limestone slab that had somehow been wedged into position in the shaft and firmly secured. After several unsuccessful attempts, they finally blasted through the slab and discovered an open shaft which veered off at an angle into the mountain. It was reported that on the floor of this shaft were found numerous tools of Spanish origin. The workers also discovered some molds into which the molten silver had evidently been poured to form ingots.

A thorough search of the shaft was made, but no seam of silver was located. A curious situation now existed: if all of the silver had been excavated from the mine, why was the shaft so elaborately sealed?

A mining engineering firm from Kansas City was called in to examine the area for any potential of silver. Like the previous miners they had no luck in locating a vein of the ore in the shaft, but they did find evidence that silver had indeed been taken out. On this same trip, the engineers discovered several small veins of silver nearby and began mining operations which continued for several years.

The Mexican priest returned to his home country and Herndon eventually abandoned the area. As the years passed, the silver mines were worked out and they too were abandoned. An old man named Grinder moved into the area and squatted on the land on which the old Spanish mine shaft was located. Grinder was well known to many of the residents of the Silver Hill area. He did odd jobs and some trapping, but as he was a rather coarse and unkempt person, most of the residents shunned him. It was clear that he was digging in the old shaft in hopes of locating the lost vein of silver.

After living near the shaft for several weeks, Grinder ordered and paid for some mining equipment he had delivered from Little Rock to the Silver Hill site. It was a mystery where he got the money to pay for what amounted to thousands of dollars' worth of machinery.

Spending all his time at the mine, Grinder worked intently down in the shaft for many hours at a time, and visitors to the area were ordered away at the point of a shotgun.

Within a year, Grinder abandoned his mining operation and sold all the equipment. To the surprise of many, he shortly thereafter purchased a 120-acre farm, paid for entirely with cash! Those who ventured into the old Spanish mine told how a completely new passageway had been opened up for several yards.

Had old man Grinder discovered the long-concealed vein of silver ore that the Spaniards had gone to so much trouble to hide? Evidently he found something that encouraged him to dig out tons of rock singlehandedly. Whatever he found, old man Grinder was not telling, and he apparently took his secret to the grave.

The Lost Tabor Mine

The Silver Hill mine was probably not the only Spanish mining activity in Searcy County. An old recluse named Tabor may have mined some silver from another one located near Tomahawk Creek.

Tabor was an eccentric who lived a hermit's life in the woods and mountains near the town of St. Joe. He was well known to area residents, for when he would come into town occasionally to purchase provisions he always paid in silver ore. When asked about the origin of the silver Tabor would cackle, and his tall and skinny frame would go into an awkward dance while he teased the locals that they would never be able to find his mine. Several of them tried to follow him back into the hills where he lived, but he always managed to elude the trackers.

Near the end of 1865, Tabor was no longer seen around St. Joe, and as he was quite elderly, it was assumed he had met his end alone in the remote wilds of the Ozark Mountains. Now and then people would venture into the Tomahawk Creek region in search of his mine but no one ever claimed to have found it. The search continued off and on for nearly fifty years but eventually the story of eccentric old Tabor and his lost silver mine was forgotten.

Hulce Taylor owned some land along Tomahawk Creek and managed to earn a respectable living by farming the bottoms and raising some cattle. One morning in 1924, Taylor took his young daughter with him and set out in search of two cows that had evidently strayed from the main herd. As they walked alongside a stretch of Tomahawk Creek they had never visited before, they came upon an entrance to what was apparently a long-deserted mine shaft. The mine had been concealed by thick overhanging vines which had recently been torn away as a result of a storm that had ravaged the valley a few days earlier.

The shaft was described as having a rich outcrop of silver ore but that is as far as the story goes. No record exists that Taylor had ever attempted to reopen the mine, and its location has long since been forgotten. Taylor's descendants have been unable to provide any information.

From the geographic location and description of the mine Taylor happened upon, it is likely the Lost Tabor Mine. Whatever may be, it has apparently been lost again and, in spite of several organized attempts to relocate it, remains lost.

Tobe Inmon's Silver Bullets

During the last two decades of the nineteenth century, historical records show significant westward migration from the states of Kentucky, Tennessee, Virginia, and Alabama. Many of the migrants made it as far west as the rich agricultural and mining areas of California, but many got no farther than the Arkansas Ozarks where the promise of good land lured them. Each person had reasons for leaving home—a sense of adventure, the potential of wealth in the California gold fields, or simply seeking a better way of life. Many who settled in the Ozark Mountains during that time had been run out of their home states, shunned and even persecuted by cliquish neighbors, and often called "poor white trash." Most of those chased out were poor and uneducated, used to scraping out a meager living from the land and subsisting on very little.

Tobe Inmon was a resident of one poor little valley in western Kentucky. He managed to eke out an existence by growing corn on a rocky hillside and raising a few hogs and chickens in the bottoms. Inmon and his family did not get along well with their neighbors, and he earned a reputation of being a recluse, neither needing nor wanting the company of others.

Inmon was accused of stealing a neighbor's livestock, and amid threats to his life he packed his few possessions, loaded his wife and two young boys onto a wagon, and left Kentucky. They headed west, driving their hogs ahead of them.

After an arduous journey over country that offered little but mud, swamps, and misery, they arrived at Moccasin Creek Valley in Pope County, Arkansas. Inmon came into the valley as a result of having gotten lost, but he took an immediate liking to what he found. The valley was rather narrow with a good running stream in the bottom and just enough floodplain for planting corn. There appeared to be good forage for his hogs and abundant timber for a cabin and firewood. It was also very remote, with the nearest neighbors living over two miles away.

Having decided that setting up a residence here was more appealing than continuing the tiring journey, Inmon went about the task of constructing a one-room log cabin and some pens for his livestock. When he had time he planted some corn on the flat area near the creek.

The nearest settlement of any importance was the town of Dover, located some twelve miles south of Inmon's Moccasin Creek cabin. It was an important stop along the old road to Fort Smith. Occasionally Inmon would haul some chickens or a hog into Dover to trade for staples like flour, sugar, and coffee.

The citizens of Dover considered Inmon a bit of a curious figure. He rarely spoke to them except to conduct what little business he had, and when he did speak he was quite surly. He preferred to conclude his business and leave town as soon as possible, never lingering nor seeking social contact. Inmon always dressed in little more than rags and always appeared unclean, and on the few occasions he brought his family into town, they too were in a most wretched and ragged condition. Those who chanced by Inmon's cabin remarked at the squalor in which the family lived, claiming the cabin had large open spaces in the chinks and appeared to offer little more shelter than the hog pen.

One day during the autumn of 1903, Inmon rode into Dover and asked for a doctor. His youngest son had fever and was unconscious. Inmon was directed to Dr. Benjamin Martin, the only doctor in town, who agreed to follow him out to his Moccasin Creek residence.

Dr. Martin was an affable man in his late forties, was well-liked by the community, and had delivered virtually every child under ten in the town of Dover and the surrounding area.

The doctor remained with the Inmon family for two days and nights treating the youngster and hovering by his bedside the entire time. Eventually the fever broke and the child was out of danger.

As Dr. Martin was preparing his horse and carriage for the return trip to Dover, Inmon appeared from around one corner of the cabin and asked the doctor about the fee. Dr. Martin, aware of the man's poverty, merely told him he could settle up sometime in the future when times got better and not to worry about it until then. But Inmon was insistent, and finally offered the doctor a small canvas sack containing perhaps thirty to forty bullets for a large caliber rifle.

During this time bullets were very difficult to obtain and most people were glad to get them when they could. Dr. Martin examined the bullets and found them to be well made, and as he was an enthusiastic hunter and sportsman, he accepted them gratefully as payment.

As the doctor packed the little sack of shells away in the carriage, Inmon explained that he had made them himself with lead he had extracted from an "old mine back in the hills not too far from the cabin." Dr. Martin thanked him again, climbed into his carriage, and returned to Dover.

On arriving at his home, Dr. Martin placed the sack of bullets on a shelf in his study, intending to use them on his next deer hunt. Over the next few weeks, however, he stayed busy treating the sick and delivering babies and as a result his autumn deer hunt had to be postponed. Time passed and he gradually forgot about the little sack of bullets lying on the shelf of his bookcase.

A full two years passed before the doctor remembered the bullets. While readying his equipment for a deer hunt, he located the sack of shells on the shelf and placed them on the desk in his study so he would not forget to take them the next morning. That evening, while reading at his desk, the doctor picked up one of the shells and turned it over and over in his fingers. Presently he scratched the tip of the bullet, attempting to pick off some of the black residue. As some of the surface coating was removed, he noticed the lead had a peculiar color to it.

On a hunch the doctor postponed his hunt and instead made arrangements to visit Russellville, a larger settlement a few miles south of Dover. Once in Russellville, he took the bullets to a friend knowledgeable about minerals and, to his astonishment, discovered them to be composed of pure silver! He sold the little sack of shells for seventy-two dollars.

On returning to Dover that evening, Dr. Martin made plans to leave for the Inmon homestead the next day to try to convince the poor farmer to show him where his so-called lead mine was located.

The next morning he flogged his poor horse the entire trip as his carriage bounced over the seldom-used road to Moccasin Creek Valley. When he arrived at the Inmon home he found it deserted;

the site had apparently been unoccupied for months. When he asked the nearest neighbor about the Inmons, he was told they had packed up and left for Texas six months earlier. No one knew exactly where in Texas they had gone.

By what little light was left in the day, Dr. Martin climbed the low hill just behind the Inmon cabin and wandered through the woods, inspecting every rock and outcrop he encountered for any evidence of mining. He searched excitedly until darkness prevented him from continuing and he finally had to return to Dover.

The next morning, however, Dr. Martin was busily outfitting himself with camping gear and provisions for an extended stay at Moccasin Creek Valley. This time he stayed for two and a half weeks, living in the deserted ramshackle cabin and exploring the hills and woods in search of the lost silver mine. After exhausting his food supply, he was forced to make the trip back to Dover, but there he immediately started planning an even more extended search.

Time and again the doctor returned to the valley in search of Tobe Inmon's mine, and each time he was disappointed. Weeks and months of searching turned into years, and over time Dr. Martin's patients found another doctor to treat them.

Eventually Dr. Martin ran out of money and had to sell his home and his practice in order to finance his continuing search for the silver. It had become his all-consuming passion, and many people in Dover believed it drove him insane.

Finally broke, broken, and disheartened, Dr. Martin moved in with a sister living in Russellville. His health deteriorated in a very short time and he died as a result of complications from pneumonia.

On learning of the story of Tobe Inmon's silver bullets, several Dover residents took up the search, and during the years following Dr. Martin's death many treasure hunters combed the hills and valleys of the Ozark Mountains around Moccasin Creek Valley looking for the source of the ore. Several ancient tools were found which were later identified as being of Spanish origin, thus giving rise to the belief that the early Spanish explorers in Arkansas had been actively involved in mining this region. But aside from the tools nothing else was found.

Could it be that Tobe Inmon had stumbled onto an abandoned Spanish silver mine? It is likely that this was the case. Poor Tobe— with all his poverty he likely had his hands on a fortune in silver and did not recognize it for what it was. And poor Dr. Martin, who did recognize it for what it was but could never locate the source of the wealth.

In the summer of 1951, a Cherokee Indian named Lawrence Mankiller brought a large nugget into Fort Smith where it was identified as a piece of high-grade silver. Mankiller stated he had found the nugget in the opening of an old mine shaft while deer hunting in Moccasin Creek Valley. He related how it had started to rain and he sought shelter in the opening to wait out the shower. While seated at the entrance of the shaft he began to poke through the rubble on the floor and retrieved the nugget.

Mankiller received an offer of several hundred dollars from a group of men who wanted him to lead them back to the mine. He pocketed the money and agreed to take them the next morning. That night, however, Lawrence Mankiller disappeared and was never seen again.

Piney Page, the late Ozark folklorist, was raised in and around the Moccasin Creek Valley. He related the story of a relative who, while plowing a corn field on the floodplain in the bottoms where Moccasin Creek joins Shop Creek, paused in his labors to take a drink from the cool clear water. While young Grover Page was lying on his stomach sipping the creek water, he spied an object on the bottom that was considerably different from the rest of the rocks. On retrieving it, he discovered it was a quarter-sized silver nugget. The Page family had the nugget assayed and, on the encouragement of the evaluation, began to explore the creek area for the source of the ore. Some distance up the narrow valley through which runs Shop Creek, a thin seam of silver and lead was discovered on a west-facing outcrop. The Pages invested in some mining equipment and proceeded to blast and drill the rock. Considerable effort was expended and initially a large amount of silver was extracted, Page recalls, but the seam was soon lost. The Pages continued to work the small mine intermittently over the next six years but the return was discouraging and they ultimately turned their attention back to farming.

A local man who lives near Moccasin Creek Valley has claimed that on dark overcast nights associated with a waning moon, strange lights appear on the ridges adjacent to the valley. He described the lights as "dancing along the ridge crests." Mexicans and Indians have long believed that mysterious lights such as these often appear above pockets of gold and silver, and to them the lights represent spirits of the dead whose mission is to guard the ore and protect it from those who are not worthy. Also, in their view, anyone who removes the ore for selfish profit will be cursed. If one believes such folklore then the presence of dancing lights in Moccasin Creek Valley may indicate that the silver is still there, protected by the spirits. But it still evades discovery, just as it did in Dr. Martin's day, over seventy-five years ago.

Perhaps someday the spirits will decide to relinquish their hold on the silver treasure that lies in these hills, and will smile upon the searcher who stumbles onto Tobe Inmon's mine.

The Mystery
of the Turtle Rock

Piney Page was the source of another tale of lost treasure in Pope County. Growing up in the rural part of county, Page heard many stories about lost and buried Spanish gold and silver in the area of Piney Creek between Pilot Rock Mountain and Ford Mountain, but the one that fascinated him most was the one told by an uncle about the mysterious turtle rock.

Around 1910, as Page recalled it, an old-timer named Mose Freeman went out to gather his corn crop from the floodplain of the Big Piney Creek where it makes a horseshoe bend between the two mountains. When he arrived, he noticed two men had camped in the wooded area next to his field. After he got the better part of his crop in, Mose decided to go visit the two men and see what news they might have from the big settlements to the south. Visitors were scarce in this valley and Mose always looked forward to having company.

But as Mose regarded the two men, he determined that they were acting suspicious and seemed to be trying to stay out of his sight. He described one of them as being a short and mean-looking half-breed with a scar that traversed the entire length of his face and the other as a tall, gangly fellow who seemed to take orders from the short one.

Presently the two men came out of the woods and furtively approached Mose, saying they wanted to ask him some questions. They wanted to know if he knew of the existence of any old carvings of snakes or turtles on exposed rocks in the area.

Mose allowed as how he had never seen anything such as they described and went on gathering his corn. The men soon disappeared back into the woods.

One morning a few days later, the two strangers were seen leaving the vicinity riding in a wagon piled high with camping gear and pulled by two sickly-looking horses. The men seemed to be in a hurry and acted nervous if anyone approached. Both were armed with rifles which they displayed aggressively if anyone ventured too close to the wagon.

The day after their departure, Mose Freeman and one of his sons went down to the deserted camp in the woods to look around. The camp was a poor one and they saw nothing of any significance. Out in the woods a short distance from the camp, however, Mose discovered several holes that had been dug around a large beech tree. The tree had the weathered figure of a snake carved into the trunk, head pointed downward. History records that the Spaniards used images of snakes and turtles to indicate the locations of buried wealth. The head of the snake supposedly always pointed to the treasure.

About twenty paces north of the old beech tree, Mose found a large rock that looked as if it had recently been dug up, turned over, and then set back down in its original location. With the help of his son and some poles they used as levers, Mose turned the rock back over. On the newly exposed side was a large carved image of a turtle! The rock was laid over a freshly excavated hole about two feet deep, and in one corner of the excavation they found a pot-sized hole from which a container had evidently been removed. Whatever the two strangers had unearthed during their search will probably never be known because they were never seen in Pope County again.

Talk of turtles carved on limestone slabs and associated buried treasure is heard often in the area, and several old-timers recall having seen such a carving at one time or another, but it was before they knew what the symbols meant.

In 1976 a geology professor associated with a small college in Missouri was conducting a field studies class in the Ozark foothills. He and his students spent several days in Pope County examining the unique stratigraphy of the Ozark limestone and collecting fossil specimens. The students were required to record their observations in a field journal and to keep a photographic record as well. After eight days in the field, one of which was in the Big Piney Creek area, the professor and his class returned to Missouri.

While the professor was in his office one afternoon going over the materials turned in by the students, one particular photograph caught his eye. The young woman who had submitted the materials he was examining had included a picture of a large limestone slab, on the top of which the dim outline of a turtle could be seen! The only visible landmark in the photograph was an adjacent oak tree that appeared to be of great age.

The professor had heard many stories of buried treasures in the Pope County Ozarks and he became quite excited about the photograph. When he contacted the student, however, she could not remember the exact location of the rock.

The professor has returned to this same area with other classes several times since the photograph was made, but so far he has been unable to locate the turtle rock. The search goes on.

Norristown Mountain Silver

Not far from Russellville near the Arkansas River lies Norristown Mountain. For years the mountain was a major landmark in the area, overlooking homesteads along the prairie that extended from its base to the tavern set just above the old steamboat landing on the river.

Many generations before the arrival of the whites, a tribe of Osage Indians who inhabited the area considered the mountain sacred. It has been written that the largest Indian burial ground in the state of Arkansas lies at the foot of Norristown Mountain and extends for many miles along the river.

As white settlers moved onto and around the mountain, attracted by an abundance of rich farmland and access to river transportation, the Osage were gradually pushed out. Many were resettled in Oklahoma, then known as Indian Territory. While they chose not to confront the white settlers in armed battle for the precious lands, the Indians did send a delegation from their tribe to Washington, D.C., to negotiate for the ownership of the mountain and the strip of land that was their burial ground. Their request was granted, and the property in question remained in their possession for nearly one hundred years. As the older members of the tribe died off and the younger ones sought their fortunes elsewhere, only very few remained to live near the mountain. Today only a handful of those who live nearby are descendants of the original inhabitants. Each year for many years, however, several dozens of the descendants of the original inhabitants journeyed from Oklahoma to the mountain, remained a few weeks in celebration, and then departed.

As time went by, the entire area was eventually purchased by

Peter Lovely. Lovely was a friendly man, who got along very well with the few Indians remaining in the vicinity, and he and his wife freely granted them permission to continue to use the sacred mountain for their gatherings and celebrations. From time to time the Indians would visit the Lovely residence and present Mrs. Lovely with beautiful hand-crafted silver ornaments. When she inquired as to the origin of the silver from which the gifts were made, the Indians always pointed toward the mountain.

One afternoon as Mrs. Lovely walked along the bank of the Arkansas River, she witnessed the burial ceremony of an aged Indian who at one time had been a prominent leader of the tribe. The ceremony was rather elaborate and lasted for nearly two hours. Just prior to filling the grave with dirt, the Indians, one by one, walked by the grave and dropped in offerings. In each case the offering consisted of hand-made silver jewelry much like that received by Mrs. Lovely. When they had finished, Mrs. Lovely estimated that they had deposited half a bushel of silver.

After the burial, Mrs. Lovely engaged an elderly squaw in conversation. The old woman told her what a great chief the old man had been and how Indians had come from hundreds of miles away to participate in the burial ceremony. When Mrs. Lovely remarked at what must have been a fortune in silver lying in the grave, the old squaw told her that it had come from the old mine on the mountain. "If the white man knew what was in the sacred mountain," she said, "his horses would all be shod with silver shoes."

Word eventually spread about the possibility of a silver mine on Norristown Mountain, and for years a great deal of prospecting and digging took place. It was said that the Indians had taken elaborate precautions to conceal their mine, and to this day there are reportedly only two or three Indians who know its exact location. To date, however, the only rock of any value officially associated with the mountain is a thin seam of coal.

In 1926 there arrived in Russellville a man identified as a "half-breed Spanish prospector." The man was observed for several days searching the area of the old burial ground. From time to time he would consult an aged map he carried with him. Following several days of searching, he employed two men from town to do some digging. He led them, along with a mule carrying shovels and a crate, to the burial ground during the dark of night and instructed them to dig in a preselected spot. Working under the dim light of a lantern, the two men had to dig several holes before they unearthed a shovelful of silver artifacts.

The half-breed and the workers removed all the silver and placed it in the crate. Once the crate was loaded onto the mule the man instructed the two diggers not to reveal to anyone the events that had taken place that night, and promised he would return the next day with a large reward for their efforts. Several days passed and the half-breed did not return. The two men became upset at not receiving their promised reward and told the story to others.

One man who has lived in the area for many years and claims to be a professional dowser related how he had dowsed for and found several small chunks of silver on the mountain. He believes the little pieces of silver he has picked up were part of the residue of mine tailings that the Indians scattered around the mountain-top as they tried to conceal evidence of mining activity. The old man is currently using his dowsing skills to try to locate the main vein of ore from which the small nuggets came. No one has actually seen the silver nuggets he claims to have found, but since he has been dowsing on the mountain for the past twelve years, he has been able to afford a forty-acre tract of land near Conway, and he has gotten a new pickup truck each year for the past four years. These purchases have been made with cash.

The Osage say that the silver will never be found by one who wishes to profit from it and that it can be removed only by one who will use it for the good of the people. They say the time will come in the far distant future when the silver will be needed, but until then it is not to be found.

The Lost Mine
of the Cossatot

In southwestern Arkansas the moody Cossatot River flows out of the Ouachita Mountains onto the level plain where it eventually joins the Little River. During the past several thousand years the Cossatot (named from an Indian word that means "skull-crusher") has relentlessly carved its way down through the soft sandstone cap of the Ouachitas, now and then exposing rock reminiscent of a bygone era when volcanic activity dominated both above and below ground. It was during one of these ancient volcanic episodes that seams of gold formed in the masses of igneous rock far beneath the surface. Then followed a period where this environment became submerged beneath a shallow sea and thick layers of sandstone strata were deposited. Eventually the sea retreated and the Ouachita Mountains were squeezed and folded upward to altitudes some investigators claim rivaled the highest peaks of the Rocky Mountains. Numerous streams like the Cossatot flowed from the upper reaches of the Ouachitas down to the lower levels of the Gulf Coastal Plain. In Sevier County, Arkansas, the Cossatot eroded away enough sandstone from one area to expose some volcanic rock and an accompanying seam of gold. This seam was apparently discovered by Spanish explorers under De Soto and extensively mined. Since that time, the gold mine of the Cossatot has lived on in fact as well as legend.

During the mid-nineteenth century, Dr. Ferdinand Smith brought his family from Frankford, Missouri, to the rugged, sparsely settled country in Sevier County along the Cossatot River. The reasons for his move have never been clear, but some have suggested he was run out of Missouri as a result of the mysterious deaths of some of his patients. Others said he merely wanted to acquire some land for farming and found what he wanted in southeastern Arkansas. Whatever the reason for the move, Dr. Smith was welcomed in Sevier County, where up until that time there had never been a doctor. He became instantly popular in the settlements along the river, making himself available to sick and injured people who more often than not paid their bills with eggs, livestock, and garden produce.

Dr. Smith also had an interest in local history, wherever he lived, and he found the residents of Sevier County more than willing to talk to him about the region's past. In this manner he heard the fascinating story of a lost gold mine located upstream on the Cossatot that was linked to the mysterious appearance of a blond woman in the company of Indians who frequented the region. Years later, Dr. Smith related the story as he had pieced it together from the older Choctaw Indians who had settled the Cossatot area.

Many years prior to the arrival of the Choctaws in Arkansas, a trading post had been established at a site now known as Lockesburg. The trading post stocked a good supply of food, tools, and clothing which was sold or traded for hides. The post served mainly the hunters and trappers and a few farmers who frequented the locale. About once a month, a blond, fair-skinned woman appeared at the trading post accompanied by three or four young Indian braves. She was described as being clothed in garments of leather and adorned with gold jewelry of rustic design. She always rode in on a splendid white horse with the Indians following behind on foot. It was apparent that the Indians were subservient to her, as they always responded to her commands without hesitation. On these visits she would buy basic foodstuffs and mining tools, which she paid for with gold nuggets. The gold was of a remarkably high quality and had obviously been mined. On the few occasions the woman spoke it was in Spanish with a heavy Castilian dialect. When asked where she had gotten the gold she always refused to answer, and her Indian companions also remained mute to the question. Many attempts were made to follow her after her visits to the trading post, but she always managed to elude her trackers.

Once in a while someone would meet her and her companions returning from the trading post along a trail that has since become the old Fort Towson Road. Following one trip from the store, she was seen entering Pig Pen Bottoms, a briery, snake-infested part of the floodplain of the Cossatot River. The observer told others at the trading post what he had seen, and a small expedition was formed to go into the bottoms in search of the mysterious blond. The party had trouble finding a passage into the forbidding area. Once inside they immediately became lost. They wandered for hours before finally finding a way out, and returned to the trading post around one o'clock in the morning, exhausted, scratched, and unsuccessful. This incident apparently put the woman on guard, for she was never seen again and there exists no record of what became of her.

Dr. Smith eventually purchased a parcel of land just south of Rolling Shoals Ford on the Cossatot. Pig Pen Bottoms was located between the ford and Dr. Smith's farm, and a large dense thicket of greenbrier extended from the bottoms onto his property. Some men were hired to clear the area so it could be placed into production. When the tangle of brush had finally been removed, a very old mine shaft was discovered in an outcrop of rock. The shaft was nearly vertical and, judging from the huge piles of excavated rock lying around the opening, had been extensively worked. Down in the shaft there were several ancient and rotting timber supports. Dr. Smith's workers tried several times to explore the old shaft, but it was nearly filled with water and passage was impossible.

Older residents of this area have no recollection of any mining whatsoever taking place in the bottoms, but history records that Spanish explorers under De Soto visited this region of the Ouachita Mountains in search of gold and silver, and though it has never been documented many people believe the Spanish mined gold from this area and shipped it back to Spain.

For years the shaft remained inaccessible to those who longed to explore its depths and retrieve any riches that awaited. During a severe drought in the early 1920s, the Cossatot River dried up to a mere trickle and the water table throughout southwestern Arkansas dropped. The water in the shaft of the old mine receded considerably and a group decided to attempt an entry.

Using ropes, two men carrying shovels and lanterns were lowered into the shaft. As far down the passageway as they could explore, they observed rotting timbers that served as mine supports. Undoubtedly, considerable work had gone into the excavation of the shaft. Farther down, when they had descended nearly one hundred feet, the men ran into water and had to turn back. When he was hauled out of the shaft, one of the men displayed a tool, a heavy hammer, which he found lodged between the wall of the shaft and a support timber. It was later identified as having been cast in the town of Seville in southwestern Spain, thus providing more evidence of Spanish mining activity in the region.

The deeper recesses of the shaft went unexplored until another drought occurred in early 1927. The water table was even lower than it had been during the earlier drought, and a group of boys familiar with the story of the lost mine made a descent into the shaft. This time there was no water in the bottom of the old mine to stop them, and after going well over 120 feet into the mine they encountered a deep layer of sediment that had been deposited at the bottom, undoubtedly carried into the opening by flood waters from previous years.

For several days the boys, occasionally aided by their fathers, removed many buckets full of the sand and silt deposit. As the work proceeded, the diggers noticed that the passageway was growing narrower, suggesting that the end was near. By this time they had excavated several tons of dirt and had found several more ancient mining tools, each bearing the mark of Spanish origin. But as their optimism grew, rain began to fall. The excavation was halted while the diggers went home to wait out the rain. Luck was not with them, however, for the rains were the beginning of a series of severe thunderstorms that struck most of the state of Arkansas that year and gave rise to the Great Flood of 1927, which placed much of the state under water. The Cossatot rose and overflowed its banks, spilling over the vast floodplain on which the mine was located. The river raged, carrying its heavy burden of silt and sand, and after many days of flooding the waters finally receded once again into the channel. But for many miles along the Cossatot the floodplain of the river had received a new deposit of the sediment which is so highly valued by farmers. This same valuable silt had completely covered the ancient mine shaft. All traces of the shaft were obliterated, and it was only after several years of searching that the opening was rediscovered: it was finally located under four feet of the alluvial deposit.

Though several parties tried to reexcavate the sediment-filled shaft, none was successful. Water was a constant problem: no sooner would some progress be made in unplugging the shaft than the spring rains would bring more flood waters and it would fill up again.

Several of the residents of Gillham, Arkansas, claim to know where the shaft is located but very few are concerned about renewing excavation operations. They have seen or heard too much about past failures. They also speak freely of the power of the river and claim that, because of the unpredictability of the Cossatot, no one will ever penetrate into the depths of the old mine. The gold, if it exists, is still buried under tons of river silt.

Golden City, Arkansas

The summer of 1886 was the driest in the memory of the old-time residents of western Arkansas. Creeks dried up, and the water table dropped to a point where existing wells no longer provided badly needed moisture for livestock. In Brushy Creek Valley in southern Logan County, about forty miles southeast of Fort Smith, the situation was particularly desperate. John Redman was trying to run a few head of cattle and operate a small sawmill but could not obtain enough water to do either effectively. This narrow valley, located in the northern part of the Ouachita Mountains, had a plentiful supply of timber and good meadows for grazing livestock, but the drought was beginning to take its toll. Redman contracted with a local man, Raymond Brigance, to blast a deeper well through the sandstone strata on Redman's property. While Redman and Brigance were cleaning debris out of the newly excavated well, they discovered what they believed to be particles of gold in a quartz vein that had been torn loose from a deep pocket of granite. Samples of the ore were shipped the next day to Little Rock for assay, and the report confirmed Redman's earlier guess: the rock contained a high grade of gold.

About a week after the gold discovery was confirmed, a dapper man named Dr. Guy Lewis arrived in the Brushy Creek Valley seeking an audience with Redman. Lewis identified himself as a geologist, originally from Oregon, and a professional gold miner. Within a week after his arrival, machinery was being erected at the site of Redman's mill preparatory to deepening and widening the shaft. In the search for more gold, this shaft was eventually to reach one hundred feet into the earth.

The news of gold in Logan County spread rapidly throughout

the state and country, and soon fortune hunters were making their way into the little valley by the dozens. Miners, geologists, mining engineers, and laborers arrived from Colorado, California, Utah, Nevada, Ohio, New Jersey, and Missouri. Many miners abandoned the rich gold fields of California to try their luck in the newly opened Arkansas opportunity. Following the influx of miners was the usual assortment of lawyers, land speculators, saloon operators, and prostitutes. Almost overnight, scores of houses and stores were built. The sixteen-room Bartley Hotel became a meeting place for lawyers and real estate moguls where thousands of dollars were exchanged each night in land transactions. No less than three mercantile stores were established, and in a matter of weeks a post office was authorized. At Dr. Lewis's suggestion, the new town was named "Golden City."

Around Redman's mill, where a month earlier there had only been a few small farms, the population swelled to around five hundred. A town picnic was held to celebrate the new prosperity, and people were invited from all over western Arkansas. It was estimated that eight thousand people filled the valley for the festivities.

Growth, prosperity, and new-found wealth seemed to be the order of the day; surely Golden City was to be an important commercial center. The population continued to swell, money continued to flow, and more and more shafts were sunk into the ground. Lewis, Redman, and a young lawyer named Oscar Miles from nearby Booneville were quietly busy buying up land and leases from one end of the valley to the other. Lewis was the first to get involved in the land speculation activity, having started almost as soon as he arrived for his visit with Redman. Then he hired Miles to handle the legal end of the business. The Redman-Lewis-Miles consortium now controlled over ninety percent of the land in the valley. As the town developed, Lewis saw to it that a new church and school were built and even formed a literary society. He was very interested in making Golden City attractive to potential citizens and investors. Telephone lines were installed and a railroad company surveyed a route from Golden City to Fort Smith. Several real estate offices appeared and dozens of lawyers hung out their shingles. Many prominent geologists and mining engineers came to Golden City to offer their expertise for a price. Among them were Charles Whitney from Colorado, Charles Samuels from New Jersey, and Colonel A.J. McDonald of the Emily Mining Company of New York. Each week saw another shaft drilled and tons of rock shipped out for processing. All the shafts were sunk on property either owned or controlled by Lewis, Redman, and Miles.

One day when the mining boom had been going on for nearly a year, two men in expensive suits arrived at the home of Oscar Miles in Booneville. They approached the young lawyer, who was napping in a hammock, and identified themselves as attorneys representing a St. Louis–based land company that was interested in purchasing some land in and around Golden City, and wanted to offer $250,000 for the Lewis-Redman-Miles holdings. Without even bothering to rise from his hammock, Miles refused the bid, stating flatly that the lands in question were worth well over a million dollars. He bade the men good day and resumed his nap. For the rest of his life, Miles was to regret his decision.

The next morning the news broke that the Redman gold mine was a hoax. Earlier in the week, Redman and Lewis had gone out of state to sell some leases and left a man named Bill Carroll to guard the mines and the property. On the evening before the two St. Louis lawyers visited Miles, Carroll had gotten drunk and told listeners that on two occasions he had watched Lewis and Redman plant gold-bearing quartz in the shafts. He further stated that the gold used in the salting had been brought to Arkansas two years earlier by Redman's son, who had been to Colorado on a prospecting trip. A hasty investigation determined that Carroll's charge of salting was probably accurate.

On returning to Golden City the next week, Lewis and Redman heard the accusations against them. Angered, they collected several henchmen, rode out to Carroll's residence, and called him out. Carroll refused to leave his house, so the gang broke in and dragged him out into the yard amid the screaming and crying of his wife and children. They tied Carroll to a horse and led him into the woods to hang him. As Carroll was being strung up, several members of the mob began to discuss the potential consequences of their action should they get caught. Afraid of what might be in store for them, the gang broke up and left Carroll in the woods, shaken but alive. Redman and Lewis disappeared from the area forever. Redman was never heard from again, and Lewis reportedly died a natural death in Cripple Creek, Colorado, in 1908.

As news of the salting spread throughout the valley, most of the miners drifted away and back to the productive gold fields of the west. Merchants likewise disposed of their goods, boarded up their shops, and moved on. Within weeks, Golden City became a ghost town of empty streets, houses, and stores.

Today there is virtually no evidence that Golden City was a bustling and energetic mining capital of the state. A few farms dot the valley of Brushy Creek and cattle are seen contentedly grazing the hillsides and creek bottoms, but the mine shafts have been filled in and not a single one of the original buildings remains.

To this day controversy surrounds this episode in the history of frontier Arkansas. It is still not clear who the real culprits were in the Golden City scheme. Some researchers claim Redman, Lewis, and Miles were all ignorant of the salting which they attribute to Redman's son. Some say that Lewis, Redman, and Redman's son conspired to make a fortune by buying and selling land in a "wealthy gold-producing area." Still others say that Lewis was duped by Redman. However, the majority opinion is that Lewis masterminded the entire scheme and was willingly aided by Redman. Reports surfaced that Lewis, a noted geologist of that time, may have doctored the original assay reports, making it seem as though the mine was producing fantastic quantities of gold. The only definite fact is that both Lewis and Redman each made a neat fortune relative to their land speculation activities. It would therefore be logical to assume the two men knowingly entered into a conspiracy to defraud potential buyers of lands and leases. Redman's son was most certainly an accomplice.

Virtually everyone familiar with the Golden City story agrees that Oscar Miles was an innocent participant who was lured into a get-rich-quick scheme concocted by Lewis and Redman. He remained in Booneville and lived out his life in the area, the frequent target of good-natured kidding by his neighbors for his gullibility in being taken in by the fraud. Over the years, however, Miles regained his credibility and went on to become a successful lawyer in western Arkansas.

But the story does not end here. Some people still maintain that the Golden City episode was not a hoax at all, and that in fact gold is still to be found in the quartz and granite outcrops beneath the crumbling sandstone layers in Brushy Creek Valley. Two reputable mining engineers ventured the opinion in 1986 that Redman actually did find gold, but that the existing technology of one hundred years ago was incapable of retrieving enough of it to make it pay. The engineers claimed to have discovered some gold nuggets in the area and say they intend to enlist backers to finance a reopening of the Redman shaft.

There is evidence, then, to suggest there may still be some potential for gold existing in Brushy Creek Valley. The year 1986 marked the centennial of Golden City, now a ghost town, and the event passed quietly and unnoticed. It remains to be seen if renewed speculation will generate a rebirth of the glory days when the specter of wealth made Golden City the promised land of western Arkansas.

The Lost Soldier's Bluff

During the Civil War, a company of Confederate cavalry troops was on its way to meet another company at the little community of Sugar Grove, Arkansas, some few miles to the east. They were leisurely picking their way through a small valley bordered by the low rolling sandstone folds of the Ouachita Mountains. Brushy Creek Valley supported a few farmers who grazed their cattle in the creek bottoms and meadows; the hillsides provided abundant timber for a small sawmill operation.

As they rode, one of the soldiers, a Corporal Henry Fletcher, became ill and dropped back, telling his companions he would join them after a short rest. Fletcher sought the shade of a nearby low sandstone bluff from which issued a dripping spring. He unsaddled his horse and staked it out to graze and then walked over to the spring to slake his thirst. While he was drinking, his eye was attracted to a glint of golden color in a quartz vein that was running through an outcrop of granite. The quartz was quite brittle, and Fletcher hammered some of it loose with the butt of his pistol and placed it in his knapsack. After resting awhile, he resaddled and caught up with his companions at Sugar Grove, telling them nothing about his discovery.

Several weeks later, Fletcher had an opportunity to visit Fort Smith, Arkansas, with his regiment, and while there he took his mineral-laden piece of quartz to have it assayed. It turned out to contain a high grade of gold ore.

Because of his commitment to the Confederate Army, Fletcher was unable to return to Brushy Creek Valley for nearly a year and a half. When he was finally mustered out of the military, he outfitted himself with some mining tools and two mules and returned to the valley in search of the sandstone bluff from which he removed the gold.

On arriving in the valley, Fletcher became confused. He had difficulty remembering the landmarks, and a recent flood had changed the appearance of the valley floor. In addition, some timbering by the valley residents had laid bare portions of the hillsides. Disoriented, Fletcher nevertheless undertook his search for the bluff that contained the gold-bearing quartz. Three weeks of searching yielded nothing and exhausted his already meager resources. Fletcher returned to Fort Smith to get a new grubstake in order to resume his quest, but each expedition met with failure.

Years passed, with Fletcher continually on his search. By now the story of Fletcher's lost bluff with its vein of gold was widely known throughout western Arkansas, and he would sometimes encounter other treasure seekers roaming the valley. Gradually his health deteriorated, and when he contracted pneumonia he was hospitalized in Fort Smith. After several months of illness he died, insisting until the very end that his story about the lost bluff was true.

It was just a few years following the death of Henry Fletcher that gold was reported discovered at Redman's Mill in Brushy Creek Valley.

A local farmer who still lives in the valley has talked with several of those who still continue to search for the Lost Soldier's Bluff and is well acquainted with the story. He also claims to know where the bluff is located. He says that although he has dug gold ore out of the quartz matrix on several occasions, there is not enough there to make large-scale mining operations profitable. He is also very concerned that renewed mining activity in the valley would disrupt the farming and ranching activities of his neighbors. He remembers the stories of the Golden City episode and does not wish to see a repetition of it.

Henry Fletcher spent most of his adult life hunting the gold he believed to exist in Brushy Creek Valley, and many others have invested time and resources in the search. Renewed interest in the geology and ore-bearing potential of this part of the Ouachita Mountains is exciting contemporary prospectors. Will they be successful? Or will their search merely add to the growing legend of the Lost Soldier's Bluff?

Spanish Silver
in Benton County

In Benton County, Arkansas, there is a cave associated with a fascinating legend of hidden gold. It lies between the towns of Gravette and Sulphur Springs near the Arkansas-Missouri border. Oldtimers in the area remember it as Black Cave, but it is advertised as "The Spanish Treasure Cave" on faded and peeling billboards along the highway—reminders of an unsuccessful attempt to make a tourist attraction out of the legendary site. Rarely visited by travelers, the cave was once the focus of attention of most of the residents of Benton County.

As history has it, some representatives of the Spanish army made exploratory forays from deep in Mexico across Texas and into the Oklahoma-Missouri-Arkansas border area. The Spaniards robbed and pillaged all along the way, and though the region between Mexico and the Ozarks was sparsely populated at the time, they eventually amassed a small fortune in gold. By the time they arrived in what is now Benton County it was deep into winter, and when a storm came up the party of nineteen soldiers sought shelter in one of the many limestone caves in the area.

One particular cave was ideal in that it opened onto an area that provided abundant firewood. There the Spaniards were content to wait out the weather as long as necessary. While they remained close to the mouth of the cave, which was only about six to seven feet high, they noticed that the cave ran deep into the mountainside and the light from their modest campfire was not able to penetrate its depths.

But trouble awaited them outside. Local Indians had been stalking them for several days, apparently because they believed the soldiers had stolen one of their women. Intent on revenge, the Indians spotted the smoke from the Spaniards' fire venting from a small sinkhole. The next morning they launched a ferocious attack. It is believed that all the Spaniards were killed, but before they were wiped out they carried their stolen gold deep into one of the corridors of the cave and concealed it.

Nothing more was heard of this incident until early in the autumn of 1885. An old Spanish gentleman arrived in the area around Sulphur Springs carrying three ancient parchment maps, all with intricate directions on how to reach the cave. He was precise and mannerly in his dealings with the Benton County citizens, and while his command of English was poor, he managed to communicate his need to locate a specific cave.

Two men, one named Callister and the other named John Harwick, took the old man out into the woods over a period of several days to search for the cave, but they seemed to have no luck in locating it. Eventually the old man was able to make the two men understand that this cave would be covered with a rock that had the image of a deer hoof carved into it. After several more days of searching and talking to residents, they located a family named Wetzel who were aware of such a rock. Rufus Wetzel and his wife and family of nine children lived in a log cabin in a remote part of the woods outside Gravette. Rufus Wetzel was not inclined to show the men the rock, but Mrs. Wetzel relented and took them back into the woods to find it.

The rock was about a half-mile from the Wetzel cabin, and when the group saw it the old Spaniard became quite excited. The rock was large, and several other men had to be enlisted to help before it could be removed from the cave opening.

Once inside the cave, the men discovered that the interior was filled from bottom to top with dirt brought in from outside. The men who helped remove the large rock were hired to excavate the fill dirt out of the passage, but after several days' work they were amazed to find that they had removed only a small part of the material. They were content to continue their labors, however, because the Spaniard paid them well.

As they excavated they found ancient Spanish tools and armaments in the dirt. Days turned into weeks, and still the men continued to dig. The more fill dirt they encountered, the more convinced they were that some great treasure was concealed at the end. Why else would anyone go to this much trouble?

During the excavation the old Spanish gentleman contracted a fever and had to be confined to a pallet. It soon became apparent he was suffering a severe case of pneumonia. He said he needed to go south to Texas where the climate was much warmer. He left a sufficient amount of money to compensate the men for their continued digging, and as he left he told them he would be in touch with them as soon as possible.

He gathered up the maps and the old tools and armor that had been removed from the cave and took them with him. He explained that once the men broke through the fill dirt they would find the cave branching out into several corridors, one of which contained the treasure in a secluded place. Once he recovered from his sickness he would return and they would share the wealth. With that, he departed.

The men continued to dig for several more days but soon tired of the labor. They divided up the money the Spaniard had left and promised to resume the excavation when and if he returned. He was never heard from again, however, and the story of the lost Spanish treasure soon faded from the memory of the Benton County residents.

In 1922 a Benton County man named Parkins left his home and went to Oklahoma to find work. He ended up in Paul's Valley, working as a carpenter. There he made friends with a fellow worker who always asked him questions about Arkansas. Eventually the talk turned to caves, and the friend said he knew about a treasure cave up near the Arkansas-Missouri border. The man said that many years earlier, during the winter of 1886, a very sick old Spaniard had passed through Paul's Valley on his way to Texas. He fell seriously ill and was taken in by this man's father, who intended to nurse him back to health. The old gentleman became sicker and it was soon clear he would not live much longer. On his deathbed he confided to the family that he had some old maps with him that showed the way to a Spanish treasure in a cave in Arkansas. If anything happened to him, he asked, could they please send the maps to an address in Madrid, Spain? The family agreed to do so, but the man died before he was able to give them the address.

The old Spaniard was buried in the city cemetery, the one that is still found outside Paul's Valley today. The man took Parkin out to the cemetery and showed him the Spaniard's grave. A rotted wooden marker bore the barely readable inscription "Age unknown. A traveler from Spain."

When Parkins inquired about the maps, the friend said that they had remained in the possession of the family for a long time but that he no longer knew where they were.

The dirt that filled the front part of the Benton County cave was eventually removed, revealing passageways that wove deep into the limestone mountain. People entered and explored these passageways but were never able to locate any treasure.

Long-time residents of the Gravette area can recall their grandparents speaking of a great earthquake that shook the area in 1812. They suggest that as a result of the huge tremor much of the interior of the cavern was destroyed, perhaps forever concealing a fortune in Spanish gold.

Tragedy at Happy Bend

Happy Bend, Arkansas, located in Conway County near the center of the state, exists mostly as a memory now. Little is left of this 130-year-old community but a few residences, some small farms, a church, and a cemetery. Cattle graze in meadows where investors once hoped to locate a prosperous and growing town. Before the Civil War there were a small mercantile store, a blacksmith shop, and the Wilson Hotel in Happy Bend. But something horrible happened which soured people from moving into the community and after which the town withered away.

Lewisburg, Arkansas, adjoins the Arkansas River some ten miles southeast of Happy Bend. Before the Civil War it was a bustling and prosperous commercial center, serving for a time as the seat of government for Conway County. Steamboats plying up and down the river stopped at Lewisburg to load and unload freight. Quite often the town was boisterous and rowdy, especially when visited by horse thieves who ranged the Fourche Mountain region to the south. Many saloons and gambling houses lined the streets of early Lewisburg, and robbery and murder were commonplace.

Into this setting rode one W.O. Wilson. No one ever knew what the initials stood for; all that was known was that he was born and reared in Alabama and then run out of his community for stealing from a merchant. For years Wilson traveled throughout Missouri, Kansas, and Indian Territory. He brought with him a reputation as a horse thief and murderer who loved to brawl, often challenging two men at a time to fight him barehanded. He had been accused of murder several times but was never brought to trial.

Wilson was an intimidating figure. He was large and stocky,

sporting thick muscular arms, shoulders, and chest. He had thick bushy eyebrows that met above his nose and wore a full beard that made his head look bigger than it actually was. He always wore a black derby hat and a black coat with tails.

Shortly after his arrival at Lewisburg, Wilson bought a parcel of land at Happy Bend that was located on a route well-traveled by those going from Little Rock to Fort Smith by land. On his property he built a two-story, eight-room hotel. He planted flowers around the hotel and procured a black slave woman to do the cooking and cleaning, and in a very short time the inn gained a favorable reputation. In spite of his threatening appearance, Wilson was always the charming host, often sitting and conversing with his guests well into the evening.

Soon after the first year of the inn's operation, strange stories began to circulate about travelers checking in and never being seen or heard from again. When confronted by his neighbors about these suspicions, Wilson always remained pleasant and invited an inspection of his property. Nothing was ever found to suggest wrongdoing.

Wilson continued to prosper over the next few years—to prosper, in fact, far above and beyond the degree one might expect in a small-town hotel operator. Now and then a new story would surface concerning the mysterious disappearance of a visitor to the inn, and several times the law was called out to investigate, but nothing ever came of it.

One day an influential rancher and businessman named Paschal, from Galla Rock, checked into the hotel and vanished. Once again lawmen were called in. While searching the grounds, a deputy was informed by two young boys that they had found a dead horse in a thicket not far from the inn. The deputy identified the dead horse as having belonged to Mr. Paschal. It had been tied to a tree and evidently starved to death. The lawmen figured that Wilson had hidden the horse in the thicket intending to return for it, but his neighbors' constant surveillance kept him from carrying out the plan. Wilson and the slave woman were arrested and taken to Lewisburg, where they were bound and guarded on the second floor of a store. The woman refused to answer any questions from the authorities and cast fearful glances at Wilson which left the impression that she was more terrified of him than of her interrogators.

On the following evening, Wilson managed to escape from his second-floor confinement and slip down to the riverbank, where he stole a skiff, pushed out into the water, and fled downstream. Pursuers who arrived at the shore just as he entered the river opened fire, and another group of men launched a boat in an effort to catch the fugitive. When they caught up with Wilson they found him lying in the bottom of the boat, dying from the wounds inflicted by the riflemen.

The next morning the slave expressed visible relief on hearing of the death of her former master. When she calmed down she told a most amazing story. She revealed the existence of a cleverly concealed trapdoor in the floor of one of the ground-level guest rooms of the hotel which led to a deep underground cellar. Searchers had failed to discover this trapdoor during their earlier visits. The slave woman said that Wilson would club an unsuspecting guest on the head with a heavy mallet and carry the limp form to the cellar. There the victim would be stripped of all valuables—coin, watches, jewelry, and other goods—which Wilson and the slave would place in a flour sack. He would also take their spurs and knock out any gold teeth they may have had. Then he would knot the sack and have the woman hold it while he turned his attention back to the unfortunate victim. To the absolute horror of the woman, Wilson would then hack the unconscious victim into small pieces with a meat cleaver. He would make her put the dismembered corpse into a weighted sack and drag it over to Point Remove Creek, about a mile away. Here the sack would be tossed into the swirling waters of the creek, to disappear forever into the soft bottom. Wilson would then send the slave back to the hotel. The woman believed that once she was out of sight Wilson always buried the sack of stolen valuables, because he would return to the hotel without it after about thirty minutes. She estimated that he had buried several dozen sacks over the three years she had been with him.

When the news of Wilson's grisly activities reached the residents of Happy Bend, they were so horrified and repulsed they set fire to the inn and burned it to the ground, determined to remove it from sight forever.

Law officers searched long and hard for the place where Wilson buried his stolen goods but were never able to find anything. Today, treasure hunters armed with electronic detecting equipment have had as little luck. A few coins and a spur have been recovered near the creek just north of Happy Bend, but nothing else substantial has been found. Since the inn has been destroyed for well over a hundred years, no one in Happy Bend today is certain of the original location. It is known, however, that the place where the bodies were dumped into the west fork of Point Remove Creek was "at a point just north of the Happy Bend settlement and a little to the north and west of Goose Pond." This is the same point at which treasure hunters located the coins and spur.

Today Happy Bend is a quiet community of approximately twenty families. Interstate 40 passes some ten miles to the south, but there are no exits off that busy highway to Happy Bend, so it remains relatively secluded and isolated. Hunters flock to the area during deer season, but otherwise very few people have reason to travel the dirt roads to Happy Bend. Now and then a resident of the town will encounter a treasure hunter exploring the river banks and the floodplain of Point Remove Creek.

Recent studies of Point Remove Creek suggest that the continued searches for W.O. Wilson's buried treasure may be in vain. The creek has flooded several times in the last one hundred years, and with each flood the channel has changed course and tons of silt have been deposited atop the fertile floodplain that extends outward from the creek. The creek today is actually several hundred feet from where it was a century ago.

But because dreams of buried treasure and wealth do not die easily, the dreamers still come to Happy Bend, each of them certain he will be the one to find W.O. Wilson's cache of coins and jewels.

The Miser's Hoard

During the Civil War, an elderly resident of Mountain Home in Baxter County named Napier was believed to have amassed a substantial fortune which he had converted to gold coin. Napier had a reputation of being a cranky old tightwad who negotiated the price of anything he bought. He walked everywhere he went, always dressed in the same black suit and carrying a cane. He owned and ran several small farms in the area and lived in a well cared for two story house in town. One day a group of outlaws that normally preyed on travelers to Mountain Home rode onto Napier's property, barged into his house, and tied up Napier and his wife and children. The outlaws threatened to burn down the house unless the old man told them where he kept his money. Napier refused and, after constant threats, the outlaws tortured him by applying hot irons to his skin. Still he refused to reveal the location of his money. Eventually he and his family were dragged out of the house and deposited in the yard. As the family watched, the outlaws burned down the Napier house and barn before riding away.

Napier moved his family into a house on one of his farms, but he remained in town, visiting the site of his former home and drawing water each day from the brick-walled well located between the burned house and the road.

Years passed and old man Napier passed away. A man named Bucher bought the Napier property and built a fine new house on the site of the burned one. Bucher drilled a new well closer to the new house. However, like Napier, he kept his milk and butter cool by storing them in the old well.

Stories soon reached Bucher about old man Napier's wealth,

which many believed was still hidden on the property. Bucher made several attempts to locate Napier's money around the site of the old house and barn but with no success.

Around 1920, one of Napier's granddaughters returned to Mountain Home to visit the old property. She observed that none of the original buildings was left standing and said the only thing she remembered from her grandfather's homeplace was the old well down by the road. She also confirmed the stories of his hidden wealth but said no one in the family ever knew where the old man hid it.

Several years after the granddaughter's visit, around the time when automobiles came to be more numerous in Baxter County, a stranger stopped at the old Napier homeplace and asked for some water for a leaky radiator. He was told to help himself to all the water he needed from the old well.

The second time he drew the bucket up, he found a gold coin in the bottom of the container. The discovery caused a great deal of excitement in Mountain Home. With the consent of the owners of the old Napier place, some townspeople tried to enlarge the well opening in order to lower someone down to retrieve the cache of coins that was presumed to lie hidden below. On the second effort to widen the opening with a charge of dynamite, the explosion caused the walls to collapse, perhaps forever burying Napier's hidden fortune.

Other Tales
of Arkansas Treasure

The Fisherman's Mine

Gordon Lambrecht has reported the existence of gold in Baxter County in a 1977 issue of a county historical newsletter. Sometime in the early 1940s, Lambrecht claims a man named Don Blevins introduced him to another man named McChord who liked to explore around the back country of Baxter County. The men struck up a friendship and spent many hours hunting and fishing together.

One day McChord asked Lambrecht if he would like to go with him to a secret place where they could dig for gold. Intrigued, Lambrecht agreed.

The two men rode in McChord's old pickup truck to Cotter, where they rented a boat from a man at a commercial boat dock. They transferred some supplies from the pickup to the boat and started upstream. After about a half-hour of travel upriver, they turned the boat into a small stream and followed it for approximately five hundred feet until it became too shallow to proceed any further. They banked the craft and walked another six hundred feet up a hill along a trail that McChord claimed he had hacked out of the forest himself.

At the top of the hill there was evidence of some recent excavation which McChord said was his gold mine. He instructed Lambrecht to start digging in one certain area.

After they shoveled for a while, the two men returned to the small stream where they continued to dig and pan for ore along the banks and sometimes out in the middle. Lambrecht was impressed with McChord's knowledge of mining and geology and did as he was instructed. After several hours of labor, the two men had accumulated a small sack of what McChord said was gold ore.

The men returned to the boat dock around sundown. Later that evening McChord cashed in the sack of ore and paid Lambrecht twenty dollars for his labor.

Rattlesnake Cave in Scott County

There is a mysterious cave in Scott County, Arkansas, that many believe was the site of an ancient Spanish mine. In the early 1900s, a man named Crosby was hunting with two companions along the side of Mill Creek Mountain in Scott County, about fifteen miles south of Waldron and close to State Highway 71. The men had wounded a deer, and in the process of tracking the animal located the opening of the cave. They peered into the cavern and saw that the passageway disappeared far back into the mountain. The men returned to their homes and the next morning arrived back at the cave carrying torches with which to explore the interior. Deep within the cave they found a crudely made stone stairway which allowed for easier passage to the lower levels. They also found several pieces of a rotted wooden ladder and many very old discarded mining tools.

For several months the men revisited the cave in search of some sign of gold or silver but were unable to find any. In time they abandoned the project.

Stories of the old Spanish mine are still told by residents of the area today, but very few have attempted to explore the interior, because the cave has become a haven for rattlesnakes.

Jesse James in Arkansas

Besides lost mines, many Arkansas legends passed along over the generations have been about such valuables as coins, bills, and jewelry hidden throughout the state by eccentrics, outlaws, and soldiers from both the Union and Confederate armies.

Jesse James and his gang of desperadoes were well known in Arkansas and regularly visited various parts of the state, and Jesse and Frank James spent time in Little Rock both before and after their outlaw careers. The James gang also operated for many years along the Arkansas-Missouri border in the Ozarks. In his later years Frank James confirmed his having directed a stage robbery in the Ouachita Mountains between Hot Springs and Malvern. The outlaws, dressed as Union soldiers, robbed the stage of its mail pouches and took money and jewelry from the passengers. They also took two of the best horses from the team pulling the stage. Frank James said the gang immediately attracted pursuit from local lawmen and they had to bury their loot just before they rode through Hot Springs. After hiding the goods they laid a large rock over the site, and both he and Jesse scratched their names on it.

In 1928, Alvin Gilpin found a large sandstone rock in the Ouachita Mountains near Hot Springs which had chiseled on its face the names "Frank and Jesse James" along with the amount "$32,000." In addition, the large rock bore the figures of a cross, a Bowie knife, and a three-pronged fork. Gilpin removed the stone and kept it for many years as a curiosity. Several years later a friend spotted the stone in his yard and inquired about it. After Gilpin explained how he had found it in the mountains, the friend said that many times stones such as this marked a location where stolen goods were buried. Gilpin tried many times to relocate the exact spot where he had found the stone, but with no luck.

Outlaws often hid their stolen loot when they were on the run and were sometimes unable to retrieve it because of death, capture and imprisonment, or simply not being able to find it. The James gang was known to be very familiar with the many limestone caves of the Ozark Mountains and are believed to have secreted stolen money in several of them. In their haste they were undoubtedly unable to return to some of them to secure their loot, and it is reasonable to believe that this wealth may still lie in some of the caves.

Crystal Hill Gold

While it is certain that De Soto camped near what is now Little Rock and sent men out into the Ozark and Ouachita Mountains in search of gold and silver, there is very little evidence that any actual mining by the Spaniards took place in and around the encampment.

In 1909, a man named Trammell was prospecting on and around Crystal Hill, a short boat ride upriver from Little Rock. He spent several weeks exploring the potential of the mountain and one day was rewarded with the discovery of gold in a quartz exposure. A small-scale gold rush ensued and the low mountain attracted hundreds of prospectors.

Several boatloads of mining equipment were brought up the Arkansas River all the way from New Orleans to the Crystal Hill site and several mining camps were established on the mountain. One large camp, operated by a Captain Hillaire, sank several shafts into the rock core of the mountain. Traces of gold were found with each effort, although never in amounts large enough to warrant continuation. Hillaire subsequently employed Trammell to guide him to the original Crystal Hill site he had discovered. Several more shafts were excavated at this site and enough gold ore was retrieved to justify the construction of a small smelter on the hill. The mine was worked for several more months until it was no longer profitable. It was soon abandoned, but up until the residential development of the Crystal Hill area, weekend prospectors would report discovering gold nuggets every now and then.

About ten miles north of Little Rock are the remains of the old Kellogg lead mines. The mining company excavated and processed ore here before shipping it to Europe. Somewhat mysteriously, the mines were abandoned, and little is known of what became of the owners and operators. Records indicate the company went bankrupt.

It is common knowledge, however, that silver as well as lead was taken from each of the several shafts associated with the mining operation. One report contains details of a lump of lead-silver ore that weighed 108 pounds!

For many years following the closing of the mines this area was clandestinely worked by freelance prospectors and miners, and even now there are those who claim to have dug some silver there.

Stone County Silver

Cow Mountain near Timbo in Stone County is reputed to have had an Indian silver mine located somewhere at the top. Jimmy Driftwood, a Timbo resident and a three-time Grammy Award–winning singer and songwriter, tells this story he heard from his father.

Many years ago as this part of Stone County was being settled by whites, an old Indian who lived in the area was caught and his life was threatened if he did not leave the country. As he was too old to fend for himself in the wild, and as he was used to begging food and clothing off the white settlers, he promised his captors he would lead them to a rich silver mine in Cow Mountain that would make them "wealthy men for the rest of their lives" if they would just let him live in the area in peace. His captors agreed to the proposition and on the morning of the next day followed the old Indian to the mountain. As they approached the ridge, the Indian insisted on blindfolding them for the remainder of the trip, saying they could remove the blindfolds once they reached the mine.

True to his word, they found themselves at the ancient mine from which the Indians had taken their silver for many generations. The men filled their pockets and sacks with as much of the silver as they could carry and, once again donning the blindfolds, left the mountain.

Two days later the old Indian disappeared. It was rumored that other Indians in the area had learned he had led the whites to the silver mine and killed him.

The white men tried several times to relocate the mine on the top of the mountain, with no success.

New Mexico

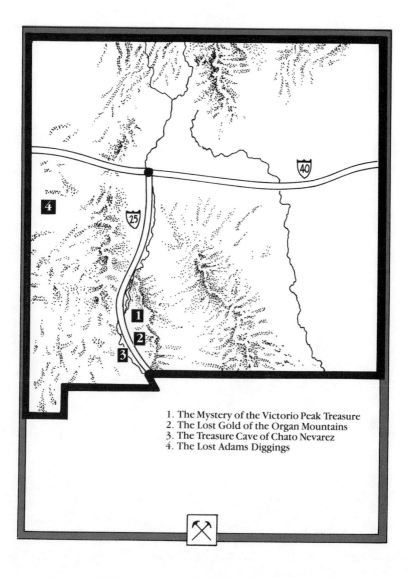

1. The Mystery of the Victorio Peak Treasure
2. The Lost Gold of the Organ Mountains
3. The Treasure Cave of Chato Nevarez
4. The Lost Adams Diggings

The Mystery of the Victorio Peak Treasure

Victorio Peak is an unspectacular rocky pinnacle that rises about five hundred feet above the desert floor near the center of the Hembrillo Basin, a low-lying area just west of the rugged San Andres Mountains in Dona Ana County, New Mexico. The basin is remote, being at least forty miles from any significant settlement, and it opens into the *Jornada del Muerto* ("journey of death")—a vast, waterless plain extending northward from Las Cruces for about a hundred miles. Bleak, treeless, and forbidding, Victorio Peak has provided the setting for one of the most baffling and intriguing mysteries of our time.

Human drama has surrounded this peak for a long time. Spanish conquistadors under the leadership of Francisco Vasquez de Coronado traveled, explored, and searched for gold and silver in the shadow of the San Andres Mountains. Artifacts from the Spanish army such as pieces of armor and spurs can still be found in this area today. The region was also visited by groups of Spanish missionaries who wanted to establish colonies and convert the local Indians to Christianity. Farming was difficult there, and the padres encouraged the Indians to mine gold and silver instead. The Apache Chief Victorio was another character who frequented the Hembrillo Basin area; he hid out there during the late 1870s as he perpetrated raids throughout the New Mexican Southwest.

In the latter part of the eighteenth century one Felipe La Rue, the son of a wealthy French nobleman, joined the Franciscan monastery. Given the wealth and position of his family, it may seem curious that Felipe chose to take the vows of poverty and lead a life of self-denial. But Felipe had a history of rebelling against established authority, and his becoming a monk was a form of rebellion against the worldly status of his family. Once ensconced within the framework of the church, Felipe continued to resent authority and continually challenged the precepts of his religion. Believing that Felipe would do well to serve some time in the primitive conditions of the New World, his superiors transferred him to Mexico and assigned him to menial duties in the fields.

Soon Felipe began once again to challenge the established policies of the church. The padres, in an attempt to counteract his dissidence, tried everything from whippings to forced labor, but the more punishment they meted out, the more volatile the young monk became. After a time he convinced a number of other monks and several Indian converts to accompany him on a journey to the north in order to establish a colony where the members could worship and live as they wished without the strict rules and regulations of the mother church monitoring their every move. In the middle of a dark night, Padre La Rue took his followers, along with a number of stolen mules and supplies, out of the monastery in Mexico City and fled toward the north.

It took them several weeks to reach El Paso del Norte, where they replenished their supplies and received information about the lands to the north. After a few more days of travel La Rue and his followers camped at Hembrillo Springs near the heart of the basin. Here La Rue found plenty of water and game and noted that the region was effectively isolated from outside intrusion. He ordered his followers to start building dwellings and a small church. They planted corn and dug primitive aqueducts to transport the spring water to the fields and to a cistern.

In the meantime gold had been discovered in the nearby rocky hill that dominated the landscape of the basin. Initially La Rue assigned two of the monks to dig the gold, but as it became apparent the ore located within the mountain was very rich and extensive, La Rue assigned two dozen monks and Indians to the chores of digging, crushing, and smelting the gold. Gold bars began to accumulate and soon they were stacked like firewood along one wall of the natural cavern that existed deep within the low mountain.

Three years passed. Eventually the leaders of the monastery in Mexico City learned of the whereabouts of the dissident colony established by Padre La Rue. They also learned of the rich gold mine that La Rue had discovered and insisted that it belonged to the church.

Eventually the church authorities sent out an expeditionary force of soldiers to Hembrillo Basin to take La Rue prisoner and return him to Mexico City. A cadre of monks accompanying the expedition was to remain at the basin to oversee the mining operations and ensure that the gold was transported back to the mother church on a regular basis.

Learning of the expedition's approach, La Rue ordered that the entrance to the mine be concealed and said that no one was to inform the newcomers of its location. When the soldiers arrived, La Rue was taken prisoner and queried as to the location of the gold mine. He refused to speak. Stripped and tied to a post in front of his followers, he was whipped until his torn flesh hung from his body, but still he refused to reveal the location of the mine. The soldiers continued to torture him until he lost consciousness and later died. Several colonists were also tortured and killed, but legend claims that the location of the mine was never revealed. Finally the soldiers chained the remaining colonists together and marched them back to the monastery, forever abandoning the colony at Hembrillo Basin.

During the 1870s, the Mescalero Apache Chief Victorio used Hembrillo Basin as a hiding place from which he would lead his warriors in raids throughout the *jornada* and the Rio Grande Valley. Victorio would attack wagon trains, churches, immigrants, mail coaches, and anything else that promised riches. Often he would take prisoners back to Hembrillo Basin, where he would subject them to elaborate torture before they were killed.

On April 7, 1880, Victorio was engaged in a battle at Hembrillo Springs with a troop of Negro cavalry which had been pursuing them for several days. The Apaches were successful in turning back the soldiers and the nearby peak was thereafter known as Victorio Peak, named in honor of the chief. Howard Bryan, a journalist for the *Albuquerque Times,* believes Victorio and his Apaches fought hard to protect their cache of treasures within the mountain.

In November 1937, a group of five men and one woman from Hatch, New Mexico, went on a deer hunting trip into the Hembrillo Basin. While the woman remained in camp, the men decided to scout the area around the springs for sign of deer. Not wishing to hunt with such a large group, Milton Ernest "Doc" Noss separated from the others and decided to try his luck over by Victorio Peak. Noss was climbing around on the slopes of the peak when a light rain began to fall. In search of shelter, he hiked up to the top of the rocky hill. Spying a rock under which he believed he could wait out the rain, Noss stumbled over a shaft which appeared to lead straight down into the mountain. Ignoring the rain and dropping to his hands and knees, he peered into the shaft, which was obviously man-made and very ancient. Just inside, as far as the light penetrated, he spotted a wooden pole with footholds carved into it. When the rain finally let up Noss returned to the camp, whispered his discovery to his wife, and informed her he wanted to come back soon and investigate the opening further.

Several days later Noss and his wife, Ova, returned to Victorio Peak with ropes and a flashlight. At first Noss tried to descend into the shaft on the aged wooden pole but found it too hazardous. He secured the ropes and lowered himself into the ancient mine.

What Doc Noss found in that mine has become one of the most controversial topics in all of New Mexico history—a web of intrigue, unimaginable wealth, murder, and mystery that involves such participants as the United States Army and Air Force, one of the most prominent attorneys in America, and several leading military and political figures.

According to Noss, he descended sixty feet by rope through an extremely narrow shaft until he arrived in an opening about the size of "a large room." On the walls his flashlight revealed what he referred to as "Indian drawings," both painted and carved. The shaft continued sloping downward at an angle for another 125 feet where it leveled off. Following the shaft, Noss entered into a large natural space inside the mountain apparently created by a great earthquake of long ago. Noss said the space was "big enough for a freight train and contained several smaller rooms along one side." He proceeded along the floor of the large room for several paces until he came upon a human skeleton. Noss noted that the hands had been bound behind the back. Before Noss was to leave the room he was to encounter another twenty-six skeletons, all bound and most of them secured to stakes driven into the ground.

In one of the smaller rooms Noss found an old Wells-Fargo chest, guns, swords, saddles, jewels, and a stack of leather pouches containing gold coins that would take sixty mules to transport. He also discovered a box of letters, the most recent ones dated 1880. Noss filled his pockets with several of the gold coins and exited the small room. Back in the main part of the cavern against one wall he encountered "thousands of bars of gold, stacked like cordwood." After further exploration, Noss laboriously returned to the surface and told Ova what he had seen. He showed her the coins and the jewels he had brought up and when she inquired why he didn't bring up any of the gold bars, he told her they weighed over forty pounds apiece and he could barely get back up out of the shaft as it was. Ova continued to pressure Noss and, after a brief rest, he returned to the cavern and brought back one of the gold bars.

Over the next two years Noss returned to the shaft many times and retrieved a total of eighty-eight of the gold bars, each weighing variously between forty and eighty pounds. On several occasions he hired men to go into the shaft with him to help carry the gold out. Benny Samaniego, now deceased, stated in an interview in 1963 that after he entered the shaft with Noss he saw "stacks of gold bars, skeletons, armor, old guns, and statues." He said all the skeletons had been tied to posts as if they had been left in the cave to die.

Once Noss employed a young boy named Benny Sedillo. Sedillo also described the bars of gold in huge stacks and discussed how difficult it was to return to the surface carrying even the smallest of the bars. He also claimed Noss threatened to kill him if he ever revealed the existence of the cave to anyone.

After two years of tediously removing the gold bars from the cave, along with dozens of artifacts, jewels, and coins, Noss decided that the task could be made much easier if he widened the opening. In 1939 he got some dynamite and set off an explosion in the narrowest part of the entrance. The result was disastrous. Instead of widening the passage, the blast caused a cave-in, plugging the entrance and halting any further recovery.

Disheartened but not discouraged, Noss decided to begin selling the treasure he had accumulated while he pondered ways of reopening the mine. During this time he took into his confidence a man named Joseph Andregg, and the two of them transported several gold bars and a quantity of the coins, jewels, and artifacts to Arizona, where they sold them on the black market.

Noss tried several times to reopen the shaft, but each attempt met with failure. He was becoming very frustrated at not being able to retrieve the riches that lay within Victorio Peak and often took out his frustration on his wife. Life for them became difficult, and Doc Noss and Ova soon divorced.

On February 15, 1946, Doc Noss finally got around to filing a claim on the Victorio Peak site. He was still trying to discover some way to break through the clogged shaft. In 1949 he entered into a partnership with a miner from Alice, Texas, named Charles Ryan. Ryan brought respectable credentials as a miner, and Noss was convinced he would be able to reopen the shaft. Noss showed

Ryan the fifty-one remaining gold bars and several of the artifacts that were taken out of the cave in order to convince him he was serious. As the men were preparing to transport some equipment out to the Victorio Peak site, Ova Noss filed a counterclaim on the area. The court decided that until the legal claimant on the site was determined, no one would be allowed in the area.

Further frustrated by the delay, Noss argued frequently with Ryan. Eventually Ryan decided to pull out of the agreement and asked Noss to refund his original investment. Noss became incensed and threatened Ryan. A fight ensued which resulted in Ryan's shooting Noss in the head, killing him instantly. Ryan was charged with murder but was later acquitted.

More years passed and Ova Noss held onto her Victorio Peak claim. In 1955 the White Sands Missile Range expanded its boundaries to encompass the Hembrillo Basin. Now and then Ova Noss would hire some men to accompany her to the peak to clear out some of the rubble clogging the shaft, but they were always escorted out of the area by military policemen, despite the fact that she held a valid claim.

For several years Ova Noss corresponded with military officials about her right to work her claim, but she was always denied permission to enter the range. In 1961 she contracted with four prospectors to enter Hembrillo Basin surreptitiously and try to clear the shaft. The men were to get a percentage of anything that was retrieved from the peak. On October 28, 1961, the four men arrived at Hembrillo Basin where they were surprised to discover a team of four air force officers and four army enlisted men digging in the shaft. The officers ordered the prospectors to leave the area immediately, claiming it was government property.

Once notified of this situation, Ova Noss contacted her attorney, who in turn contacted state government officials. Inquiries were made to a Colonel Jaffe, judge advocate at the missile range, but he denied that any digging was taking place at the Victorio Peak site. Ova Noss contacted another attorney in Kansas City, who continued to put the heat on the United States government.

In the ensuing weeks a remarkable story surfaced about another entrance to the fabulous treasure cache. In 1958 an Air Force Captain named Fiege and an unnamed companion were exploring the Hembrillo Basin area when they discovered a natural opening on the side of Victorio Peak. The men entered, followed a passageway for several dozen yards, and encountered one hundred gold bars stacked against one wall. Each man retrieved a gold bar. In the summer of 1961 Captain Fiege, Major Keely, Captain Swanner, and Colonel Gorman, all associated with White Sands Missile Range, obtained permission from the U.S. Army to work the Noss claim. On August 5, 1961, the Fiege party returned to the site accompanied by the commanding officer of the range, a secret service agent, and fourteen military policemen. For some reason Fiege could not relocate the opening he had discovered even after several hours of searching. A subsequent lie detector test indicated Fiege was telling the truth about the opening and the gold bars, and as a result the U.S. Army ordered a full-scale mining operation established at Victorio Peak. This operation was what the four prospectors hired by Ova Noss encountered in October of that year.

Within weeks, Ova Noss's attorneys converged on the New Mexico state capitol in an effort to get the United States government to halt the diggings at Victorio Peak. During the negotiations, a document was discovered that showed the acting director of the Denver Mint had obtained a permit from Holloman Air Force Base Commander John G. Schinkle to dig for the Noss treasure. Apparently judge advocate Jaffe was aware of the digging on Victorio Peak but had lied to Ova Noss. After hearing all the arguments, the military agreed to cease all mining operation in and around Victorio Peak.

In 1963, the Gaddis Mining Company of Denver, Colorado, under a $100,000 contract to the Denver Mint, obtained permission to dig at Victorio Peak from July 13 through September 17, a period that was in between testing schedules at the military range. Thousands of tons of earth were removed from the mountain by dynamiting and bulldozing, but according to all reports, no entrance to the treasure cache was gained. By the time they had finished the hill was ravaged.

In 1972, F. Lee Bailey, a nationally prominent attorney, became involved in the case. He was accompanied by Attorney General John Mitchell and soon-to-be Watergate figure John Erlichmann. Bailey claimed to represent fifty unidentified clients "who knew the location of a cave with one hundred tons of gold stacked within." They had retained Bailey to find a legal means to locate and remove the gold from the federal reservation. Ova Noss was not one of the fifty claimants.

On March 5, 1975, a federal judge in Albuquerque ruled that the army might in fact prohibit entry to the treasure site, but that sometime in the future the army should work out an arrangement with the claimants to continue the search.

One such arrangement was made in 1977. The army agreed to recognize six claimant groups and permitted a two-week search. Ground radar readings employed during the search indicated the existence of a huge cavern within Victorio Peak exactly where Doc Noss said it was. It also revealed about four hundred feet of dirt and rock debris filling the entrance. When the two-week search yielded no entry to the cavern, the claimants bitterly complained that the allotted time period was far too short to accomplish anything.

Some researchers who have spent considerable time on the mystery of the Victorio Peak cache are convinced that the United States Army retrieved much of the gold said to be hidden in the mine and then instigated and perpetrated a cover-up. They point out that the army spent hundreds of thousands of dollars working in and around the peak, conducting mining and digging operations as well as road-building activities. It also placed a locked steel door over the original shaft discovered by Doc Noss.

It seems likely that the Padre La Rue mine, Chief Victorio's treasure cache, and Doc Noss's discovery are all one and the same. There can be no doubt that the treasure exists: the gold bars have been photographed, affidavits have been obtained from those who have seen the cache, and Ova Noss showed this author an ancient Spanish sword, a silver goblet, and a golden cup, all of which she claimed came from the cache within Victorio Peak. Ova Noss died in 1979, but her son continues the search for the treasure. Indeed, he and Ova Noss have invested over a half-million dollars thus far in pursuit of the cache.

Currently there are no active claims on the Victorio Peak site, and the United States Army has locked the entrance to Hembrillo Basin. The military patrols the area on a regular schedule. It has been rumored that the military continues in its attempt to find the cavern; surreptitious low-level flights have occasionally spotted military vehicles and heavy equipment on and near the peak. Inquiries directed to army officials at White Sands Missile Range are repeatedly ignored.

New Mexico historians are interested in gaining access to the interior of Victorio Peak, not for the potential wealth within, but for the historical artifacts they believe are still there. Meanwhile, F. Lee Bailey and his clients as well as relatives of Ova Noss continue to pursue their right to dig into the peak.

Hembrillo Basin remains quiet save for the hum of insects and the call of quail and dove. As one stands in the basin in the shadow of Victorio Peak, a haunted feeling overrides all other senses. The feeling is so strong that one is tempted to look around to see if others are near, others like Padre La Rue, Victorio, and Doc Noss.

The Lost Gold
of the Organ Mountains

Demetrio Varela was born in the year 1824 to poor parents in the farming region along the floodplain of the Rio Grande near what is now Las Cruces, New Mexico. Because he was one of several children and because the family could not provide enough food for all of them, Demetrio left when he was fourteen to work in the mines in the mountain ranges to the north. For the next twenty-two years he labored in the mines, always taking care to send money home to his family. Around the time the Civil War began Demetrio learned that his family had fallen on hard times, so he returned to the little farm to help them with their few acres of corn. He soon became bored with farming and cast about for other ways to earn a living. He became acquainted with an old Indian who earned a decent living tracking lost or stolen cattle and returning them to their owners. Such *rastreadores*, as they were called, were in demand in the Southwest. Occasionally Demetrio would aid the old tracker, but as he gained experience and a reputation for himself, he gradually hired out to the neighboring ranchers. Tracking cattle was preferable to hoeing the long rows of corn out on the sweltering floodplain.

For several years Demetrio earned a good living as a *rastreadore*, and as a result of his now widely known skills in working with livestock he was offered a job as foreman of a large ranch near Las Cruces which was owned by a widow named Doña Chonita. Her late husband, a successful rancher, had left her with a large land-holding and an excellent herd of cattle.

Demetrio enjoyed his job as ranch foreman and spent many happy years at it. The ranch prospered and life was good. Just about the time Demetrio and Doña Chonita were thinking of adding to the herd there came a drought that thinned out the crops and grass and reduced the large cattle herds. Even through Doña Chonita's ranch was irrigated by the waters of the nearby Rio Grande, the river remained dry for months at a time. Gradually the ranch started losing money, and one by one the owner had to let the hands go, leaving only Demetrio and herself to tend the cattle. Things were so bad that Demetrio began to consider returning to the mines to earn a living.

The autumn of 1878 had given way to winter, and Demetrio dreaded the thought of working the mines in the cold weather. Just as he was on the verge of quitting his ranch job, he received a message from a wealthy rancher named Armijo who lived several miles away but had not been as hard hit by the drought. Some of Señor Armijo's prize cattle had been stolen, and he wanted to hire Demetrio as a *rastreadore*. Demetrio told Señor Armijo he was getting ready to leave for the mines, but the old man offered him an attractive stipend to track his cattle. Thinking that the money he would make from this job might help save Doña Chonita's ranch, he agreed.

The cattle thieves had gotten a full day's head start by the time Demetrio took up pursuit. He left the Armijo Ranch with two cowhands and picked up the trail almost immediately. The men rode hard, trying to close the distance between themselves and the cattle rustlers.

Around noon of that day the temperature began to drop rapidly as the wind picked up. Occasionally light flakes of snow whipped the faces of the pursuers, but the men just turned up their collars and went on.

The tracks led them into a deep arroyo, where they found the cattle had been butchered and the meat apparently loaded onto pack mules which had been waiting there. The pack train of meat was then driven northeastward toward San Augustin Pass in the Organ Mountains. Demetrio and the men believed that the cattle thieves intended to trade the meat to Indians for hides. They thought that if they rode hard all night they would overtake the rustlers around dawn of the next day. As the wind continued to rise and the temperature dropped, the men mounted up and headed for the pass. They rode northward for an hour along a trail that paralleled the Organ Mountain range just to their east. The men could see the jagged peaks of the Organs looming in the distance, the black serrated edges seemed to rise straight up into the sky.

The wind continued to rage and was soon joined by a driving snow. Just as the men approached San Augustin Pass the snow became a severe blizzard. Holding their hats tightly on their heads to keep them from blowing away, squinting into the driving snow and sleet, the men tried to continue, but they could not see ten feet ahead of their horses. They gave up the trail and turned eastward toward a narrow canyon in the Organ Mountains in search of shelter. They discovered a small clump of oak trees near a deep overhanging ledge that appeared to offer some protection against the storm. They tied their mounts up for the night and proceeded to gather firewood.

While the snow continued to fall and the wind howled up and down the narrow canyon, the men heated tortillas and coffee over the warm fire and tried to make themselves comfortable for the night.

Before long two feet of snow had accumulated, and more was falling. The fire was nice, but Demetrio was getting cramped, seated in one position for so long. He rose to stretch his tired muscles and walked around the shallow cave. He felt they had been lucky to find it when they did.

Demetrio saw that more wood would be needed for the campfire, so he set out to locate some. He had gone but a few feet along the steep rock face of the cliff when he came upon a haphazard pile of rock and debris that appeared to be intentionally stacked against the wall. On examining it closely, he noticed that it was piled in front of a small opening in the cliff face. Hands numb with cold, he began pulling the rocks from the opening and found it was just large enough to enter if he crawled in on his stomach. He yelled over to his *amigos* that he was going to investigate the cave, and they warned him to watch out for a bear.

Slowly Demetrio worked his way into the opening. After crawling about twenty feet on his hands and knees he reached a place where he could rise to his full height and walk around. He pulled a small tallow candle out of his pouch, lit it, and with its faint light began to inspect the interior. Noticing thick timber supports along the walls and ceiling, he realized he was inside an ancient mine shaft.

Because the light from his candle did not penetrate very far into the darkness, Demetrio made slow progress into the mine, occasionally slipping on the wet floor and stumbling on rocks that must have fallen from the ceiling. As he explored the ancient shaft, Demetrio wondered who might have operated the mine and when, for he was unaware of any mining activity in the Organ Mountains.

Suddenly he came to an abrupt halt. Looming before him was a shape he could not identify. He pulled his pistol from its holster as he inched forward, mindful of the warning of a bear. In the dim light just ahead was a shape nearly shoulder-high and huddled against one wall of the cave. Demetrio approached cautiously, his pistol at the ready and his heart thumping in his chest.

As the light from the small candle gradually illuminated the shape, Demetrio saw that it was not a bear but rather a pile of leather sacks that had been stacked against the wall of the shaft and covered with a half-inch of dust. Demetrio replaced his gun in the holster and allowed his heartbeat to return to normal. In a few moments he walked over to the sacks and pulled one off the top. With his knife he cut the cord that bound it, reached inside, and pulled forth several small pieces of quartz that were thickly veined with yellowish metal. Demetrio uttered a short prayer as he recognized the gold that lay in his hand. He opened another of the sacks and saw that it too contained more of the gold-laden quartz. His heart began to beat rapidly again at the thought of the fortune that lay before him in the dark shaft.

Demetrio placed the handful of nuggets in his pocket and returned the sacks to the pile. Lifting his candle high above his head, he continued into the shaft another ten paces and reached a low stack of small gold bars. Each of the bars was eight inches long and Demetrio estimated there were eighty of them. He picked one of them up and tucked it in his shirt.

Several more yards into the mine shaft he came upon an ancient ore-crusher and forge. As Demetrio pushed on the bellows, the aged leather cracked and broke, joining the dust that had lain on the floor of the shaft for centuries.

Demetrio sat down, his head ringing with the excitement of his find. At first he thought he needed to rush outside and tell his friends of his discovery, but the longer he sat the more he was sure he must keep this information to himself. As his candle burned low, Demetrio lit a cigarette, leaned back against the old ore-crusher, and pondered his new wealth. He thought about how hard he had worked all his life. He thought about how the gold could save Doña Chonita's ranch. He thought about all the things he could now provide for his family, things that they never had in all their lives. As he pondered these things he realized he was rubbing the gold bar he had placed inside his shirt.

Demetrio also thought about something else, something important. He remembered the Mexican belief that only certain people are ordained to find and retrieve buried wealth. For others to do so was bad luck and they would be cursed for the rest of their life. Demetrio thought about the good things he intended to do with the gold and decided that he must be the one destined to locate the long-buried treasure. He said a prayer of thanks for his good fortune.

When the candle started sputtering he realized it was time to leave the mine shaft. He secured the gold bar inside his shirt and under his waistband and snuffed out his cigarette. He patted his pocket where he had placed the golden quartz and then slowly made his way back to the entrance.

When he finally crawled out of the opening he saw that his friends had constructed a shelter made of pine boughs as a protection against the blowing snow. The campfire burned high and a large stack of firewood had been gathered. As Demetrio walked toward the fire the men asked him what he found inside the cave. He told them he was just exploring and looking at some interesting rock formations and then dismissed the topic, hoping they would not be curious enough to investigate. He sat down by the fire, poured a cup of coffee, and proceeded to warm his feet and collect his thoughts.

Because of the head start the cattle rustlers had on the pursuers, and because the snow had covered the trail they were trying to follow, Demetrio and the two ranch hands decided to return to the Armijo Ranch. While he was embarrassed about not being able to catch the rustlers, and dreaded the inevitable encounter with Señor Armijo, Demetrio consoled himself with thoughts of the wealth waiting for him. During the trip back to the ranch he decided that in early spring, when the weather cleared up, he would return to the mine and retrieve the gold.

During the next few days at Doña Chonita's ranch, Demetrio kept to himself as he made plans for his future. He had buried the gold bar and nuggets, but he kept digging them up to look at them. He thought he might go crazy thinking about his fortune and not being able to do anything about it immediately. He also thought about the curse and convinced himself that it would not happen to him.

He was feeling particularly restless one morning when two friends stopped by to ask him to accompany them to a place near Sierra Blanca, Texas, where they had filed a mining claim. They were aware of Demetrio's mining experience and felt he would be helpful in initiating an excavation. Since Sierra Blanca was about 125 miles to the southwest and at a considerably lower elevation, Demetrio decided it would be a good place to live until the weather cleared up around the northern part of the Organ Mountains. He left with his friends, intending to return in two months.

Near the end of the second week at the mining claim, Demetrio was placing dynamite in preparation for setting off a charge. The explosion went off prematurely, and the blast drove minute pieces of shattered shale into his eyes. He was rushed to the hospital in El Paso, but it was too late to do anything to save his sight.

Every night in the hospital Demetrio thought of his gold in the Organ Mountains, wondering if he would ever be able to hold it again, ever be able to relocate the mine shaft. He also thought about the curse he had worried about for so long. Each night Demetrio prayed.

After a two-week stay in the hospital Doña Chonita arrived to carry him back to the ranch. There Demetrio would lie for hours in his bed thinking over and over again of the hidden gold. He wondered why he had been allowed to get so close to the fortune and then placed in a position of never finding it again. Doña Chonita tended him, but after a few years she died from a fever. Eventually he was taken in by relative who lived in El Paso.

Nearly helpless without his sight, Demetrio spent most of the rest of his life sitting on his relatives' patio, pondering what life would have held for him had he still possessed his eyesight. After several years had passed and he realized that the fortune in gold really had eluded him, he began to tell his story. Word of the lost mine of the Organ Mountains soon spread and not long afterward a group of adventurers from the East came to Demetrio with a proposition. If they accompanied him from the original Armijo Ranch to the Organ Mountains, would he guide them to the mine using descriptions of landmarks encountered along the way? If so, the men agreed to split the gold with him, should it be located.

The old spirit of adventure surged through Demetrio. He readily consented, and the party left the next morning. For two days the men rode on horseback from the old Armijo Ranch and searched the area. When Demetrio recalled a particularly large tree he had once used as a landmark, they discovered the tree was no longer there. In the intervening years many of the small streams had altered their courses and the trail had been rerouted to accommodate automobile traffic. The narrow canyon in which the mine had been found so many years earlier could not be identified. It was a disappointed group that finally returned to El Paso.

Demetrio received several more offers over the years to guide men to the lost mine, but, saddened and disheartened from his last experience, he refused them all. He could not bear to relive the disappointment. He did continue to tell the story of the sacks of gold and the stack of gold bars, but the excitement was gone. When he finished with his story he would turn away, tears filling his eyes as he recalled what might have been.

Those who are intimate with the story of Demetrio Varela believe he stumbled onto an ancient Spanish gold mine and cache, probably operated by the Catholic friars sent into the area in the seventeenth century. It has since been substantiated many times that the Spanish operated several mines in and around the area of the Organ Mountains. The gold nuggets and ingots were loaded onto pack mules and burros and transported to church head-quarters near Mexico City. It has been recorded, however, that during the Pueblo Indian uprising in the year 1680 many of the mines had to be abandoned with haste. The friars had orders to seal and camouflage the entrances to the mines so no one else could discover their existence. It is likely that Demetrio found one of these Spanish mines.

Demetrio Varela's curse was to lose his eyesight and live with the fact that he could never reach the wealth that lay hidden in the old shaft in the Organ Mountains. He died in 1916 at the age of ninety-two, and after a small funeral was buried in El Paso.

The Treasure Cave
of Pedro Nevarez

Between the years 1639 and 1649, a band of outlaws led by the infamous Pedro Nevarez preyed on travelers and supply trains going between Mesilla and Hot Springs, New Mexico, in the Rio Grande Valley. Nevarez preferred to attack the supply trains coming up from the interior of Mexico with food and mining equipment destined for the mission priests farther north. These supply trains were normally unescorted by soldiers and were easy victims for the robbers. Sometime the outlaws would attack individual travelers, rob them, and torture them to death.

Some said Nevarez was a Mexican and others claim he was a half-breed Indian, but the record is unclear. His outlaw band was, in fact, made up of both Mexicans and Pueblo and Apache Indians. When not raiding, they maintained a semi-permanent camp deep in Soledad Canyon in the Organ Mountains, a few miles due east of Las Cruces.

One day in the spring of 1649 one of Nevarez's scouts announced an approaching caravan of pack mules headed north and led by a group of missionaries. The church men had traveled from the monastery at Acolman, located about forty miles northeast of Mexico City. The Acolman monks belonged to the Augustinian order, eschewed violence, and seldom traveled with an armed escort. The pack train would soon pass near a place in some low mountains by the river where the outlaws lay in waiting. Near evening the monks were beginning to seek a good location to spend the night by the river, when the renegades charged from a nearby ridge and swept down on the hapless and unarmed caravaners. In their fright the monks ignored the pack mules which had scattered up and down the floodplain. Seeing that the missionaries offered no resistance or threat, the outlaws rounded up the mules and drove them off toward the east.

Once out of sight of the missionaries, the bandits tore open the packs to find a wide assortment of religious objects including golden chalices, urns, and candlesticks along with several sacks of silver coins. Some of the booty was divided up and Nevarez gave his men orders to cache the remainder in a nearby cave, sealing it against the discovery of those who might later come to avenge the missionaries.

The monks, frightened and unable to proceed, returned to El Paso del Norte to report the robbery to their superiors in Acolman and await instructions. In a few weeks a company of soldiers arrived from Durango. While at El Paso del Norte, the soldiers disguised themselves as missionaries and, leading a makeshift pack train, proceeded northward toward the territory of Nevarez and his outlaw band.

Not suspecting anything, Nevarez and his men roared out of a canyon in the Organ Mountains and descended upon the travelers. As the outlaws approached the pack train, the soldiers threw back the missionary robes and produced their weapons. A brief fight flared, with several men on both sides killed, but the element of surprise was effective and the outlaws were defeated. Those who had not escaped or killed by the soldiers were taken prisoner, roped together, and forced to walk all the way to Mexico City. Pedro Nevarez was quickly tried and sentenced to hang. While awaiting his fate in a dim jail cell he tried to bargain with a guard for his release. In exchange he told the guard about a place in the Organ Mountains where the wealth from many robberies was cached. The description was written down by a monk from the nearby Acolman monastery who was charged with attending him. In spite of his promise of riches to anyone who would release him, Nevarez was hanged within the week.

The matter probably would have remained closed and forgotten had it not been for a remarkable incident that occurred one day in 1930 in El Paso. Near the center of that city there was a shop that specialized in repairing and restoring old trunks, strongboxes, and safes. On this day the proprietor of the shop was given a well-worn and quite ancient Spanish safe to repair. He was told that it had come from the old monastery at Alcoman. As he was removing the ruined interior wall of the safe, he discovered a Spanish manuscript that had been hidden between the inner lining and the outer steel wall of the box. The manuscript eventually came into the possession of a foreign languages professor at the University of Texas, who translated it into English. It turned out to be the description of the cache of stolen goods dictated by Pedro Nevarez only days before his death in 1649. One version of the translation states:

Go to El Paso del Norte and inquire where the Organ Mountains are. The mountains are located up the river two days' travel from El Paso del Norte by horseback. It is a large mountain range with some peaks on it. You will find in these mountains two gaps. One is called Tortuga and the other is called Soledad. Before entering the first gap turn to your right and go to about the middle of the slope of the mountain where you will find a very thick juniper tree. From this tree proceed downhill 100 paces to a spot covered with small stones. Look there for a blue stone a great deal larger than the others. A cross was made on this stone with a chisel. Remove this slab and dig about a man's height and you will find a hole full of silver taken from the packs of six mules. You will find at the bottom of this hole some boards. Remove the boards and you will find coins from three mule trains we captured and buried there. Following this go to Soledad Canyon and follow up the pass until you reach a very large spring which is the source of the water that runs through the canyon. The spring is covered with cattails. Proceed to the right to about the middle of the slope of the mountains. Look with great care for three juniper trees which are very thick and set not very far apart. In front of these trees is a small precipice in which can be found a large flat rock on which a cross has been carved with a chisel. Between the trees and the rock exists a mine which belonged to a wealthy Spaniard named Jorge Colon. The mine is so rich that silver ore can be cut with a knife. The opening of the mine is covered by a large door we constructed from the timbers of the juniper. On top of this door is placed a large red rock. It will take 25 men to remove this rock. Just inside the door can be found gold crucifixes, images, platters, vases, and other items. Passing this, continue down into the mine shaft and you will encounter a tall stack of silver bars. Beyond this lies mining equipment. Thousands of families will be benefited from this wealth.

Coincidentally, another description of a location of some of Nevarez's buried loot surfaced. After the surprise counterattack by the Spanish soldiers on Nevarez's band, one of the wounded renegades escaped and was discovered unconscious the next morning outside the residence of a priest who ministered to Indians at the mission in Doña Ana. Before he died, the outlaw confessed to the priest that he was a member of Nevarez's gang and that they had been tricked by the Spanish soldiers. He also described the church valuables they had taken in a previous robbery and where they were buried. The priest wrote down the words of the dying man and filed away the information. Sometime around 1879, the Apache Chief Victorio went up and down the Rio Grande valley attacking settlers. He raided the mission at Doña Ana and, after securing much stored food and many silver coins, proceeded to tear and burn down the church. Books, letters, and church documents were scattered over the area in the wake of the raiding Indians. Among the papers retrieved was a letter written by a priest to the monastery in Acolman in 1649 but apparently never delivered. The letter contained the dying outlaw's description of the buried treasure:

In Soledad Canyon there is a natural cave in the brow of a hill opening toward the south. There is a cross cut into the rock above the entrance to the cave and directly in front of a young juniper tree. For better directions, there are three medium-sized peaks toward the rising sun whose shadows converge in the morning 250 paces east of the cave entrance and a little to the south. Two hundred and fifty paces from this point directly north can be found an embankment from where by looking straight ahead you can see the *Jornada del Muerto* as far as the eye can see. The distance from this point to the cave should be exactly the same as the distance to the place where the shadows of the peaks converge. One hundred paces from the entrance to the cave down the *arroyo* you will find a dripping spring. The entrance to the cave has been covered to the depth of a man's height and ten paces beyond the entrance there is an adobe wall which must be torn down in order to gain access. At the bottom of a long tunnel the cave separates into two parts: the left cave contains two mule loads worth of coined silver and the right cave contains golden candlesticks, images, and crucifixes taken in a robbery.

Dr. Arthur Campa, a renowned folklorist and scholar of Hispanic culture in the Southwest, met a man named Ben Brown who told him about a discovery he made while out hunting one day in 1913. Brown had spent most of his life in and around the

Rio Grande valley near the Organ Mountains and was quite familiar with the story related by the mortally wounded member of Nevarez's band of renegades, having heard it from a former employee.

Brown was a miner and was currently managing several profitable mining operations in and around the Organ Mountains at the time. He told Campa about an experience he had one day while deer hunting. Brown had shot a deer, but the animal was only wounded and led him on a chase of several hundred yards until it finally disappeared. Disappointed at not being able to retrieve his quarry and exhausted from the pursuit, Brown sat down in the shade of an old juniper tree on the slope at which he had arrived. He rested for a while, scanning the distance for some sign of the wounded deer. Then he began to notice something unusual about the slope: it was covered with loose rock and soil, unlike the rest of the hillside. Brown immediately wondered why someone would go to such trouble to modify the landscape.

Trying his best to recall the buried treasure story told to him some months earlier, he stood up and began to examine the area. Immediately he identified the three conical peaks. From the juniper where he was standing, he walked 250 paces in the direction of the rising sun. He marked the point at which he stopped and then turned north and proceeded to pace off the same distance in that direction. At the point where he stopped he found himself standing on a low promontory where he could look out across the *Jornada del Muerto*.

He returned to the tree and walked downhill to the *arroyo* exactly one hundred paces and stopped where the dripping spring was supposed to be located, but he saw nothing. Using a flat rock he dug into the dirt at his feet and encountered moisture only six inches deep.

Brown began to think he might have discovered the location of the treasure that had been buried by Pedro Nevarez over 260 years before.

Before dawn the next day, Brown returned to the site with some digging tools. As the sun rose he waited to see if the convergence of the shadows of the three peaks would occur. At about midmorning it happened and he marked the point with a cairn of rocks. He then paced off 250 steps to the west, stopped where the fill material merged with the solid rock of the mountain hillside, and commenced to dig straight down into the rubble. In about an hour and a half he had excavated a hole about six feet deep when his shovel struck solid rock. As he widened the hole he realized he had encountered a large flat stone and as he cleared the dirt from it he was fascinated to see a crude symbol of a cross carved onto its face!

By this time Brown was exhausted from the work and the excitement and thought it best to quit for the day. He threw some dirt over the rock to conceal the cross and returned to his home in Las Cruces.

The next morning he filed a mining claim on the area in the office of the county clerk, loaded his car with camping gear and supplies, and returned to the dig. He set up a primitive camp, marked his mining claim with the customary rock monuments, and cut down the juniper tree in order not to leave landmarks for anyone else who might be searching for the treasure.

Through slow and laborious work, Brown removed the large flat stone that sealed the entrance to the cave. Then he discovered that the cave itself had been filled in with rock debris and topsoil. Nevarez and his men had certainly gone to great lengths to conceal their treasure cache.

Now the truly difficult work had begun. Bucketful by bucketful Brown removed the fill dirt from the passageway—crawling in, scooping the dirt into a bucket, sliding the bucket along as he crawled back out, and then carrying it to the top of the excavation where he dumped it. After the second day of excavating the cave in this manner he discovered a Spanish copper coin that had the date of 1635 on it. He felt encouraged.

Several days and tons of dirt later he reached the adobe wall described by the outlaw. Using a crowbar he chipped away at it until it was rendered to small clods of dirt and hauled to the surface. Just beyond the wall the cave was open for about ten yards and he could stand upright to his full height, but just beyond that short open space he encountered more fill dirt. Brown continued to remove the dirt one bucketful at a time. During this part of the excavation he uncovered a well-worn remnant of a tool he described as having a pick blade on one side and a hatchet blade on the other. Some weeks later he sent the tool to the Chicago Field Museum of Natural History and was informed that it was made of hand-forged Spanish steel.

During the excavation Brown also had to maintain his other mining operations in the Organ Mountains. His excavation work on the Nevarez treasure cache continued, but one full year later he was still removing soil from the interior of the cave. The production from his other mining claims fell so low that Brown had to take other jobs in order to provide for his wife and two daughters. Over the next few years he worked at other mining claims, as a forest ranger, and even as a musician. When he could manage the time, he would return to the cave for more excavation work.

Brown was still removing dirt and debris from the cave twenty years later when he met Dr. Campa. He and Campa became good friends, and Brown spoke openly about his search for Nevarez's buried treasure. He said that most searchers for the treasure were convinced that the dying outlaw had identified Soledad Canyon in the Organ Mountains but that was a mistake. Brown said although the right canyon had the same name as the canyon in the Organ range, it is in fact in the Doña Ana Mountains, a small range some fifteen miles west of the Organs and commencing about five miles north of Las Cruces. On a subsequent visit Brown actually took Campa to the cave and showed him the excavation. Campa writes:

The tunnel against the hillside had the appearance of a natural cave, very similar to the subterranean formations (in) . . . Carlsbad Caverns, except there was no moisture and the floor was covered with topsoil. For a short distance we walked upright; then we stooped and finally began crawling on all fours. About two hundred feet down into the earth we came upon a point where the cave split into a Y going in two directions. I took one side and Ben followed . . . the other. This was as far as he had cleared . . . (but) I could see that the (passage) continued indefinitely. Back (at) the surface . . . Ben pointed out the landmarks of the three peaks . . . the *jornada* . . . and the spring.

Leaving the excavation, Brown told Campa that he was trying to locate financial backing in order to buy some machinery that would facilitate clearing the soil out of the cave. However, he never got the funding, and at the same time he became active in mining perlite and tungsten nearby. His profits from these undertakings were such that he decided to devote full time to the effort. He was now earning a good living and spent less and less time with the exhausting excavation.

Campa and Brown parted company and did not see each other again until the mid-1940s. Brown told Campa that he had been prospering from his active mines but had not given up on the

Nevarez treasure. Several years later Brown wrote Campa that he needed to see him because he had a lot to tell him about the Nevarez treasure cache. Because of academic obligations at the University of Denver where he taught, Campa was unable to reach Brown. Not long afterwards Ben Brown passed away. Whatever secrets he discovered about the buried treasure of Pedro Nevarez were buried with him.

The Lost Adams Diggings

Not much was ever known about Adams, not even his first name, and much of his life remains as mysterious as the fabulous lost placer mine he is associated with. It is known that he was born in Rochester, New York, on July 10, 1829, but little else of his background has ever surfaced.

In 1861 Adams worked for a freight company that made regular runs between Los Angeles and Tucson. In August 1864 he dropped off a load of freight in Tucson and was returning to California leading twelve horses, a large freight wagon, and a trailer. He was also carrying two thousand dollars in cash, the payment for the freight he had delivered. One evening on his return journey he set up camp near Gila Bend, and prior to bedding down he turned his horses loose to graze nearby. At dawn he was awakened by the sound of Indians running off his horses. He saw five young Apaches herding his animals toward a nearby gully. Strapping on a pistol he pursued them, killed two of the Indians, and retrieved the stock. By the time he returned to the camp with the animals he discovered his wagons set ablaze, his harnesses cut to pieces, and his provisions and money stolen. The theft of the horses was apparently a diversion to facilitate the looting of his camp.

Penniless and without provisions, Adams pondered what to do. He knew of a friendly Pima Indian village a few miles away and set out toward it, hoping he would be able to barter for enough supplies for the return trip. At the Pima village, Adams found a group of twenty miners from California panning for gold in the nearby river. Because none of the miners had horses they were very interested in the animals Adams had with him. As Adams and the miners were involved in negotiations they were joined by a

123

young Mexican dressed as an Apache.

The Mexican told Adams that he and a brother had been kidnapped by the Apaches from a ranch deep in Sonora and raised by the Indians. Recently the Mexican had had a quarrel with a member of the tribe and killed him. Fearing retaliation he fled, eventually arriving at the Pima village in Arizona. The Mexican had been born with a deformed left ear that resembled a flat knot and was given the name "Gotch Ear."

Gotch Ear had been watching the excited miners with amusement as they pulled an occasional small nugget out of the river during their panning operations. He confided in Adams that he knew of a canyon to the northeast where one could gather enough gold in one day to make a full load for a horse. He said he had seen nuggets as large as acorns lying in the stream that flowed through the canyon. Adams told this story to the miners and, intrigued by the possibilities of great wealth, asked Gotch Ear if he would lead them to the canyon. They offered him two of Adams's horses, a good saddle, a rifle, and a saddlebag filled with ammunition. Gotch Ear agreed to lead an expedition to the canyon which he said was a two-week journey by horseback.

Because Adams had the only horses, he was selected leader of the party. On the morning of August 20, 1864, the twenty-two men, some riding and some walking, set out for the canyon of gold. Adams tried to note landmarks along the way but he had little sense of geography and direction and was unable to retain much of what he saw. This lack of attention to detail was to plague him in later years when he tried to relocate the fabled canyon.

After several days the caravan crossed over a pass between Mount Ord and Mount Thomas in eastern Arizona. Adams recalled later that during the journey the party had skirted the White Mountains and crossed two major streams, the Black River and the Little Colorado. Others suggest one of the streams might have been the San Francisco River and still others suggest the Gila River. The group eventually crossed a well-used wagon road that the guide said led to Fort Wingate somewhere to the north.

Late in the evening of the fourteenth day the guide led the group to a campsite by a spring. The next day, he told them, he would take them to the gold.

The following morning as the men were preparing breakfast they observed that their campsite was a small cultivated and irrigated pumpkin patch, apparently worked by local Indians. In later years searchers for the canyon of gold tried to relocate this pumpkin patch but with no success.

After the men had secured all the equipment on the horses, Gotch Ear led them away from the trail and into a canyon to the north of the campsite. The canyon seemed endless as the party worked its way along the rocky bottom. At one point along the trail the guide showed them a concealed opening in one wall of the canyon which he referred to as "the little door." A huge boulder partially obscured the opening so that it was difficult to spot it from the canyon trail. Entering this opening the men rode downward along a rough boulder-strewn trail through a canyon so narrow that they could touch both walls from horseback. Adams described the narrow canyon trail as having the shape of a perfect Z.

Eventually the narrow pass opened out into a valley filled with pine trees and cottonwoods which had a small stream running through the middle. At the northwestern end of the valley the men could see a waterfall. Beyond the far ridge could be seen two rounded mountaintops which the guide referred to as the Peloncillos.

Turning, the guide waved an arm in the direction of the valley and told them that there they would find the gold. Several of the men immediately dismounted and began to pan for ore in the small stream. Within minutes the valley was filled with excited shouts of discovery as they found gold nuggets in abundance in the clear water.

After supper Gotch Ear told Adams he would take his leave. He was paid off and the men waved farewell as he disappeared into the narrow zigzag canyon on his way out of the valley. The guide was never seen again, but rumors surfaced months later that two Apache warriors were seen riding the horses which Gotch Ear had been given to guide the men into the canyon.

Adams, exercising his influence as leader of the group, suggested that the men pool all the gold and divide it equally at a later date. Several of the men who did not have the necessary panning equipment were given the task of constructing a log cabin for shelter against the approaching winter. At one end of the cabin they made a hearth, using large flat stones. Under one particularly large stone they dug a hole which was to be used for storing gold nuggets.

During the cabin-building the valley was visited by Apache Chief Nana and thirty of his braves. They rode in and formed a line in front of the cabin. Nana inquired as to the intentions of the

125

men and Adams replied they were interested only in panning for the gold in the little stream. Nana replied that this valley belonged to the Apache, but that if the men treated it with care they would be allowed to search for the gold, as it was of no use to the Indians. They were welcome to hunt and to graze their horses on the lush grasses that grew in the valley, Nana said, but under no circumstances were any of them to venture to the upper end of the valley beyond the falls. That part of the valley was sacred, and any violator of it would be severely punished. Nana referred to the canyon as *Sno-ta-hay*.

Two weeks after their arrival, provisions began running low. Adams decided to send a group of men to Fort Wingate for food and mining supplies. One of the miners, John Brewer, was selected to lead an expedition of six men to the fort. Adams and Brewer calculated it would take eight days to reach the fort, buy supplies, and return to the valley.

As the men continued to pan gold from the little stream, the richness of the take never diminished. It was estimated that by this time they had accumulated over $100,000 worth of gold. Each day they saw Apaches but always at a distance, never hostile, and always watching.

On the fourth day after the departure of Brewer and the supply party, one of the miners showed Adams a gold nugget as large as a hen's egg. When asked where he had gotten it, the man replied he had found it above the falls. He presented the large nugget to Adams as a gift and told him there were dozens more just like it in that part of the stream. Adams reminded the man of the warning given by the Apaches and cautioned him not to enter that area again. The next day, however, the man showed Adams a coffee pot half full of large gold nuggets he had gotten from above the falls. Again Adams warned the man to avoid the restricted area as they did not want to incur the wrath of the Indians.

On the eighth day following Brewer's departure Adams became concerned. He continually watched the opening of the zigzag canyon for the group but they failed to appear. On the morning of the ninth day Adams and Bill Davidson rode out of the valley to look for some sign of the returning supply party. At the little door their worst fears were realized—they found the scalped and mutilated bodies of five men along with several dead horses. The group had apparently reached this point on their return from the fort when they were attacked by Indians. Some of the recently purchased supplies were scattered about the canyon floor.

Adams and Davidson hurried back to the valley to tell their comrades. On approaching the end of the zigzag canyon, the two men heard Apache war yells intermingled with the terrified screams of the miners. As they entered the valley they witnessed about three hundred Apaches torturing and killing the miners. The cabin had been set afire and was burning furiously. Fearing they would be discovered, Adams and Davidson dismounted and hid in a dense thicket of trees from which they could watch the depredations below. By now all of the miners had been killed and the Indians were fighting over their scalps. The frenzy continued until sundown, at which point the Apaches retreated out of sight beyond the falls. During their time of concealment several Apaches passed near Adams and Davidson, but their hiding place went undetected.

After the Indians left, Davidson insisted that he and Adams sneak down to the cabin to retrieve the gold under the hearth. When they arrived the cabin was still burning and the timbers were too hot to move from the hearth. Disappointed, the two men crept out of the valley and back up the zigzag trail. The only gold they were able to take from the valley, ironically, was the large nugget given to Adams by one of the miners—the nugget that had brought the Apaches' wrath down upon them.

In the canyon the men found their horses and rode out. As they had not eaten all day they stopped to dine on raw acorns they found near the pumpkin patch. They fled toward the west but in their haste neglected to watch for pertinent landmarks and soon became lost. Two days later they killed one of the horses and broiled some of the meat. Thirteen days after fleeing the valley the men were discovered by a detachment of United States Calvary from Fort Apache and were taken to the fort, where they were treated for hunger and exposure.

Davidson, who was fifty-four years old, never completely recovered from the ordeal and died a few months later. Adams fared better but the experience left him a broken man. One day as he lay in the shade of building on the military post he was startled by the arrival of five Indians riding into the fort. He pulled a pistol and shot and killed two of them before he could be subdued. He was placed in the guardhouse to await trial for murder, but a sympathetic lieutenant arranged for him to escape and even provided him with a horse. During his flight Adams stopped in Tucson, where he sold the large nugget he carried. A year later he was known to be living in Los Angeles with his wife and three children. Because of recurring nightmares and his fear of the Apaches, he was not inclined to return to the valley of gold.

Ten years later, however, Adams became acquainted with C.A. Shaw, a retired sea captain who had heard about the fabled canyon. Shaw had an adventurous spirit and agreed to finance an expedition to return to the valley if Adams would lead it. Adams, now forty-five, was reluctant but finally agreed to participate. During the search he repeatedly lost his bearings and could never recognize any pertinent landmarks. The men returned empty-handed. Over the next ten years Shaw financed several more searches and, though he placed great faith in Adams and his story, was never able to get the old freighter to relocate the canyon of gold.

During one of the searches, Adams and Shaw had taken up temporary residence at Fort Wingate. At that time Chief Nana and his band had stopped at the fort on their way to the San Carlos Indian Reservation. Adams, recognizing the Apache chieftain, approached him and asked him how long it had been since he had been to *Sno-ta-hay* Canyon. Nana glared at Adams through narrowed eyes, hostility rising in his countenance. After a full minute the old Indian turned and stalked away without saying a word.

The Adams diggings also interested John Dowling. Dowling learned of the valley of gold from the surgeon who had treated Adams and Davidson at Fort Apache. The doctor was able to piece together a crude set of directions to the valley, based on Adams's description, which he communicated to Dowling. The surgeon tried several times to reach the valley himself but never succeeded. He was city-bred and had a difficult time in the wild mountainous environment of western New Mexico. Rather than face the rigors of the trail he gave up. Dowling, on the other hand, was at home in the wilderness. On one trip in search of the lost Adams diggings, he entered a narrow valley that matched the description written down by the doctor. The first thing he noticed was about sixty stumps, stumps of trees that might have been used to construct a log cabin. In one part of the valley he found a deep pile of charcoal and ash next to the remains of what appeared to be a rock chimney. At the time Dowling was unaware of the existence of the large gold cache under the hearth. Dowling panned the little stream for two days but never found any gold.

Adams once met a man named Bob Lewis in the little settlement of Magdalena, New Mexico. Lewis had hunted for the diggings for years, and now he was face to face with the man whose name was associated with the lost canyon. Using some first-hand directions he got from Adams, Lewis attempted another search. In the Datil Mountains of New Mexico, he discovered a narrow twisted canyon that entered a somewhat larger one. The entrance to the smaller canyon was partially concealed by a huge boulder, similar to the "little door" through which Gotch Ear led the original Adams party. Near the entrance to the smaller canyon Lewis found the skeletal remains of five men as well as several horses stuffed into a deep rock crevice. Were these the remains of the supply party led by Brewer?

St. John lies west of the Datil Mountains about fifteen miles inside the Arizona border. One day in 1888, two wagons pulled up to the main house of the Tenney Ranch, located just outside St. John. The wagons contained a man, his Indian wife and daughter, and all their belongings. In tow were several well-bred horses and about twenty head of cattle, all herded by an Indian helper. The man in the lead wagon asked Tenney if he could camp in the area for a few days. The man introduced himself to Tenney as John Brewer! In the days following their meeting, Brewer told Tenney the story of the lost Adams diggings and his escape from the Apaches. Before leaving, Brewer presented Tenney with a manuscript dealing with his experience. The following account of Brewer's escape is taken, in part, from the manuscript.

As Brewer and the supply party approached the zigzag canyon by way of the little door, they were set upon by Apaches. Early in the attack Brewer took an arrow in the left calf, dropped his rifle, and fell off his horse. He crawled to the concealment of some rocks and thence into a dense thicket of scrub brush where he remained hidden while listening to the noise of the massacre. After waiting for several hours, Brewer left his hiding place and found the horribly mutilated bodies of his companions. Frightened and bleeding, he crept down the narrow canyon to warn Adams and the others of the attack. He entered the valley and saw the devastated cabin and the bodies of the miners. He tried to approach the cabin to see if he could secure the gold cache but heard approaching footsteps and hid in a gully. He lay quietly as two shadowy figures passed by him and on into the canyon. It is very likely that the two men Brewer heard that night were Adams and Davidson. After remaining hidden for about two hours, Brewer emerged and retraced his path back out of the canyon. He wandered for several days until he chanced upon a village of friendly Indians. Brewer was delirious, raving and talking to himself. The Indians fed him and cared for him for several days, and when Brewer was able to travel they took him to the nearest white settlement. He never attempted to relocate the lost canyon of gold.

It may be that the lost Adams diggings will never be found. In the 1870s a man named Jason Baxter became involved in the search for the lost valley. Acting on information he had obtained, Baxter eventually located what he was certain was the zigzag canyon, but when he entered the valley he found that most of it had been covered up as a result of a tremendous landslide. Baxter surmised that a great earthquake had occurred in recent years and caused tons of rock to crash into the little valley, forever concealing the wealth that lay in the stream.

The lost Adams diggings have been sought by hundreds—by men on horseback, on foot, and even in airplanes—but it remains one of the most elusive lost mines in the history of the Southwest.

Oklahoma

1. Lost Gold of Devil's Canyon
2. Hidden Spanish Gold Cache in the Wichita Mountains
3. Bell Starr's Lost Iron Door Mine
4. The Lost Gold Ingots of Padre LaFarge
5. The Lost Payroll

The Lost Gold of Devil's Canyon

The Wichita Mountains of southwestern Oklahoma are made up of several jumbles of rugged rock outcrops which originated millions of years ago as a result of deep and violent underground volcanic activity. The very forces which gave rise to these huge rock structures are related to those involved in the formation of gold and silver, both of which are found in these mountains. In addition to being rich in ore, the Wichita Mountains are rich in history and lore. In the early part of the seventeenth century the Spanish explored much of the area and attempted to establish a colony. While their colonization efforts failed, their mining activities succeeded, and legends describe great wealth in gold and silver mined from the Wichitas and shipped back to the Spanish homeland. The mountains have also been claimed as the territory of numerous Indian tribes, including the Comanche, the Kiowa, and the Wichita, all of which found the abundant game and water to their liking, and perceived the rugged vastness of the range as easy to defend against encroaching white settlers.

Anglo settlement and ranching in and around the Wichita Mountains began during the mid-nineteenth century, and by 1880 several large and successful ranches had been established. The U.S. Army guarded the area against Indians with several companies of well-mounted and well-armed cavalry.

At the extreme western end of the Wichita Mountain range lies Devil's Canyon, a southwest-northeast oriented gorge flanked by Flat Top Mountain and Soldiers' Peak. The steep walls of the two mountains keep much of the canyon in shade during the day, lending a dark and forbidding atmosphere to the rocky, brush-choked canyon floor. Local legend says that the canyon is haunted by the

133

spirits of those who have died there. Indeed, over the past two hundred years dozens of skeletons have been found in the canyon along with bits and pieces of Spanish armor and mining equipment. Many Indian artifacts have also been found, indicating a large and continuous Comanche encampment at the mouth of the canyon.

The canyon was the site of a Spanish mission established in 1629 by Padre Juan de Salas. Salas, along with a few Indian converts, tried to grow corn and beans near the mouth of the canyon where a small stream empties into the North Fork of the Red River. The little settlement languished, and a prolonged drought forced its abandonment a few years later.

The canyon was visited again in 1650 by a small detachment of the Spanish army led by Captain Hernan Martín and adventurer Don Diego del Castillo. They searched the area for gold and silver and, encouraged by the discovery of rich ore, reported the findings to their superiors.

In 1657 a Spanish priest named Gilbert arrived at the canyon leading a group of one hundred men. Using directions provided by Martín and Castillo, they began mining gold from the canyon. A large shaft over a hundred feet in length was sunk into the solid rock of one canyon wall. Several mule loads of ore were taken from the mine, but it was soon abandoned because of the continued threat of hostile Indians.

In 1698, a group of Spaniards disembarked at a port near present-day New Orleans and proceeded inland toward the Wichita Mountains. The party, one hundred strong, was well equipped with mining tools and was accompanied by a detachment of fifty soldiers. Following a set of maps and charts, the group reached Devil's Canyon after a journey of several weeks. They established a permanent camp, building several dwellings of adobe and rock, a church, and a primitive smelter located in a nearby cave.

As the Spaniards mined and smelted the ore, the canyon was visited several times by Indians. Initially their visits were hostile, but when they learned the white men were interested only in the colored rock that was of no use to them, a truce was established and the Indians permitted the Spaniards to remain.

Several times a year a pack train laden with gold bullion would leave the canyon and proceed to the port on the gulf, where the ore would be shipped to Spain. The party would then return to the canyon with more mining supplies.

As the months passed, relations between the miners and the Indians became strained. Occasionally the soldiers would range far from the canyon on hunting trips and encounter Indians. Brief but violent skirmishes occurred, and the Spaniards were soon forced to post several armed guards around the settlement each night, alert for a potential attack. Indians posted high atop the canyon walls were often observed watching the miners, but no overt threats were made.

Early one winter morning a pack train composed of fifty mules carrying gold bullion exited the canyon, traveling southeastward along the trail toward the gulf. As the last mule left the canyon, about three hundred Indians fell upon the caravan. The miners and soldiers from the settlement armed themselves and ran to the aid of their comrades, but they were far outnumbered. Soon all of the Spaniards lay dead, save for three who had escaped.

The area remained quiet for several years with no one entering the canyon but an occasional hunting party. In 1765 a French explorer of the area named Brevel made friends with several Indians who told him the story of the massacre of the miners many years earlier. Brevel examined the canyon and saw the ruins of the ancient church and dwellings that had been constructed by the Spaniards. Farther up the canyon he found several abandoned mines.

During the next few years many travelers and explorers to the region reported seeing the crumbling ruins of the Spanish structures, but no one tried to reopen the mines. Then sometime in the early 1830s a party of Mexicans moved into the canyon and set up residence. Legend says that the Mexicans were led by a descendant of one of the Spaniards who had escaped the Indian attack of three decades earlier and, armed with maps and descriptions of great wealth to be found in the canyon, they located and reopened the mines. In 1833 the Mexicans were observed by Simon N. Cockrell, who worked as a scout for some businessmen wishing to establish a trading post nearby. The Mexicans remained secretive about their activities in the canyon, but Cockrell recognized mining tools and presumed they were working in the old Spanish mines.

In the summer of 1834, the Mexicans were preparing to leave the canyon with several dozen mule loads of gold ore when they were set upon by Kiowas. A fierce battle erupted at the mouth of the canyon. Several Mexicans ran to the mine shaft and rolled a huge boulder over it in an attempt to conceal it. This done, they returned toward the mouth of the canyon to aid their fellows but by the time they arrived the battle was over and the Indians victorious. As the Indians went from body to body taking scalps, the surviving Mexicans concealed themselves among the boulders along one of the canyon walls and waited for a chance to escape. After taking the scalps, the Indians turned the pack train back into the canyon, where they unloaded the ore and, as the Mexicans watched from hiding, cached it in a small cave in the canyon wall. They concealed the place with several tons of rock and debris in order to make it match the surrounding environment. Once the Indians departed the canyon, the miners rose from their place of concealment and set out on foot toward Mexico.

In 1850 a second group of Mexicans arrived at Devil's Canyon. This group was smaller than the first and was led by one of the men who had escaped the Kiowa massacre sixteen years earlier. On their first evening in the canyon they set up camp near a small pond just beyond the entrance. On the morning of the second day they walked to the place where the Kiowa had cached the gold ore after the massacre. As the men dug into the hillside, two young boys were sent to a trading post seven miles up the North Fork of the Red River to get some supplies. When the boys were about a half-mile out of the canyon they heard shots and screams coming from where the men were digging. They raced back into the canyon and saw a large band of Indians attacking the party. The boys turned and rode to the trading post for help. When they returned with a group of ten men, they discovered the entire party had been killed, scalped, and mutilated.

In the early 1870s a man named J.C. Settles established a homestead near Devil's Canyon. In grazing his cattle in and around the canyon he noted the crumbled ruins of the old Spanish church and dwellings. Settles made friends with many of the Indians who remained in the area and he often hired them to work on his ranch. One day Settles and an older Indian were running cattle toward the pond in Devil's Canyon when the Indian related the story of the battle with the Mexicans many years earlier. He also told Settles he knew of a place back in the canyon where the Mexicans mined the silver and said he could take him to it. He told Settles the miners had dug a shaft over one hundred feet deep straight down into the solid rock of the canyon floor, following a thick vein of gold. He also told how the Mexicans had rolled a great boulder onto the opening to conceal it. At the time Settles was interested in cattle, not mining, but several years later he did make an effort to locate the site. He found an ancient mine shaft with a large boulder rolled into it, not on top of it, and with great difficulty he eventually succeeded in blasting it from the opening. Inside the shaft he found a human skeleton and a coal-like substance he couldn't identify. Without having any of the material from the mine assayed, Settles abandoned the mine, never to return.

In 1900 an aged Kiowa woman was seen hiking near Devil's Canyon apparently searching for specific landmarks. When questioned, she claimed that as a young girl she accompanied the band of Kiowas that attacked and killed the Mexican miners in 1834. She said she had helped two braves hide three mule loads of gold after the battle and was now searching for it. She never found the cache.

Soon after 1900 there was a brief flurry of prospecting and mining in the Wichita Mountains. Several people examined the potential of Devil's Canyon and one man discovered an eighty-five-pound nugget of gold! He claimed to have dug it out of one of the old Spanish mines in the canyon.

At the entrance to Devil's Canyon can be found a grove of trees, some of them very old. On several of these trees are some ancient carvings, among them one of a turtle—long recognized by researchers as a symbol used by the Spanish to denote the existence of gold or silver nearby. Even more mysterious is the large turtle symbol that was found deeper in the canyon. This manifestation of a giant turtle was an abstract figure fashioned on the ground using a total of 152 stones. The head of the turtle was pointed toward the northwest in the direction of one wall of the canyon. Some claim the head of the turtle pointed to the location of one of the mines. Unfortunately, the image was demolished during the construction of a stock pond.

An old Indian legend claims that Devil's Canyon is haunted by the devil himself and that he guards the cache of gold concealed against one wall of the rugged canyon. The legend also says that a layer of human skeletons covers the gold. In 1967 a youth was hunting rabbits in the canyon when he discovered several human skeletons exposed near one wall. The area had been subjected to heavy rains the previous week and several hundred pounds of rock and debris were washed away, revealing the grisly collection. Thinking he had come upon a long-forgotten graveyard, the youth did not investigate any further. He told no one of his experience until several years later. On hearing the tale, a group of men familiar with the stories and legends of Devil's Canyon hiked into the canyon in an attempt to locate the skeletons but were unsuccessful.

Today Devil's Canyon is a part of Quartz Mountain State Park and is visited by hikers and rock collectors. Even though the area is now more accessible to weekend explorers, the spirits reputed to roam the canyon apparently still guard the lost gold.

Spanish Treasure in the Wichita Mountains

The five men carefully guided their horses through the rock and rubble of the canyon floor. Few words passed between the ranchers as they scanned the canyon walls in search of landmarks and Indians. The landmarks were important to them, for they believed they were on the trail of a great fortune in hidden Spanish gold. Indians hostile to the presence of whites were also known to be in the area. The band of Comanche currently using the mountain range as a hiding place had just ridden in from the south, where they had raided and burned several ranches, killing and scalping along the way.

As the group of white men exited the canyon, they saw another, smaller canyon that lay just to the east. The leader pulled a folded parchment from inside his shirt, spread it open, and examined it with great care. He told the others that according to the map the lost underground vault of the Spanish miners was located a short distance into the canyon just ahead of them. Taking another long look at the surrounding ridgetops, the men then goaded their mounts forward. The anticipation of locating the fabulous lost hoard of wealth was exceeded only by their apprehension of what would happen to them should they be discovered by the bloodthirsty Comanche.

As the leader steered the group toward the smaller canyon he mused over the circumstances that brought them there. Almost a year earlier he had encountered a Mexican wandering the periphery of the Wichita Mountains. The man was lost, hungry, and out of water. The rancher brought him to his home and nursed him back to health. When the stranger had three days of rest and several full meals behind him, he told the rancher that he was searching for a cave that was reputed to conceal hundreds of bars of gold which were stacked and left behind when the Spanish miners fled the area just ahead of Indian hostiles. The rancher openly displayed his skepticism at the tale and, anxious to prove what he said was true, the Mexican untied and removed a large folded band of silk from around his waist. When unfolded and spread out, the silk nearly covered the dining table. Clearly embroidered on it was a map showing many prominent landmarks found within the range. The Mexican pointed to a point on the map which he said was the location of the cache. The rancher warned him of the danger of the Comanche and said it was a bad time to enter the mountains. Undaunted, the Mexican undertook several expeditions into the range using directions provided by the rancher, but always returned emptyhanded. He told of seeing Indians several times but he always managed to hide among the rocks and remain undetected.

The rancher was now convinced that the cache existed, but he thought the Mexican was foolish to risk his life in the mountains. After several more attempts to locate the cache, the Mexican told the rancher that he didn't believe it could be found and he had decided to return to his home. He thanked the rancher for his hospitality and inquired how he could repay him for his kindness. The rancher suggested that he be allowed to make a copy of the map. His guest agreed and the rancher spent the evening copying the markings from the silk onto a large piece of parchment. The Mexican departed at dawn of the following day, never to be seen in the area again.

The rancher believed that his familiarity with the Wichita Mountain environment would provide him a better chance of locating the gold cache. The following spring he assembled four of his neighbors and told them about the map, and they all agreed to enter the hostile mountain range.

Now in the heart of the mountains the rancher refolded the map and replaced it inside his shirt. If the directions he had copied were correct, the hidden chamber should lie just within the small canyon ahead. Using landmarks indicated on the map, they arrived at a place in the canyon that appeared to have been excavated long ago and then subjected to a hasty and ineffective attempt at concealment. After posting one of the men on a nearby ridge to watch for Indians, the other three began to dig. They removed nearly five feet of loose fill dirt from what appeared to be an ancient excavation in the rock floor of the canyon. Once the fill was removed, the men encountered a man-made wall along one side of the excavation. The wall was only about three feet high but was clearly fashioned from rock and mortar. Using their tools they tore down the wall to reveal an opening into a shaft which led at a downward-sloping angle into the mountainside.

Inside the shaft the air was musty, cool, and dark. When the men lit the torches they had hastily fashioned from twisted grasses outside, they saw several ancient mining tools and many human bones. Several steps inside the shaft was a startling sight: hundreds of gold bars stacked like firewood against one wall. Each bar was a foot and a half long and very heavy. On the mine floor, at the end of the row of gold bars, lay several rotted baskets which contained gold coins. Beyond these the men saw a waist-high stack of bulging leather bags, which they approached in awe, intent on slicing one open. Just then they heard the shouts of their comrade who was standing guard on the ridge. Turning back, they clambered out of the shaft and looked up at the ridge to see the guard pointing toward the north and screaming that Indians were approaching from several miles distant. The men ran to the top of the ridge and saw in the distance a huge cloud of dust raised by the horses of what must have been at least a hundred riders. The men sped to their horses, mounted, and fled from the canyon.

They rode for several miles and took shelter in a canyon that afforded them good protection if the Indians attacked. However, all was quiet, and at noon on the second day of hiding the men ventured out and decided to return to the excavation. Warily they made their way back to the canyon—only to find that the Indians had filled in the excavation! Unwilling to go into the shaft a second time, they left the area determined to return when it was safe.

When the men finally returned home, the leader discovered that he had apparently lost the map during the flight from the Indians. He was not certain he could find the canyon again. Indian hostilities continued in the area for several more years, making it unsafe to venture into the range. A few more years passed, the Civil War began to consume the attention of the nation, and the rancher and his neighbors were called upon to serve.

It is not known if others have searched for the lost underground gold cache. Some who are familiar with the legend believe that a group of men had found the shaft sometime in the early 1840s, but they were careless and let the Indians slip up on them, slaying them all. Some believe that the human skeletons encountered by the ranchers belonged to those first discoverers. In any event, the Indians were obviously aware of the existence of the cache and did their best to keep it hidden. The Indians did not appreciate the value of gold and had little use for it except for fashioning occasional ornaments. They were aware, however, of how the gleaming yellow metal made the white man crazy with greed for the wealth it brought. They knew that when gold was discovered on Indian land it was a matter of scant time before the Indian was displaced so that whites could dig the ore. The Indians did their best to cover the mines worked by the early Spanish in these mountains, thereby thwarting others' efforts to relocate them.

Comanche and Kiowa legends tell of the ghosts of their ancestors that roam the canyons of the Wichitas, maintaining a constant vigilance over the gold. Even today, treasure hunters in the mountains report seeing strange lights along the ridges and hearing unidentifiable sounds coming from deep underground.

Belle Starr's Iron Door Cache

Like most famous outlaw figures in American history, the notorious female bandit Belle Starr has taken on the proportions of legend which, as time passes, becomes increasingly difficult to distinguish from fact. It is well known that Belle Starr headed a group of outlaws that robbed trains, banks, and ranches, and it is also well known that she hid out in Oklahoma during her heyday as the bandit queen of the Wild West. Less is known of her mysterious gold cache reputedly located somewhere in the Wichita Mountains of southwestern Oklahoma, a cache of U.S. government ore reportedly worth in excess of half a million dollars.

Sometime in the mid-1880s, Belle Starr and her gang stopped a train bound for the Denver Mint with a cargo of government gold. Though the robbery went smoothly, the gang decided to cache the take for a while until things cooled down. They selected a cave in the Wichita Mountains in which to conceal the booty. On leaving the site of the robbery, they removed a large iron door from one of the railroad cars and dragged it along behind them to the hiding place. Once the gold had been stashed within the cave, the iron door was placed over the opening, secured with an intricate lock, and covered with rock and brush.

During a second train robbery attempt several months later, all of the gang members were killed. In 1889 Belle Starr herself was mysteriously murdered, and the crime has never been solved. With her death no one remained alive who knew the exact location of the iron door cache.

Investigators for the railroad learned of the possible existence of the cache in the Wichita Mountains and, though they searched for weeks, were never able to locate it. Soon the incident was forgotten.

Soon after the turn of the century a local rancher and his son were riding from the Wichita Mountain Wildlife Refuge toward the home of some friends in Indiahoma, located on the south side of the range. Getting a late start and fearing they might not arrive at their destination before nightfall, they took a shortcut through an unfamiliar portion of the range, skirting Elk Mountain and entering a deep canyon. As the sun was setting a bright reflection from one canyon wall caught their attention. Upon investigating, they found a large, rusted iron door set into a recessed area along the canyon wall. The boy wanted to explore it further, but the father insisted they try to reach their friends' house before nightfall and promised they would return soon to the strange door.

When they arrived they described the iron door set into the mountain and asked if anyone had ever seen it. Their host became quite excited and related the tale of Belle Starr's lost treasure cache. Early the next morning the man, his son, and the host retraced the path taken the evening before. They found the canyon with no difficulty but once into it could not find the door. The host suggested it might not have been the correct canyon so they examined another, and yet another, but they had no success and returned to Indiahoma. Over the next few years the man and his son undertook several more searches. They explored many canyons of the Wichita range, hoping to catch a glimpse of the iron door, but their quest always proved futile. Each was certain that it was imperative to be in a certain location during a particular moment of sunset, in order to see the rays of light striking the metal door, but they could never find themselves in the right canyon at the right time.

Interest in the cave with the iron door resumed in 1908 when an elderly woman arrived in the Wichita Mountains after a long and tiresome wagon journey from Missouri. The woman, who gave her name as Holt, had in her possession a map supposedly showing the location of the iron door cache. She also carried a large key which she said would unlock the door. The old woman revealed that several years earlier she had tended the wounds of a dying outlaw who claimed to have been a member of the gang that rode with Belle Starr and stashed the treasure in the cave. Before the outlaw died he sketched a map showing the location of the cave and gave her the key. He also told her there was a large tree close to the cache that had a railroad spike hammered into it. A tree matching this description was identified sometime during the 1950s, but it was later cut down, and no one can recall its exact location.

In 1910 a group of four teenagers who were exploring one of the remote canyons of the Wichitas came across the iron door. One of the youths gave a detailed description of the huge door and the large rusted padlock that held it shut. The boys assumed the cave was being used by a local rancher to store supplies and so they left it. Many years later one of the four heard the story of the lost iron door cache. Now a grown man with a family, he returned many times to what he believed was the same canyon but repeatedly failed to relocate the door. He thought the canyon was located just to the north of Treasure Lake, the same general area identified by the man and his son some ten years earlier.

In the 1920s a group of men were coon hunting in the Wichita Mountains. Their dogs treed a raccoon, and the men hurried to get a shot at the unfortunate animal. As one of the hunters was taking aim he was distracted by a reflection from the opposite canyon wall. Curious, he climbed a nearby boulder to try to discern the origin of the glare and saw that it was coming from a large piece of iron set in one canyon wall. As the men had no time to investigate the hunk of iron they continued their hunt, determined to return another day. When they did return weeks later, however, they could not find the door. These men, like others, claimed the door was in a canyon near Treasure Lake.

A few years later three boys were hiking to Indiahoma through the Wichita Mountains. The three were in a hurry and decided to cut through a strange canyon to save some time. The walk through the canyon floor led them past a large rusty iron door set into the mountainside. Briefly, the boys inspected the door and the big padlock that held it in place. They tried to pry the door open to see what was behind it but were unable to move it. Unaware of the potential of great wealth that lay just a few feet away, the boys hiked on. Fifty years later one of them, by then an elderly rancher, learned the story of Belle Starr's lost iron door cache from a local Indian. Certain that it was the same door he had seen as a boy, the rancher attempted to relocate the canyon. Like all the others he failed. All he could remember was that the canyon was north of Treasure Lake.

In 1932 an itinerant farm laborer was walking from Hobart to Lawton in search of work, and his journey took him through the Wichita Mountains. When night fell he set up a poor camp at a convenient spot. On the morning of the next day he continued his walk, which took him past Elk Mountain. As he hiked he claimed he saw a "rust-stained door . . . barely exposed on the mountainside." The laborer knew the story of Belle Starr's treasure cache and was certain that he had located it. He climbed to the door and struggled for nearly an hour trying to open it. He removed dozens of large rocks from in front of it and cleared away a great deal of brush but was still unable to gain entry. He decided it would take heavy tools to wedge the large rusted piece of metal out of the cave opening. When he arrived at the next town he enlisted the help of two men who supplied tools and dynamite. When they returned to the area the door could not be found! They searched all day, covering the same trail many times, but like the others failed to relocate the door.

A man named Stephens reported in the 1940s that he had actually found the door. He was hiking in a canyon near Treasure Lake when he saw it set in a shallow recess in a canyon wall not far from the trail. He described it as being an old railroad car door, partially concealed by rocks and brush. He tried to pry the huge door open to see what was behind it but was unable to budge it. He decided to return with some tools that would enable him to gain access and as he departed he constructed a cairn of rocks at a trail crossing to identify the canyon. When Stephens returned several weeks later with tools and a group of men he was unable to locate either the cairn or the canyon.

Some day when the angle of the setting sun is reflecting off of the mysterious door, a lucky searcher may be in the right place in the right canyon at the right time. Perhaps only then will it be known if the great wealth in gold is in fact hidden behind the fabled iron door.

The Buried Ingots
of Padre LaFarge

In the heat of late August in 1804 six lumbering oxcarts
traversed the bleak and arid plains of what is now the Panhandle
of Oklahoma. The carts, pulled by tired, hungry oxen, followed
the ruts of the old Santa Fe Trail which crossed this region. The
group of men accompanying the carts, mostly walking alongside
them, consisted of seven Frenchmen, one Spanish guide, and a
dozen Indian slaves. A casual glance at the contents of the carts
would have revealed nothing but furs, evidently the products of a
season of trapping in the Rocky Mountains to the west. However,
underneath the cover of furs, five hundred gold ingots lay hidden.
In all, the carts transported nearly four thousand pounds of gold.
The leader of the party frequently scanned the horizon, always
alert and on the watch for bandits and Indians. From time to time
he would lash out at an Indian slave if one of the oxcarts moved
too slowly. The leader, whose name was LaFarge, seemed to be in
a hurry as he urged the slow-moving oxen along with his whip.

LaFarge was a native Frenchman with a troubled past. Many
years earlier he had been admitted to the priesthood and then assigned to Mexico in the New World. Though the complete facts
will probably never be known, LaFarge was convicted of killing a
nun, defrocked, and sentenced to prison. After several years he was
released from prison but continued to assume the role of a priest
and even now wore the robe and hood of a Catholic friar.

LaFarge drifted north of the Rio Grande, traveling from settlement to settlement and using his disguise to advantage. Eventually he fell in with six other Frenchmen and journeyed with them
to Taos, where they established a placer mining operation along
several of the small mountain streams found in the vicinity. None

of them had any mining experience, and they soon became frustrated with their meager take from the gold-laden streams. Even more frustrating was the news of large amounts of gold panned by Mexican miners working nearby. The Frenchmen decided it would be easier to take the gold from the successful miners than to continue the drudgery of panning for their own. Over the next several weeks the seven robbed and killed twenty-two miners and accumulated a large store of stolen gold. At this point, LaFarge hired one José Lopat, a Spaniard who had experience in smelting gold ore and forming it into ingots.

After Lopat had molded five hundred gold bars, LaFarge decided it would be best to take what they had stockpiled and quit the area before their deeds were discovered. He decided to transport the gold along the old Santa Fe Trail and head south to New Orleans, where the Frenchmen would ship back to their homeland and live a life of luxury with their newly acquired wealth. Lopat continued in the employ of the Frenchmen as a guide.

As the party labored along the trail, Lopat informed LaFarge that he had located a spring just ahead and that, as it was nearing sundown, it would be best to establish a camp for the night. Both La-Farge and Lopat noted the presence of Sugar Loaf Mountain, a prominent landmark located a short distance to the north. When the party arrived at the spring (believed to be what is now called Flagg Spring in the north central part of Cimarron County) they found four mountain men encamped there, also bearing a load of furs from a recent trapping expedition. The trappers told the Frenchmen that New Orleans no longer belonged to France and that it had been sold to the United States. LaFarge became concerned that the United States government would never allow them to ship the ingots out of the country and might even confiscate the gold. Secretly he confided his concerns to his fellows, and they eventually decided to send two of their number to New Orleans to arrange for a vessel to meet them somewhere along the coast, far from the scrutiny of government agents.

The next morning two of the Frenchmen departed for New Orleans while LaFarge and the rest of the party prepared for a long stay at the spring. It was estimated that it would take three and a half months to make the round trip, so LaFarge ordered the Indian slaves to build several dugouts and rock dwellings for shelter against the approaching winter.

By the end of December the two Frenchmen still had not returned. LaFarge decided to bury the gold bars until he could determine the best way to ship the wealth to France. He ordered Lopat and the Indian slaves to return to Santa Fe and, once they were out of sight, had the gold ingots buried, presumably in the vicinity of the spring.

Following his return to Santa Fe, Lopat learned the truth of LaFarge's criminal past. He wrote what he learned, as well as the account of his helping the Frenchmen transport the gold ingots to Flagg Springs, in the back of his family Bible. It is this chronicle in the handwriting of José Lopat that provides most of the information about the buried gold ingots of Padre LaFarge. Several more months passed and one day Lopat spotted the robed and hooded figure of Padre LaFarge walking down a Santa Fe street. LaFarge told Lopat that the others had been killed by Indians and that only he, LaFarge, knew the location of the buried gold ingots. He informed Lopat that he was preparing an expedition to retrieve the gold buried near the spring and wanted the Spaniard to serve once again as guide. Lopat suspected that LaFarge had killed the others and would likely murder him once he helped the ex-priest locate and retrieve the gold bars. LaFarge told Lopat he would be well paid for his services, but the Spaniard said he wanted to consider the offer for a few days.

While Lopat stalled, LaFarge was identified by two men as one of the group who had raided and killed the placer miners months before. Several townspeople were enlisted and soon a mob roamed the streets of Santa Fe in search of the outlaw priest. LaFarge escaped by hiding under some baggage in an ox cart, but he was discovered and captured several miles outside of Santa Fe. Two weeks later Lopat learned that LaFarge had been killed and buried out on the plains.

Buried with LaFarge was the secret of the location of the five hundred gold ingots. Based on what LaFarge had told him, Lopat believed he could find them. He made a trip to the spring but found no evidence that the gold had been buried anywhere in the vicinity.

The story of the lost gold ingots of Padre LaFarge evolved into legend over the next few decades, but no record exists of any organized attempt to locate the buried treasure. Then in 1870, a series of strange stone markers were discovered near the old Spanish trail. The markers consisted of huge stones rolled into place to form the shape of a V. Each V pointed toward the next marker, which was always five to ten miles away. The strange stone direction markers were found in a somewhat regular pattern from

Santa Fe to the settlement of Las Vegas, nearly fifty miles away. Beyond Las Vegas, searchers were unable to locate any others. Several years later, however, more stone markers were discovered along the old road to Clayton, New Mexico, in the northeastern part of the state and just a few miles west of the tip of the Oklahoma Panhandle.

Then in 1900, a rancher named Ryan was driving a herd of recently purchased horses from Clayton to his ranch in Cimarron County. One evening several horses broke away from the encampment and scattered onto the plains. Ryan began a search the next morning and after a few hours of tracking stopped to rest. As he was smoking a cigarette and regarding the countryside, Ryan spotted another of the stone markers. It consisted of large rocks like all of the others and was in the distinct shape of a large V. Ryan, who was familiar with the legend of the lost gold ingots of Padre LaFarge, believed that these man-made arrangements of small boulders pointed the way to the buried treasure. Over the next two years Ryan searched for and found several more of the markers, which led him to the general vicinity of Flagg Spring. He searched the area of the spring for several years but was never able to locate any of the hidden gold. Ryan's great-nephew, a man named Cy Strong who ranched in the shadow of Sugar Loaf Mountain, was certain the ingots were buried somewhere near the spring. Not far from the spring Strong found the remains of an ancient dugout as well as a jumble of rocks and weathered adobe bricks that apparently comprised part of a crude dwelling. In addition, several pieces of rotted oxcart wheels were found nearby. More recently, however, Strong has discovered other stone markers that suggest the treasure may be buried closer to Sugar Loaf Mountain.

Since the turn of the century untold numbers of searchers have arrived at Flagg Spring looking for the hidden gold of Padre LaFarge, but apparently no one has succeeded in uncovering it to date. Some come armed with maps and others carry sophisticated metal detectors, but to no avail.

Current gold prices would place the value of the hidden treasure at approximately $1.5 million. This tantalizing figure has inspired a group of treasure hunters to employ a low-level hot-air balloon search for markers in the vicinity of Flagg Spring and Sugar Loaf Mountain. They suggest that some important directional information might elude searchers on the ground, and that the clues might be more apparent through low-altitude surveillance.

Many residents of Cimarron County feel it will be just a matter of time before the secret location of the gold ingots is revealed and the wealth retrieved.

The Plundered Payroll

During the late 1890s St. Joseph, Missouri, was a bustling town on the Missouri River, accommodating travelers going both west and east. Trading posts, hotels, saloons, and gambling houses thrived with the crush of voyagers and residents alike. The town's many livery stables also conducted a brisk business, since nearly everyone who didn't travel by boat went by horse, carriage, or coach.

One morning the owner of one such livery stable was busy feeding the riding stock boarded in his establishment when an old man entered the wide double doors. The man, bearing the look of one who had traveled for a long time in the same clothes, waited patiently for the owner of the stable to finish his chore and then stepped forward and asked for a handout. The owner could see that the elderly stranger was quite sick and weak. He gave him some food and offered him the use of a vacant stall in which to rest for a few days. The stranger thanked the owner and offered to help out around the stable in return for his keep. The next day the old man passed out twice while attempting some chores, and several times his body was racked and ravaged by a deep and severe cough that suggested an advanced case of tuberculosis. Finally the stable owner told the stranger to rest in the stall and not be concerned with the chores. The old man grew weaker each day while the compassionate stable owner fed and cared for him. His offers to bring in a doctor were waved off by the stranger, who said he did not trust physicians and refused to let one examine him. It soon became clear that the old man was dying. The stable owner did everything he could in order to make the stranger's last few days as comfortable as possible.

One evening the old man called the owner to his bedside and, amid fits of violent coughing, said he wanted to repay him for his kindness.

The dying man said that he had been recently released from prison, where he had served nearly twenty years for his part in robbing a military payroll shipment and killing the members of the escort. His story began with the dawn of one particularly cold winter morning in 1869 when he and seventeen other outlaws waited in hiding among a grove of trees beside Mill Creek, a small stream flowing through a portion of south central Oklahoma. The bandits awaited a caravan from Fort Leavenworth, Kansas, bound for Fort Arbuckle, which carried a large government payroll in gold. Soon the caravan appeared. As the wagons slowed down while rounding the bend on the narrow trail, the outlaws unleashed a barrage of rifle fire from their hiding place, killing most of the armed escort with the first volley. After a brief firefight, all of the troopers were killed and five of the outlaws lay dead or dying. Quickly the bandits opened the payroll wagon, removed the gold shipment, and loaded it on several mules they had brought along. They pulled the wagons into a tight circle and set them on fire, hoping that any pursuing cavalry would think Indians had perpetrated the deed. Fearing imminent pursuit from the soldiers at nearby Fort Arbuckle, the raiders galloped away, leading the heavily loaded mules.

After riding for several hours, they stopped and divided the gold into three piles. Two of the piles they placed in sacks and cooking pots and buried in separate sites along the creek. They put the contents of the third pile, the largest, in several empty coffee cans and loaded them back onto the mules. Then the outlaws turned north and rode into the Arbuckle Mountains. They spent the night in a cave and, before going on, buried the gold-filled coffee cans in the floor of the cavern. They decided to split up into three groups and ride off in different directions in order to throw the pursuing cavalry off their trail. They made plans to meet in two months when things cooled down and they could return for the gold.

One group, led by a Mexican, rode south and eventually crossed the Rio Grande into Mexico. Another rode toward Arkansas to hide out, and the third group, including the old man, rode north toward Missouri. The cavalry picked up the trail of the riders going to Missouri and, aided by area law officers, caught up with them. There was a brief gunfight, and when it was over the old man had been captured and the others killed. He was tried and sentenced to prison for his part in the robbery. He stated during the trial that he had no part in the killing of the military escort and was only holding the horses at the time the shooting started.

In prison he learned that the other members of the gang that had ridden toward Arkansas had all been killed. He heard nothing from the group that went to Mexico.

As the dying stranger told this story to the stable owner, he sketched a crude map on a piece of butcher paper, showing the point where the robbery occurred, Fort Arbuckle, and the three sites where the gold payroll was buried. Another fit of coughing overcame him and he found it difficult to continue. When the attack subsided after several minutes he lay down and drifted off to sleep. Within two days he was dead.

The stable owner was convinced of the truth of this deathbed tale and he decided to try to find the buried payroll. Visions of a wagon load of gold danced in his dreams at night. Within a few days he sold his livery stable and headed south.

A few weeks later he arrived in Davis, Oklahoma, the only town of any size in the general vicinity of where the dying man said the gold was buried. Following the map, the man was able to relate certain critical landmarks to the notations the old outlaw had sketched and written, but once he arrived at the indicated site of the burials along Mill Creek, the directions became somewhat vague. He dug at several spots along the creek bank but found nothing.

His search ran into months, but the man would not be discouraged. He firmly held to the truth of the story told by the dying outlaw and was convinced that sooner or later he would locate the treasure. Eventually, however, he ran out of money and was forced to seek work in Davis. He built a rude one-room log cabin in the hills just outside of town, took a local Indian woman as his wife, and committed all his free time to searching for the buried payroll.

Months turned into years. The once-successful livery stable owner became an old man, partially blind and nearly penniless. It became hard for him to search for the hidden gold, but he persisted. His wife left him in 1930, and he sometimes went several days without food.

Years earlier he had made a friend in Samuel Davis, the founder of the town and the leading merchant in the area. He told Davis the story of the buried payroll many times. Davis, who was fond of him, would occasionally make trips out to his cabin to bring him meals. He encouraged the old man in his search for the gold, and they became partners. When it became apparent to the old man that he was too infirm to continue the search, he gave the weathered map to Davis and bade him good luck.

Davis had always been impressed by the old man's unshakable belief in the existence of the buried gold. Every now and then, he would take the crumpled old map and spend several days at a time searching the area around the Mill Creek region for the loot.

One day Davis was visiting a rancher on whose land one of the burial sites was indicated. To Davis's surprise, the rancher told him that many times in the past people would arrive at the creek to search for the gold. He said that only been a month before a group of five Mexicans had inquired about camping near the creek to do some fishing. The rancher obliged them and pointed out a good spot, but became suspicious when he did not see a single item of fishing gear among them. A few days later the Mexicans departed, and when the rancher walked down to their campsite he found a series of holes dug into the bank about forty yards away. In one of the holes he found an old iron pot which had apparently been buried for years. The rancher told Davis he could see the impressions of coins on the inside of the pot.

Davis believed the Mexicans may have been related to one or more of the outlaws that originally robbed the caravan in 1869 and escaped across the Rio Grande. He presumed they possessed directions to the location of at least one of the burial sites of the gold, but Davis also believed that the other two hiding places might still be found.

Davis spent the next several years in search of the gold when he found the time to do so. Finally, the press of his businesses precluded his continued effort, and he abandoned the search. He stored the old map in a room in his home but years later was unable to relocate it.

A seasoned veteran of treasure hunting who currently lives in Davis has searched for the lost payroll for nearly thirty years. He believes that one of the burial sites is not on Mill Creek at all but rather along Guy Sandy Creek. Unfortunately, he says, the spot is now under fifty feet of water. In 1962 the Lake of the Arbuckles was created by the construction of a dam at the confluence of Rock Creek, Buckhorn Creek, and Guy Sandy Creek.

As for the third cache in the floor of a cave in the Arbuckle Mountains, no one knows what route the outlaws took through the mountains during their escape and, as there are hundreds of caves in that range, the task of locating the one with the gold would be overwhelming.

Texas

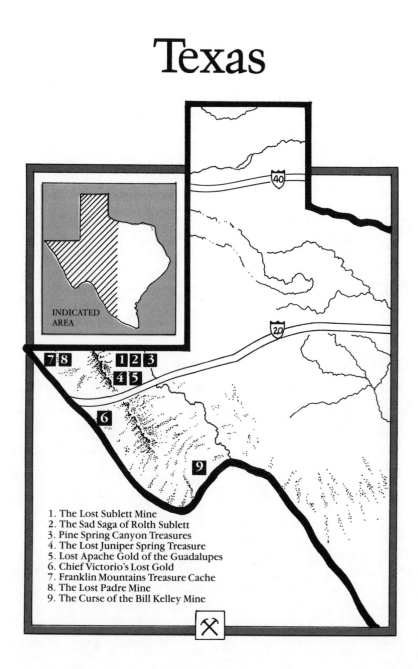

1. The Lost Sublett Mine
2. The Sad Saga of Rolth Sublett
3. Pine Spring Canyon Treasures
4. The Lost Juniper Spring Treasure
5. Lost Apache Gold of the Guadalupes
6. Chief Victorio's Lost Gold
7. Franklin Mountains Treasure Cache
8. The Lost Padre Mine
9. The Curse of the Bill Kelley Mine

INDICATED AREA

The Lost Sublett Mine

William Caldwell Sublett was one of those poor souls whose life was always beset by hard luck and trouble, but he may have discovered one of the richest gold mines in all of Texas.

As a young man growing up in Tennessee he drifted from one job to another, never able to remain very long at any of them. His wanderings took him to Missouri, where he met and married Laura Louise Denny. From there they went to Colorado, but Sublett never succeeded at anything there either. They wandered from place to place looking for work, and eventually their travels took them to Bowie County, Texas, where Sublett was able to find only part-time employment. Finally, discouraged at every turn, the Subletts departed for west Texas, lured by the promise of opportunities that reportedly existed in the growing area of the Trans-Pecos.

The call of west Texas was strong, and after several weeks of travel they arrived in Monohans. By this time they had run short of money and were too exhausted to continue. On the outskirts of Monohans the Subletts set up housekeeping out of the back of their old wagon and in an old shabby tent. While Sublett looked for odd jobs around town, Mrs. Sublett took in washing. When Sublett wasn't whitewashing buildings or mopping out saloons, he took prospecting trips in the rugged Guadalupe Mountains about a hundred miles to the west. He was warned of the hostile Apaches who lived in the mountain range but, oblivious to danger, he went anyway. Due to his predilection for ignoring the ever-present menace of the Apaches, his eccentric behavior, his inability to hold a job, and his ragged mode of dress, Sublett earned the reputation of one who was a bit crazy. People began to regard him as just another demented old prospector who had spent too much time out in the sun and who was always looking for a handout. He was soon known around Monahans as "Old Ben."

Years passed and the Subletts had three children: two girls named Ollie and Jeanne and a boy, Rolth. As the children grew older, Mrs. Sublett worried that the rough environs of the Monahans cowtown was not a proper place in which to raise them. This, and the fact that Old Ben still could not hold a job for very long, gave the family the impetus to move to Odessa, a larger town some twenty-five miles to the east. Odessa was a growing center of economic and ranching activity and, though still somewhat wild, it provided a more suitable cultural climate in which to bring up the children.

Laura Louise Sublett had suffered from tuberculosis for a long time and had been getting weaker and weaker. Soon after the move to Odessa, when Rolth was just six months old, she died. Ollie, the oldest daughter, took over the washing business and assumed the responsibility of raising her younger brother and sister. As they continued to earn a meager living, Old Ben made the rounds of Odessa, taking on the occasional odd job that fell his way. His old reputation dogged him in the larger town; with his decrepit appearance and his oft-repaired wagon pulled by two pitiful-looking horses, he was always the target of cruel jokes perpetrated by the townspeople.

Old Ben continued to prospect the Guadalupe Mountains, now about a hundred miles northwest, even though the Apache hostility was greater than ever before. The lure of wealth in this wild mountain range pulled strongly at him, drawing him to its dark canyons time and again. The massive limestone peaks and deep shaded valleys of the Guadalupe Mountains, with their aged and crumbling beds of sedimentary rock, never suggested the existence of gold or any other kind of ore, but Old Ben continued to search. So far he had returned from the mountains with his scalp intact, but his repeated visits to the savage environs added to his reputation as a crazy man. He told everyone in Odessa he would soon strike it rich and when he did he would buy drinks for the entire population. The townspeople continued to believe Old Ben was feeble and tolerated him as they would any other strange coot.

Old Ben began hanging around with an old Apache in Odessa, whom he had met while both were employed whitewashing a building. The Apache, like Old Ben, was continually down on his luck and lived a hand-to-mouth existence doing odd jobs and taking handouts. During a break while painting one day the old

Indian told Sublett he knew the location of a rich gold placer mine located in the Guadalupe Mountains. Sublett pressed the ancient warrior for details and was soon able to construct a rough map of the location based on the old man's description. After that Old Ben's trips to the mountains became more and more frequent. He was certain he could find the placer mine, and the quest to do so became an obsession.

Sublett's continued searching had the immediate result of making him neglect his family. Before long, the only income they received was what the older daughter brought in from washing. Several prominent women in the town starting calling for the authorities to take the children away from the crazy old man and place them in homes where they could be properly cared for and taught to lead decent lives.

About a week after efforts were begun to remove the Sublett children to foster homes, Old Ben returned from one of his trips to the Guadalupe Mountains and changed the direction that life was to take for him and his family. He pulled the creaky old wagon up to the Mollie Williams Saloon in downtown Odessa, walked in, and poured out a buckskin pouch full of gold nuggets! Loudly, he ordered drinks for everyone in the place and then announced to everyone present that he had just found the richest gold mine in all of North America. Old Ben, once regarded as a crazy old bum, was now a wealthy celebrity in Odessa.

The next day he sought for and found proper accommodations for his three children and outfitted them with new clothes for the first time in their lives. Life had definitely taken a positive turn for the Subletts.

Before three weeks were to pass, Old Ben already found himself low on funds and began making plans for another trip to the mountains. Once again he hitched up his team and struck out, only to return in a few days with several more pouches of gold nuggets. One man described the gold as being so pure that a jeweler could hammer it out easily.

Whenever the need arose, Old Ben would make a trip to the mountains, always alone, and each time he returned his standard of living would rise a little higher. Many citizens of Odessa tried to pry the secret of the location of the mine from Old Ben, but he remained aloof and secretive. He reminded them that only a few weeks earlier they had all been calling him crazy.

Sublett was often followed. He had expected such tactics and would go to elaborate lengths to throw off the trackers. He would leave Odessa at odd hours of the night. Sometimes he would set up camp on the Pecos River and remain there for three or four days and then return to Odessa. Sometimes he would evade the trackers entirely and come back to town within a few days with more sacks of gold.

Sublett kept his money in a bank in Midland owned by W.E. Connell. Connell observed that whenever Sublett's account ran low the old man would make another trip to the Guadalupe Mountains. Within a week Sublett would arrive at Midland and invariably deposit cash. Connell never found out where Sublett exchanged his gold for money; it remains a mystery to this day.

Connell and a Midland rancher named George Gray often talked about Old Ben and his rich gold mine in the Guadalupes. Together the two offered Sublett ten thousand dollars if he would reveal the location of the mine to them. Sublett laughed at this proposition and told them that he could go out to his mine and dig up that much in less than a week!

Incensed at his response, Connell and Gray began to meet every evening to discuss ways to find out the location of the mine. They soon hit upon a scheme. They hired a local cowboy named Jim Flannigan to track Sublett to the mine secretly and then report back to them with the location. Within the next few weeks when Sublett's account began to run low, Connell and Gray alerted Flannigan that the old man was due to make a trip to the mountains at any time. Lee Driver, the owner of a Midland livery stable and an accomplice of Connell and Gray, kept a horse ready for Flannigan to leave at a moment's notice. After about two weeks of waiting, Sublett was spotted leaving Odessa in a carriage pulled by two burros. Alerted in Midland, Flannigan took up pursuit and picked up Old Ben's tracks just north of Odessa. The carriage tracks were easy to follow in the soft west Texas sand that covers much of the Trans-Pecos, and Flannigan had no trouble staying on the trail. He remained behind and just out of sight of Sublett for nearly seventy-five miles, but somewhere on a portion of the trail that paralleled the Pecos River, Flannigan lost him. Frantic, he circled the area several times trying to pick up some trace of the wagon and burros, but had no luck. While he was trying to relocate the trail, Flannigan encountered a hunter who told him he had seen Sublett heading back into Odessa. Flannigan, feeling he had been tricked, turned and spurred his mount toward Odessa, but before he ever reached the town, Sublett had already returned. The next morning Old Ben deposited a large sum of money in

Connell's bank. As the story of Old Ben's trickery made the rounds, people began to assume the old man had a cache of ore or money located somewhere along the Pecos River.

A year or two passed and Old Ben made the acquaintance of another old prospector who went by the name of Grizzly Bill. As Old Ben did not have any friends, and as the two men were very much alike, an instant kinship was formed. It has been said that Old Ben eventually revealed the location of his mine to Grizzly Bill, telling him that there was more gold there than he could ever use in a lifetime and that he wanted to share it with someone. Grizzly Bill apparently found the mine. On one of his return trips from the Guadalupe Mountains, Grizzly Bill stopped at a tavern in Pecos to show off his new-found riches, initiating a celebration that lasted well into the night. He took on more liquor than he was able to hold and let himself be talked into a bronc-riding contest. During the ride he was thrown off the animal and died instantly from a broken neck.

Another time, on returning from a trip to the Guadalupes, Old Ben ran into an old acquaintance named Mike Wilson. He showed Wilson several sacks of gold nuggets and, apparently in a generous mood, gave him the directions to the mine. Wilson, as Old Ben and Grizzly Bill had done, arrived back in Odessa several days later with several sacks of gold nuggets. Not being able to contain his glee, Wilson announced his discovery, bought everyone within earshot several rounds of drinks, and launched a party that lasted three days. By then his gold was almost gone, so he decided to return to the mountains for another load. During his second trip to the placer mine Wilson became confused and disoriented and could not remember Sublett's directions. Wilson continually got landmarks mixed up and became lost. Eventually he returned to Odessa and sought out Old Ben for the directions again. Sublett was so incensed at Wilson's carelessness that he called him a fool and said he could not be trusted with the directions to the mine. Mike Wilson spent the better part of the rest of his life searching for the mine he had once located. Eventually he died in a small cabin in the foothills of the Guadalupe Mountains, at the last still trying to find the Lost Sublett Mine.

A story was told that sometime around the year 1895 one Rufus Stewart was doing some remodeling on a house for Judge J.J. Walker of Barstow, California. Stewart had once been a guide for immigrants heading west to California and had also been a driver for the Overland Mail. He had led an adventurous life and had been involved in several skirmishes with renegade Apaches in and around the Guadalupe Mountains. Now somewhat older, he relished telling the tales of his youth in the Wild West and was never at a loss for listeners. One day while taking a break from his remodeling job he found a listener in Judge Walker himself, who was sipping lemonade in the shade of a big elm tree on the front lawn. Here Stewart joined the judge and unfolded another chapter in the story of the Lost Sublett Mine.

In 1888, several officials of the Texas and Pacific Railroad had hired Stewart to guide them on a hunt into the Trans-Pecos area. He led the men to a place near the Pecos River that was a favorite feeding ground for deer and pronghorn. Word reached the hunting party that several Mescalero Apaches had broken free from a reservation in New Mexico to the north and were heading for the very place Stewart and his party were encamped. Stewart, who had his young son with him, was naturally cautious and posted guards around the camp each evening.

One night while he was pulling guard duty, Stewart watched as a wagon pulled by a single horse approached. Confidently, the driver steered the wagon right into camp and stepped down. By the light of the campfire Stewart recognized Ben Sublett, whom he had met previously in Odessa. Stewart was aware of Old Ben's eccentric behavior and the stories of his gold mine. He invited Ben to have coffee with him and to spend the night, and soon several of the Texas and Pacific Railroad men woke up and joined them. They all visited around the campfire for another hour, but as the night wore on the railroad men went back to their tents.

Once they were alone, Sublett confided to Stewart that he was on his way to his gold mine in the Guadalupe Mountains. He also told Stewart that this would probably be his last trip, as he was getting on in years and now had all the wealth he knew what to do with. He said he would show Stewart the mine.

Stewart told Sublett that he could not leave the men he had been entrusted to guide, and that furthermore he had serious misgivings about taking his young son into hostile Apache territory. Sublett replied that he would never be bothered by Apaches as long as he was with him. However, Stewart decided to stay in the camp.

Morning came and after feeding Sublett a good breakfast, Stewart rode several miles with him to the top of what he has since described as a blue mound toward the west. From this point Sublett, with the aid of a telescope, tried to show Stewart the approximate location of the mine. Sublett said that Stewart could still go with him, but that if he went alone to seek the mine he probably would not find it. The two men shook hands and Sublett promised he would return in three days.

True to his word, Sublett drove the wagon into the hunter's camp on the evening of the third day, and as soon as the railroad men bedded down, he poured out a large quantity of gold nuggets onto a deer hide he had unrolled by the light of the campfire.

Stewart remarked that all of the nuggets were uncommonly large. That was because the larger ones were easier to pick up, Sublett said; he left the smaller ones lying where he found them, for just another rake through the gravel would yield several more of the large ones.

The next morning after breakfast Sublett left for home. That was the last time Stewart saw him. Not too many weeks after this encounter, Stewart tried to locate the Sublett mine using Old Ben's directions. He rode to that blue mound where he tried to recall the landmarks described by Sublett. He made several forays into the Guadalupe Mountains but never found the gold.

Old Ben was known to show his famous gold mine to only one other person, his son Rolth. As a grown man Rolth tried for many years to relocate the mine but was never successful.

Throughout the rest of his life Old Ben Sublett lived comfortably and provided well for his children. When he died in Odessa in 1892 he did not leave much of the wealth he had brought out of the Guadalupe Mountains, but he did leave a legacy.

Some researchers dispute the notion that Old Ben Sublett ever actually had a gold mine in the Guadalupes. Geologists studying this mountain range say that the weathered sedimentary structure of what was once an undersea algae reef is not conducive to the formation of gold ore. Gold, they say, forms when hydrothermal solutions under pressure penetrate into the rock surrounding an underground pocket of molten rock. In order for this to occur there must first be some type of volcanic activity beneath the surface. No such activity has been detected in the Guadalupe Mountains. It is entirely possible, however, that somewhere deep within the limestone beds of the Guadalupes some evidence of ancient volcanic activity may yet be found. Just a few miles west of the Guadalupe range are several mountains of volcanic origin, and a 1987 geographic expedition to the Guadalupes noted the existence of intrusive igneous rock on the southeast facing slope, approximately where the Lost Sublett Mine is believed to be.

Other investigators believe Sublett did not have a mine at all but rather stumbled onto an ancient Spanish gold cache left by the conquistadors who explored and mined much of the Southwest. Still others think he discovered a Mescalero Apache gold cache. Both Geronimo and Mangas Coloradas, noted Apache chieftains, have said that the Guadalupe Mountains were the source of the gold of the Mescaleros.

The notion has also been advanced that Sublett actually participated in holdups of mail and freight wagons traveling between El Paso and points east and that his gold was plunder from these robberies.

Whatever the source of the gold, people are still searching for the Lost Sublett Mine of the Guadalupe Mountains. Today much of the mountain range lies within the boundaries of a national park, and treasure hunting is forbidden by law. But these laws are not important to those who come for the quest, the dream, of being the one to discover Old Ben's lost placer mine.

The Sad Saga of Rolth Sublett

In 1887, as a nine-year-old, Rolth Sublett accompanied his father William Caldwell "Old Ben" Sublett to one of the most famous lost mines in all of western history: the Lost Sublett Mine of the Guadalupe Mountains in west Texas. Old Ben wanted to share the location of the mine with his only son and wanted his help in retrieving the nuggets from the bottom of the deep shaft, but Rolth's young mind turned to other things that interested him more. While Old Ben was preparing for a descent into the vertical crevice, a bear cub wandered into camp. Enthralled by the little animal, young Rolth was oblivious to the wealth at the bottom of the mysterious opening. His unique playmate was much more appealing than the mine, landmarks around it, or the fabulous fortune in gold nuggets his father kept bringing forth from deep within the mine. Old Ben lowered Rolth into the mine on a rope ladder, but the boy was frightened by the dark interior and was anxious to return to the surface. Disappointed that his son showed so little interest in the mine, Old Ben never brought him again on his many trips to the Guadalupes.

Five years later Old Ben Sublett lay dying in a hospital in Odessa, Texas. He was eighty years old and had led a remarkable life, one filled with years of hardship and hard work followed by years of adventure and wealth after his discovery of gold. Sublett never had any close friends and his two grown daughters were married and gone, leaving only fourteen-year-old Rolth to minister to him in his failing health. Rolth visited his father daily and often stayed by his side at night. Rolth was old enough now to appreciate the significance of his father's gold mine and what it could mean to him in the future. He asked his father for directions to the mine but the dying man refused him. Finally, when it was clear the old man could not live much longer, Rolth begged him for the location of his gold. Old Ben said that any directions he provided would be useless. Just before he died he told Rolth he would just have to go out and find it on his own.

Though he had amassed a fortune in his lifetime, Sublett did not leave much of it when he died. As he had gotten older he ceased the long and taxing journey to the Guadalupe Mountains and lived off what he had accumulated. At the end hospital bills took most of the rest. Rolth used what little was left to get by and when that was gone he was forced to go to work. As his father had done many years before him, Rolth took odd jobs around Odessa, not lasting very long at any of them. All the while he kept thinking of the fortune in gold somewhere in the Guadalupe Mountains and wondered if he could ever again locate the mine.

Soon tiring of the menial jobs he had undertaken, Rolth outfitted himself with some camping gear and a horse and wagon and headed for the Guadalupes. After three days of travel he arrived at Pine Springs, Texas, nestled in the shadows of El Capitan Peak at the southernmost part of the range. He made a meager but comfortable camp at one of the springs and the next morning began his search for the Lost Sublett Mine. Much of what he saw as he walked along the foothills of the mountain range seemed familiar, but it remained vague enough in his distant memory to keep him confused as to which direction to take. Each time he arrived at the entrance to a canyon he was certain that it was the one his father had taken him into, but after exploring around in it he would find nothing familiar.

After five days of searching he ran out of food and had to return to Odessa. He did not remain there long, but sold some of his belongings and proceeded to outfit himself for yet another trip to the Guadalupes. Again he traveled to the mountains to search and again he returned with nothing. He took a job for a while raking out some cattle pens and related the story of his father's lost mine to the owner. Intrigued, the man advanced Rolth enough money to purchase more supplies to make another trip to the Guadalupes. He told Rolth that this investment entitled him to a partner status if the boy found anything.

Encouraged by the investment and the man's faith in him, Rolth made yet another journey westward to the mountains. This time he remained for two weeks before returning to Odessa. Though he came back emptyhanded, he was encouraged because, as he told his new financial backer, he was beginning to recognize some of the landmarks in and around the mountains. He asked the man for additional funding and got it.

For the next forty-five years, Rolth Sublett journeyed hundreds of times to the rugged Guadalupes in search of the riches of his father's lost placer mine. Those who knew Rolth said that finding the mine had become an obsession with him, dominating his thoughts and his conversation. There are many who claim that Rolth's preoccupation with relocating the mine drove him just a little bit crazy, to the point where he neglected everything else, much as his father had done so many years before.

With his optimism, energy, and drive along with his power to persuade, Rolth encouraged many others to back him financially over the years in order that he might devote himself full-time to the search. But each trip to the mountains ended in failure, and his backers left him one by one.

When Rolth was in his late fifties, he was interviewed by the noted folklorist and writer, J. Frank Dobie. Dobie, who had researched and written about dozens of similar tales of lost mines, was convinced that Rolth was telling the truth about his father's gold. Rolth told Dobie that it was a two-day journey to the mine by wagon once they crossed the Pecos River. He claimed he had a vague recollection of how the mine looked. He said it was down in a crevice and the only way to get to it was by a rope ladder that his father always removed when he finished bringing up the gold.

The late Tío Ben Wattson also believed in Rolth's version of the Lost Sublett Mine. Wattson and his wife, Pauline, worked for the various ranches, restaurants, and filling stations in and around the Guadalupe Mountains. Wattson was a sometime resident of Pine Springs and recalled seeing Sublett pull his horse-drawn wagon into Pine Spring Canyon many times to set up camp preparatory to a search. Wattson was several years older than Rolth but had sometimes worked for him as a cook when Sublett had a client along with him. Wattson also spent many days searching for the mine with Rolth and was convinced of his sincerity.

Wattson described Rolth as a "short man, but real wiry and muscular, always moving. He had salt-and-pepper hair that had turned real gray at an early age, making him look older than he was." Wattson said Rolth always wore knee-high cowboy boots with his khaki britches tucked inside in the manner of the ranch hands in the area. Rolth appeared to have boundless energy and never seemed exhausted after a full day of hiking and climbing.

The late Walter and Bertha Glover, early settlers of Pine Springs and longtime operators of the Pine Springs Cafe, knew Rolth well and recalled how he would visit them on his many trips to the canyon. He always arrived in the same horse-drawn wagon and was usually accompanied by a grubstaker. Rolth always referred to these men as "financial partners" and would introduce them around to everyone in Pine Springs. Walter Glover, who never believed in the existence of the Lost Sublett Mine, said that Rolth just liked to act important and show off. Walter described Rolth's financial backers as "just more suckers for one of his harebrained lost mine schemes." Walter thought Rolth earned a pretty good living conning investors into believing gold existed somewhere in the Guadalupes. Other than his lost mine searches, Glover referred to Rolth as "the laziest S.O.B. I have ever met."

Bertha Glover was always willing to give Rolth the benefit of the doubt and thought Walter was too hard on him. She noted that Rolth and his backers always set up camp at one of the springs where there was plenty of water and would spend three to five days searching the southeastern slope of the range from Pine Springs to Rader Ridge, some ten miles to the northeast. The search pattern never varied.

Rolth often told interviewers that he believed his father's lost placer mine was located in the Rustler Hills, some forty miles to the east of Guadalupe Peak and Pine Springs. Most believed that Rolth made up this story to throw other searchers off the trail.

For people who have researched this legend, there can be no doubt that the Lost Sublett Mine exists. For evidence they cite the wealth accumulated by the elder Sublett from his frequent visits to the mountains. They also point to Rolth's experiences and the hundreds of trips he made to the range in search of the treasure. True, he often had financial backing for these trips, but many times he searched alone and at his own personal expense. Skeptics claim that Rolth parlayed the supposed existence of the mine into a money-making enterprise by conning local ranchers and businessmen into financing him, but those who knew Rolth well claimed that, although he was eccentric, he was a man of integrity and would not stoop to exploiting others.

As he exhausted the number of people who could finance his searches, Rolth moved to Artesia, New Mexico, where he tried his hand at various businesses. Every now and then he would make another journey to the Guadalupes but these gradually became rare. Soon he was too old and infirm to make the trips and contented himself with settling down in that quiet community. He never tired of telling stories of his searches for the lost mine to any and all who would listen. For years he stuck to his conviction that he would eventually find the mine.

The gold of the Guadalupe Mountains had relieved Old Ben Sublett's hand-to-mouth existence. But it eluded Rolth Sublett his entire life. Knowing that it existed, having actually seen it, but never being able to relocate it tortured him to the point of obsession for most of his adult life. But as he grew older he also grew more philosophical. He once told an interviewer that he was probably never meant to find the gold, and that maybe if he had it would have brought him nothing but trouble. Rolth claimed he never had much luck at managing what little money he ever possessed. At least, he said, he was content in knowing the mine did exist and was still waiting for the right person to come along.

Rolth never lived to fulfill his dreams of relocating his father's treasure. Weakened with old age and pneumonia, he died in Artesia, where he is buried.

Rolth once said he was sorry he missed having a normal life because of his obsessive and continuous search for the lost mine. He had very few close friends, and people avoided him because of their belief that he was crazy like his father. But whatever else he was, Rolth Sublett was part of one of the greatest western legends of all time.

Pine Spring Canyon Treasures

Pine Spring Canyon is one of the best-known and most completely explored canyons in the Guadalupe Mountains. The small settlement of Pine Springs, Texas, can be found at the mouth of the canyon on Highway 62-180, close to where the Butterfield Overland Mail established a station in 1858. The site was selected in part because of the availability of fresh water from a nearby spring.

In prehistoric times Pine Spring Canyon served as a home for native Americans, as evidenced by the many artifacts and rock paintings discovered there. Later, during the operation of the Butterfield Overland Mail, outlaws preyed on the coaches traveling east and west along the route and sought refuge among the protective walls of the canyon. Because of this, Pine Spring Canyon has figured prominently in many of the treasure tales of the Guadalupe Mountains.

In 1902, a man named Abijah Long contracted with Jim White, the man who discovered Carlsbad Caverns, to mine bat guano from several caves in the Guadalupe range. Long energetically pursued this mining operation and made his first shipment in 1903. Initially the company did well, with guano selling at ninety dollars per ton, but after the first few shipments it failed to make any profit. After several more months, Long abandoned the mining activity but continued to live in the Pine Spring Canyon area. During this time he was visited occasionally by Rolth Sublett, and together the two men often searched for the famous Lost Sublett Mine. Research suggests that Long may have been acquainted with the elder Sublett at one time.

Long continued to camp in and around the Pine Spring Canyon

area, often visiting with Walter and Bertha Glover, longtime residents of Pine Springs. Eventually Rolth Sublett moved on to other business enterprises but Long continued to explore and prospect in the canyon. Once, in 1916, Long was gone for two days exploring back in the far reaches of the canyon. When he returned he contracted with Walter Glover for the use of three horses to pack out some mineral samples. Long returned after another two days in the canyon and was later observed loading several sacks of what were presumed to be ore samples into the trunk of his automobile. That very afternoon Long drove away and was not heard of for fifteen years.

In 1931 a Wells-Fargo representative appeared at Glover's door inquiring about Long. The agent related an amazing story which Glover has repeated many times. It seems that after driving away from Pine Spring Canyon, Long went to El Paso and sold some gold at the American Smelting and Refining Company. Several years after that transaction, agents from Wells-Fargo came across the records of the gold purchase and became interested. They undertook an elaborate search for Long that led them to Pine Springs. During questioning, Glover told the Wells-Fargo agent that a few weeks after Long departed he had found an opened wooden box in front of a shallow cave near the far end of Pine Springs Canyon. Glover related that he had passed the box many times while searching for stray cattle in the area. He had, in fact, examined the box once but found it empty. The Wells-Fargo man asked Glover if he would lead him to the box, and together the two men rode up the rocky trail and retrieved it. The box was of a type that was often used to transport sacks of gold nuggets during the era of the Overland Mail. The Wells-Fargo agent deduced that the chest had been taken from one of the mail stages during a holdup and cached back in the canyon. Loaded, the chest was estimated to weigh more than 350 pounds. The old redwood box remained in Glover's store for many years and was finally donated to the Smithsonian Institution.

Several months after the visit of the Wells-Fargo agent, Glover learned that Long had been located in Oregon. He admitted to discovering the chest full of gold hidden in the cave in Pine Spring Canyon and selling the contents for $90,000. With the money he purchased a fine ranch in Oregon and stocked it with prime cattle. The Wells-Fargo representatives tried to prosecute Long and arrange to have the money returned, but it was eventually determined that in recovering and selling the contents of the chest Long had committed no crime, and he was never tried.

A former resident of Pine Springs has suggested that the old Wells-Fargo chest was the actual source of Ben Sublett's gold. For years this old-timer has suspected that Sublett never actually mined any gold in the Guadalupes but had merely located this cache and from time to time took away a few pouches of the gold nuggets. This could explain, he says, why Old Ben's trips to the mountains from Pecos never took any longer than just a few days. The theory has also been advanced that Old Ben may have had a hand in robbing one of the Overland Mail stages and cached the box himself. Being shrewd, he took small portions of its contents over a long period of time in order to avoid suspicion.

The Wells-Fargo chest discovered by Abijah Long was not the only one found in Pine Spring Canyon. In the mid-1920s, two men appeared at Glover's store and got directions to the canyon. The men were never seen again, but several days later Glover rode up into the canyon and found several freshly dug holes. Near one of the holes lay the shattered remains of another old Wells-Fargo chest. It had apparently been broken open in order to obtain the contents.

In 1963 a hiker discovered two very old graves far back in Pine Spring Canyon. The graves were side by side and haphazardly covered with large rocks. The hiker had seen them several times during subsequent visits to the canyon but never attached any significance to them. During a meal at the Salt Flat Cafe one afternoon the hiker casually spoke of the graves, sparking some interest from one of the other customers. The man asked the hiker if he thought he could locate the graves on a map. Two years later the hiker encountered the man he had spoken with in the cafe. The man told the hiker that he had gone out to the canyon the next day and dug up the graves. In each he found a cache of rifles, presumably taken from one of the Overland Mail coaches. He told the hiker that disguising such caches as graves was a common trick of early bandits because graves were easily located and most people would respect a grave and leave it alone.

Tío Ben Wattson often sat in the old porch swing in front of the Pine Springs Cafe gazing out into the distance at the high pine-topped ridges of the Guadalupe Mountains to the north. Tío Ben worked occasionally for Walter Glover, owner of the Pine Springs store and cafe, but most of the time he could be found either exploring the vast range or contentedly perched on the old mesquite-wood porch swing.

Tío Ben looked like an escapee from a Wild West show with long white hair streaming down to his shoulders and a full white beard. At the end of one arm he had a hook instead of a hand. Tío Ben was the living personification of adventure, having been a wanderer and dreamer nearly all his life. In 1962, when I met him, he claimed to be ninety-nine years old. His wife, Pauline, told me years later he was born October 6, 1863, on an island in Lake Michigan. He ran away when he was eleven and earned a living shining the boots of train passengers. Compassionate railroad employees allowed him to bed down in the caboose on long trips across the country. Several years later he arrived in New York City and was captivated by the sea that stretched out to the horizon from that eastern shore. Ben managed to hire on with a freighter as a cabin boy and for the next four years saw much of the world. He returned and, at seventeen years of age, hiked from New York to Texas. On arriving in the foothills of the Guadalupe Mountains in 1880, he was abducted by bandits who made him a virtual slave, forcing him to tend their horses and perform the cooking and camp chores. While serving these desperadoes he witnessed several robberies and killings. One night, after working up the necessary courage, Tío Ben secreted a store of water and food, escaped from the outlaws, and made his way on foot to Pine Top Mountain. There he remained hidden and from his vantage point in the mountains was able to observe all that transpired in the outlaw camp below. On rising and discovering that their cook had vanished, the bandits searched the area briefly, broke camp, and departed. Tío Ben never saw them again. He hiked through the mountains toward the north and west and arrived in Silver City, New Mexico, where he found work in the mines and on ranches. Years later he returned to the Guadalupe Mountain area, where he spent the rest of his life.

Tío Ben loved to tell the stories of his youth, particularly his adventures as a captive of the outlaw band in Pine Spring Canyon. Several times he had watched the outlaws return to the camp with booty from a recent stage robbery. He often observed them burying their stolen goods and then disguising the caches as graves. He said he had returned frequently to the sites of these buried caches and was confident the money, bullion, and firearms he saw deposited therein were still secure. When asked why he never recovered any of it for himself, Tío Ben confessed to believing in *El Patrón*.

Tío Ben acquired a belief in *El Patrón* from the Mexicans he lived and worked with over the years. It is a belief that the spirits of the dead watch over buried treasure that was acquired by wrongful means. There are many Mexicans living in the Southwest who claim to know the whereabouts of buried treasure caches but refuse to retrieve them or tell anyone else of their location. To do so, they insist, would insure a life of bad luck for them and for their families and perhaps even tempt death.

Tío Ben also related the story of the buried chest found in the ruins of the old Butterfield Stage Station located just a few hundred feet from the store. Late one afternoon he was sitting in his customary position on the porch swing when an old automobile topped the western horizon. Ben watched it approach, wondering if it were going to stop for gas. Smoking badly, the old car lumbered past the cafe. About fifty yards down the road the brake lights went on as the car slowed. Turning around in the road, it returned to the cafe and pulled to a stop in front of Tío Ben.

Opening a very creaky door, the driver paused a moment as if to ready his legs for walking, and then stiffly stepped out onto the gravel. Tío Ben asked the man if he wanted some gas and he replied that he needed directions, not petrol. Ben invited the man to pour himself a cup of coffee from the pot on the store counter and join him on the porch. The man gratefully accepted the invitation and settled into the homemade swing next to Ben. He was a Mexican, perhaps fifty years old, who had obviously worked hard during his lifetime. He looked weary from long travel, and Ben noticed that his car had California license plates. After several sips of coffee he voiced his thanks to Ben and began his request.

The man told Ben that many years ago his father had worked for the Butterfield Overland Mail at the Pine Springs station as a horse wrangler along with the station manager, a cook, and a blacksmith. At that time a large chest filled with gold bullion had been deposited at the station awaiting pickup by an eastbound stage. The chest was very heavy and was always guarded by two men. Word reached the station that hostile Mescalero Apaches were sweeping through the area looting and killing and it was recommended that everyone seek the protection of Fort Davis, a three-day journey to the southwest. Unable to transport the heavy chest, the two guards buried it deep in the northeast corner of the station and took care to disguise the hiding place. The station was then abandoned in favor of the protection of the fort. On route to the military post the group was attacked by Mescaleros, and the two guards and station manager were killed. The wrangler, the blacksmith, and the cook escaped.

The three men finally reached the fort and were advised to remain there for a few days until the Apache threat diminished. The blacksmith and cook were offered jobs at the military post and chose to stay. The wrangler was afraid to return to the station and took a job at a nearby ranch. He often thought of the buried chest at the station and at times was tempted to return and recover it for himself, but because of his belief in *El Patrón* he was afraid to make the attempt.

Years passed and he moved to California, where he got work on a large ranch, married, and raised a family. In his old age he lay dying of pneumonia on a cot in a ward at a local hospital. He called his oldest son to his side, told him the story of the buried chest, and gave him directions to the old stage station. Because of the constraints of job and family the oldest son was not able to make the journey to Pine Springs to search for the buried chest. Now, as he told Tío Ben, all his children were grown and gone, his wife had been in her grave for several years, and he thought it was time to look for the buried fortune.

Tío Ben told the man that the ruins of the old station were just up the road and that he had passed within a hundred feet of it when he drove in. However, he said, many treasure hunters had dug all around the station and it was unlikely anything remained to be unearthed. The man thanked Tío Ben and took his leave.

The next morning, after finishing his chores, Tío Ben decided to take a walk over to the old station to see if the man was still camped there and to inquire how his search was going. On arriving at the station he could find no sign of the man but he noted a ring of stones and the still warm embers of a fire on which he had apparently cooked an early breakfast. Approaching the ruins of the station, Ben noted a large pile of dirt near the northeastern corner of the structure. Next to it was a deep hole dug at a slight angle until the bottom was actually under one wall. At the bottom of the hole could be seen the rectangular outline of a large chest that must have lain there for many years. Some broken pieces of wood, iron straps, and hinges were scattered behind the ruins. Apparently the man had located the chest but found it too heavy to lift from the hole. He had had to break into it in order to remove the contents.

Did the chest contain gold bullion, as the man had suggested? Obviously great effort had been expended to bury it nearly five feet in the ground. The Mexican had apparently taken care to obtain the contents and leave the premises as quietly and as soon as possible.

Pine Spring Canyon contains many small caves, and isolated graves are still being discovered. How many of these contain cached treasures is anybody's guess. Tío Ben has long since gone to his own grave, and the Butterfield Overland Mail has become a topic for history classes, but the legend remains a vital element of this fascinating landscape.

The Cache of Juniper Spring

Jesse Duran was a simple goatherder who never owned much of any value in his life, but on one cool, misty spring morning in 1930, he accidentally discovered a cache of fabulous wealth secreted in a limestone cave in the Guadalupe Mountains of west Texas. The discovery was to change his life dramatically and initiated a search for the treasure he found that continues today.

Jesse was tending his goats up on Rader Ridge, a somewhat narrow, low ridge that juts out from the southeast face of the Guadalupes to the El Paso–Carlsbad highway for a couple of miles. It had been misting off and on for the previous two days, and Jesse watched his goats from the shelter of a large Texas madrone tree. Around midmorning he decided to walk over to Juniper Spring and fill his canteen. The spring was about a mile to the southwest and downhill from where he sat. As he made his way across the slick limestone along an old game trail, he stepped onto a large flat rock, which shifted under him, revealing a small cave just behind it. In the dim light of that cloudy morning, Jesse looked into the cave and recoiled in fright at what he saw. Just inside were three skeletons and what was left of their clothes rotted and hanging loosely from the bones. The skeletons were leaned up against the right side of the cave, and across from them several rifles leaned against the other limestone wall. As his eyes grew accustomed to the darkness, Jesse saw, on the floor of the cave, several small strongboxes of the type used by Wells-Fargo and the Butterfield Stage Company. One box was opened and was half full of gold and silver coins.

Jesse did not touch anything in the cave. Frightened, he replaced the large flat stone, went to the spring to fill his canteen, and returned to his goats. He spent the rest of the afternoon worrying about what he should do with his discovery.

Later that evening he knocked at the door of Frank Stogden's ranch house. Stogden, who was entertaining three neighboring ranchers, invited Jesse in, and they all listened while he recounted his experience of the morning. All the while he spoke Jesse appeared nervous and apprehensive.

Stogden and the other men wanted to make plans to ride out to the cave at first light, but Jesse hesitated, saying he was afraid of the spirits of the dead that resided in the cave. This belief that the spirits of the dead guarded buried treasure and would bring harm to the family of those who removed the wealth was a strong one with the Mexican people. Jesse presumed the three skeletons represented three persons who were murdered and that the treasure was stolen. He felt nothing but evil would befall him for leading the men to the wealth, and this undoubtedly kept him from removing any himself.

The ranchers became irritated with Jesse and his reluctance to lead them to the cave, but not wanting to risk further refusal, they agreed to wait until the following morning to discuss the matter once again. The next day, however, Jesse Duran could not be found, and he was never seen in the vicinity of the Guadalupe Mountains again. (Several years later, Jesse's sister, who lived in Carlsbad, New Mexico, revealed that her brother's fear of the spirits of the dead was so strong that he fled to California, where he worked in the fields until he died in the 1970s.)

Rancher Stogden and the other men arrived at Juniper Spring about midmorning of the next day. A rain the night before had obliterated all signs of Jesse's presence in the area, so the men dismounted and combed the rugged environment on foot. Jesse had said he discovered the cave while walking down the slope from Rader Ridge toward the spring along an old deer trail. He had slipped on the stone while still a quarter of a mile from the spring, approaching it from a northeasterly direction.

That day the men found nothing. But soon others in the area heard the tale and joined the search. As far as anyone knows, the treasure is still sitting on the floor of that small hidden cave.

Research on Jesse Duran's tale and subsequent hunts for the cave suggest that this cave does indeed exist and in all probability did and does contain a treasure of strongboxes filled with gold and silver coins.

The Guadalupe Mountains are pocked with hundreds of small

caves such as the one Duran described. In fact, within a mile of Juniper Spring there are at least five such caves that I have located and explored. It is also a fact that the Butterfield Stage Line ran just one mile to the south of Juniper Spring, and the Pine Springs Station where the stage stopped to change horses is located a mere two miles to the southwest. During its brief existence, this stage transported money and supplies from the East to newly settled lands in the West. Desperadoes often lurked in the remote Guadalupe Mountains to pounce on the vulnerable stages as they made their way up the grade to the Pine Springs Station. Records show that on several occasions stages in this area were robbed of strongboxes containing money. Given these facts, it is logical to assume that Jesse Duran's cave was a cache of stolen goods from the stage line. Other strongboxes (all empty) have been reportedly found in and around the Pine Spring area. The people who hid the stolen goods may have been captured or killed or for some other reason never could return to the hiding place.

Jesse Duran's character is a staunch testament to the validity of this story. I have spoken often with old-timers in the Guadalupe area who knew him, and each stated that he was an honest, sincere, trustworthy, and hard-working man who was not inclined to making up stories. Jesse was a devout Catholic and had the respect of all who knew him.

There is some evidence that others may have located this cave. Eugene Anderson, a writer who has done extensive research on the Juniper Spring treasure, tells of Sam Hughes's experience with this cave. Sam Hughes is from a noted family of ranchers at Dog Canyon on the north side of the Guadalupe range. One day in 1945, Hughes was hunting deer in the Juniper Spring area when he accidentally slipped and fell into the entrance of a small cave. Being unaware of the Jesse Duran story at the time, Hughes picked himself up and continued with his hunt. Later in the day Hughes related the incident to Noel Kincaid, foreman of the vast Hunter Ranch and an occasional searcher for the Juniper Spring treasure. Kincaid asked Hughes if he could relocate the cave, and Hughes said he believed he could, even though he was unfamiliar with this part of the Guadalupe Mountains. Kincaid and Hughes hunted for the cave for an entire day but found nothing. Hughes kept insisting the small opening to the cave was just a few hundred yards northeast of Juniper Spring.

One day in 1966 when I was comparing notes on lost and buried treasure with the late Lester P. White, he told me of finding "a little cave in an outcrop about a mile northeast of the Frijole Ranch headquarters and not too far from a spring." The Frijole ranch house was once the home of Noel Kincaid. White said he discovered this "little cave" quite by accident while he was resting next to an old game trail he was following out to Rader Ridge. He said that the angle of light at the time and the shadows cast by one particular rock just down the trail from where he sat suggested an opening behind it. On walking over to the rock he found that it was perched up against an opening to a cave. White peered into the interior and saw "two skeletons and a bunch of old rotted clothes and boots." Lester had found skeletons in these mountains before and was not particularly interested in these two, so he turned away and resumed his hike. When I asked if he could take me to this cave he assured me he could, but after an entire afternoon of searching the area we found nothing. Lester confessed some confusion and said, "The angles and shadows are all different."

I have been fooled several times in the Guadalupe Mountains by "angles and shadows." Once, in the face of the limestone rock about a half-mile northwest of Juniper Spring, I found a crevice with a small cache of old tools and spurs in it. I went there many times and spent many hours in and around that crevice searching for and retrieving artifacts. But on a recent trip I could not locate it. I know I was within fifty feet of the entrance to the crevice, but still it eluded me. I suspect that something similar has happened with the Lost Juniper Spring Treasure and its searchers. Someday, when the angles and shadows are once again just right, someone will stumble onto the small cave with its grisly skeletons and strongboxes of gold and silver coins.

Apache Gold in the Guadalupe Mountains

In 1926 San Antonio was an exciting town, noted for the colorful mix of Mexicans and Anglos that characterizes it even today. It was growing and gaining a reputation as one of the more important cities in Texas, and it was also a crossroads where newcomers arriving from the gulf on their way north would encounter Easterners on their way to the real and imagined opportunities in the West.

On one humid summer day of that year, a crippled old man walked slowly and carefully through downtown San Antonio, scrutinizing the addresses on the front of the buildings he passed. Every few steps he would pause, unravel a crumpled piece of paper in his hand, and reread it. Presently he found what he was searching for: the office of a chiropractor.

Self-conscious because of his poor clothes and broken and halting English, the old man introduced himself to the doctor as Polycarpio Gonzalez and managed to communicate to him that he had gone deaf. He told the chiropractor that he had been to many doctors in the past but none could help. A relative suggested he go to a chiropractor and gave him the name of the man who now stood before him. All he wanted, Polycarpio said, was to be able to hear music again. Using an improvised sign language, the chiropractor told the old man that he would try to help him and so began giving him treatments.

As Polycarpio was leaving the chiropractor's office after his fourth visit, he asked permission to rest awhile in the waiting room before going home, for he was very tired. While he was resting the receptionist turned on a radio. In a moment Polycarpio's eyes widened and he straightened up and began shouting, "I hear music! I hear music!" Excited and emotional, he jumped up and began a strange dance. The chiropractor, hearing the commotion in his outer office, came out to investigate and began celebrating with the old man.

When Polycarpio had exhausted himself and sat back to recover, the chiropractor inquired about the unusual style of dancing he performed, remarking that the steps were completely unknown to him.

"I learned from the Apaches," was all Polycarpio would say. He was so happy he could hear that he did not wait to explain more, but rather hastened out of the office to tell his family.

The next day he returned to the office and asked to talk privately with the chiropractor. Once they were alone the old man said how much he appreciated all the chiropractor had done to help him get his hearing back. He said that he now sat for hours just listening to the music he had missed so much for so long. He went on to say, "You know that I have no money to pay you for your services and I know that you told me not to be concerned, but I feel that I owe. You are a good man and I must pay you somehow." And at this point, Polycarpio Gonzalez recited an amazing story.

When he was eleven years old his mother had sent him to a Colonel Boone, an Indian fighter stationed at Fort Stockton, Texas. Colonel Boone's duties were to protect travelers and settlers from the Apaches that roamed that part of west Texas. Boone was a highly experienced soldier with many skirmishes behind him. It was never clear why Polycarpio was given to the colonel, but the officer immediately enrolled him in the school located on the post.

When school was not in session, Polycarpio was allowed to ride with the soldiers out on the scouting missions. One evening he was riding with thirteen troopers far south of Fort Stockton and just north of the Chisos Mountains. It was getting dark and they had just decided to make camp near a rocky ravine when they were set upon by fifty Apaches. All of the troopers were killed in the fighting. Polycarpio received a bullet in the leg and the Indians found him hiding in the brush. By Apache custom, the youth was taken alive and raised as one of their own. (During this time, many warriors fighting under Geronimo, Cochise, and Victorio were Mexicans who had been stolen as youths during raids in Chihuahua.)

Polycarpio was not afraid. He willingly learned what the Indians taught and in time became a fighter among what many consider to be the greatest warriors of all time. Polycarpio said the Indians were very kind to him and to all children. They also taught him their language and dances.

With the Indians, Polycarpio often camped at Manzanita Spring near the southern slope of the Guadalupe Mountains. Here the women would harvest and roast mescal and prepare stores for the winter and the men would fashion weapons and speak of war with the white soldiers.

While camped at Manzanita Spring, Polycarpio was told by the elders of the tribe that the Guadalupe Mountains were the source of the gold the Apaches used to fashion ornaments and sometimes trade for provisions with the Mexicans. He was told that one of the numerous mines was a walk of only several minutes away. The next day one of the elders invited Polycarpio to go with him to the gold mine to get some ore for trading purposes. They walked a game trail that paralleled the drainage arroyo that ran from Smith Spring located at the head of the canyon. A little more than halfway up the arroyo, the elder halted and pointed to a jumble of rocks at the bottom.

"That is where the shaft is located," he told Polycarpio.

Polycarpio and the elder slid down the steep sides of the arroyo and stood in front of the jumble of rocks. Displaying strength that belied his great age, the old Mescalero Indian moved a few of the larger rocks and revealed the opening of a shaft. From behind another rock he produced a rope and secured it to a nearby juniper tree. He lit a torch and the two descended into the shaft. It was nearly fifty feet to the bottom, but once there the elder showed Polycarpio how to knock off chunks of the rich gold ore that was embedded in the quartz protruding from one wall of the shaft. The older Indian told the youth that the gold was useful in trading for guns and ammunition with the white gunrunners. Other than for trading and for fashioning ornaments, the Indians had no uses for the gold.

Back at camp, scouts told of the approach of a cavalry unit which had attacked and killed several warriors during a skirmish just to the south in the Delaware Mountains. After two days the chief called the group together and said they could remain at Manzanita Spring no longer. He sent Polycarpio along with several of the younger braves to fill the old mine shaft. They rolled and carried large rocks for two full days and completely filled the shaft. The entrance was also covered with rock and other debris so that it appeared like any other part of the arroyo bottom.

Then the old chief called Polycarpio aside and told him it was time for him to go back to his people. He said he was taking the tribe into the Sierra Madres of Mexico to join up with Chief Juh's band of fighters. At first Polycarpio was inclined to go with the Indians, but the chief insisted he remain behind. He was eighteen years old and the year was 1877.

Polycarpio told the chiropractor that he never felt any desire to tell a white man about the Apache gold until now. He said, "You are the first I have found it in my heart to tell. I owe you more than gold for bringing back my hearing, but if you wish I will take you to where the gold is located. Like the Indians who showed me the location, I want none of it."

Stirred by this story, the chiropractor made arrangements to go with the old man, and within the week they had acquired supplies and departed by automobile for the Guadalupe Mountains in far west Texas. They arrived in the mountains, leaving their car at the little settlement of Pine Springs, borrowed horses, and rode the short distance to the site of the old Apache campground at Manzanita Spring. It was evening, and they set up camp in the very spot where Polycarpio had camped with the warring Mescaleros nearly fifty years before.

They ate dinner while Polycarpio regaled the chiropractor with more stories of his adventures with the Apaches. Presently they went to sleep, with Polycarpio promising to show the doctor the location of the mine in the morning.

Wearied by the long drive from San Antonio, the doctor awoke late in the morning. He sat up and found the old man placidly sitting on a rock sipping strong black coffee and staring out at the vastness and majesty of the Guadalupe Mountains. They fixed a hasty breakfast and began the hike up the arroyo. As they walked, Polycarpio shifted his eyes from one landmark to another, stopping from time to time to study his surroundings. Soon he left the trail and slid down the high bank of the arroyo, beckoning for the chiropractor to follow. At the bottom, the old man went to a jumble of rocks against the opposite side and pointed, saying, "Here is the mine from which the Mescalero Apaches took their gold."

The men began to remove some of the rocks and soon revealed the outline of a shaft. They hauled rock until about five feet of the shaft had been excavated, and at that point the chiropractor said that it would be impossible to remove any more bare-handed. He suggested they return to San Antonio and arrange to hire some men and equipment to remove the large rocks from the shaft. They left that afternoon.

Back in town, the chiropractor found that it was difficult to contract for the labor and equipment he needed. It was also going to be much more expensive than he had thought. One delay led to another, several weeks elapsed, and one day the chiropractor received word that Polycarpio had died in his sleep.

The chiropractor made one more trip to the Guadalupe Mountains. He relocated the old mine shaft quite easily and then ventured into El Paso, some one hundred miles to the west, to try to enlist an excavation crew. He had no luck and, discouraged and disappointed, he returned to his practice in San Antonio and eventually gave up hope of ever retrieving any of the Apache gold.

Years passed, and violent thunderstorms have dropped their rains on the Guadalupes many times. These waters have gathered and rushed down the arroyos that extend out from the great crest. The rapidly moving streams of runoff carry great loads of fine gravel and sand that are deposited along the way. In this manner the ancient gold mine of the Mescalero Apaches has been covered. Another flash flood may eventually uncover it, but at this writing the lost mine of the Apaches that was visited by Polycarpio Gonzalez and the San Antonio chiropractor lies hidden at the bottom of the arroyo that runs by the ancient campground of mighty warriors.

Chief Victorio's Lost Gold

In September 1958, as I entered my junior year at Ysleta High School in far west Texas, my Spanish teacher was to be Miss Myrtle Love. This would be her last year of teaching and she was looking forward to her retirement. I dropped by to visit with her on the day before school was to begin. I knew she was interested in stories about the people and places of west Texas and I wanted to tell her of a summer camping expedition wherein I had spent several days exploring around the old settlement of Indian Hot Springs, ninety-five miles downriver from El Paso on the Rio Grande. The settlement had been a major route used by cattle rustlers in moving stolen livestock into Mexico as well as a favorite camp for the great Apache Chief Victorio. All of the seven springs were still flowing and most of the original buildings were still standing. Miss Love asked if I had heard the story of the lost gold of Chief Victorio which was supposedly still hidden in a cave in the Eagle Mountains near Indian Hot Springs. When I told her I hadn't, she proceeded to tell me.

One day in 1929, Miss Love received a telephone call from the El Paso County sheriff, who knew of her interest in the lore of west Texas. He said that there was a man in the county jail who had a very interesting tale to tell and that he would arrange a meeting with him if she so desired.

The man's name was Race Compton, and he had been found sleeping in a boxcar at the railroad yard. As he had no money on his person and had the general appearance of a hobo, he was charged with vagrancy. When she was admitted to the small interview room, Miss Love found an elderly man, probably in his sixties, who had the weather-worn appearance of one who had spent

191

the better part of his life outdoors. He was bewhiskered and had gone too many weeks without a haircut. His hands were calloused and hard from years of hard work but they were steady. He was very well-mannered and in measured tones told Miss Love how he came to be in El Paso.

He was there, he said, to obtain some dynamite and digging equipment which he needed to gain entry to an old cave that had been sealed up and which reputedly contained millions in gold. As he spoke, Miss Love recorded the following story.

In 1859 the Butterfield Stage Line was doing a brisk business. Coaches passed through west Texas carrying mail, payroll, and sometimes gold. Throughout the Trans-Pecos region a network of stations had been established to provide fresh horses for the coaches and meals for the passengers and drivers. One such station had been built at Eagle Springs, Texas, located in the northern foothills of the Eagle Mountains about fifteen miles southwest of Van Horn and twelve miles northeast of Indian Hot Springs.

Bigfoot Wallace, who later gained fame as a daring and adventurous Texas Ranger, was a driver on one of these coaches. His partner was Joe Peacock, a nineteen-year-old who despite his youth had already been involved in several skirmishes with outlaws and Indians and had killed several men. At that time Apache raiders were particularly active in this part of west Texas and Chief Victorio, the bloodthirsty leader of the Mescalero Apaches, had a reputation for hating all white men.

Within minutes after pulling into the Eagle Springs station, Victorio and a band of some twenty warriors charged out of the mountains and attacked. Two of the passengers and one of the men who operated the station were killed, several horses were taken, and Peacock, who had been impaled in the leg by an arrow, was thrown across the back of a horse and taken captive by the raiders. Traveling day and night without stopping, the Indians rode straight to their stronghold in the Tres Castillos Mountains in northern Chihuahua, some twenty miles from the Rio Grande. Here they felt safe from pursuit by the Texas Rangers and the United States Cavalry.

Peacock had his wound treated by a young Apache girl called Juanita who was said to be the daughter of Victorio. His wound was not serious and as soon as he was able to walk, he was forced to work in the Indian camp gathering firewood and performing other tasks normally reserved for women.

During the several months he remained a prisoner of the Mescalero Apaches, Juanita became more and more attracted to him. Several times Victorio threatened to kill the young white man but each time Juanita begged for his life to be spared. Eventually young Peacock was allowed to go about his camp duties without a guard, as escape from the mountain stronghold was virtually impossible.

At night Peacock and Juanita would meet secretly. Displaying uncharacteristic boldness for an Apache woman, she tried to persuade Peacock to marry her.

But Joe was cautious. He did not want to refuse her and incur the wrath of a rejected woman who thus far was the only reason he was still alive. He managed to stall, saying he was very concerned about his mother back in Texas and needed to see that she was safe and well cared for. Juanita accepted this explanation but continued to pressure the young Texan. One night she told him that if he would agree to wed her she would tell him where Chief Victorio hid his stolen gold.

This intrigued Peacock. During his imprisonment he had watched the Indians come and go with bars of smelted gold, obviously stolen from some pack train. He knew they carried the gold bars into Mexico and used them to trade for rifles and ammunition. On occasion he sometimes watched the tribe's artisans hammer out golden armlets and other kinds of jewelry worn by the Apaches.

When he asked Juanita about the gold, she told him it was kept in a cave with a small opening which was located in the Eagle Mountains near where he was captured. One could get to it, she said, from the old Indian trail that led from Eagle Springs through the mountains toward Indian Hot Springs. Juanita said she had been in the cave many times with her father and remembered seeing dozens of gold bars stacked against the back wall. In addition, she said, there were numerous buckskin sacks containing gold coins and nuggets. She said it would require fifty mules to transport all of the gold in the cave.

She also told Peacock that recently Chief Victorio and several braves on their way to the cave had encountered some soldiers. There was a brief skirmish in which one Indian was wounded and two of the soldiers were killed. The Indians went on to remove what gold they needed from the cave, and then Victorio, fearing that whites were on the brink of discovering it, ordered the braves to conceal the entrance with large rock and debris so that it looked no different from the rest of the mountainside.

Being familiar with the area she described, Peacock felt he could locate the cave with no trouble. That night he made plans to escape.

Several more weeks passed with no opportunity for Peacock to escape. Then one day Victorio and a large contingent of warriors left for a major raiding action deep into Chihuahua, leaving only women and children in the camp. That night Peacock met again with Juanita and promised to return for her as soon as he could. She got a horse for him and provided him with a deer gut full of water and some jerked meat. In the dark of night he made his way out of the mountains and across the desert. Several days later he arrived at Eagle Springs.

After resting for a week, he began to hunt for Victorio's hidden cave. He rode up and down the trail several times in the area described by Juanita but had difficulty interpreting the landmarks. Unfortunately there were several places along the trail that matched her descriptions.

For days he searched but was unable to locate the cave. He knew of the Apaches' skill in camouflaging a cave or mine to match the surrounding environment, but he felt he was just on the verge of making the discovery. Weeks passed and still he was unsuccessful. Soon he was out of supplies and needed to find employment. He returned to his old job with the stage line. When he found the time he would continue the search for the lost cave, but he was becoming more and more discouraged.

Eventually he earned enough money to buy a small ranch just north of the Eagle Mountains. He kept his job with the stage line and worked the ranch when he had time. Because he was so busy he had very little time to search the mountains for Victorio's hidden gold.

In 1880, Peacock was riding with a company of Texas Rangers under the command of Lieutenants Baylor and North. They were responsible for patrolling the area and keeping a watch out for Victorio and his men, who had been making raids in the area. Then a message came that the Apaches had been found and attacked by a force of Mexican soldiers led by General Terrazas, and a full-scale battle was taking place in the plain just south of the Tres Castillos Mountains. The ranger company crossed the river to go to the aid of the Mexicans.

By the time they arrived, the Indians had been routed and Victorio killed. (Terrazas credited one of his marksmen with bringing down the famous Apache chieftain, but the Indians claimed Victorio died by his own hand.)

During the fight with the Mexicans, twelve of Victorio's warriors along with the tribe's women and children managed to escape. When last seen they were riding toward the Eagle Mountains. The rangers immediately took up pursuit.

Three days later they caught up with the Apaches in the mountains. The Indians were able to withstand the rangers' fierce charges for a while, but finally ran out of food and ammunition. They made a break during the night and fled northward for the security of the Sierra Diablo Mountains. They had just entered the mountains when they were overtaken by the rangers and every member of the band was killed. Peacock searched the faces of the dead women for Juanita, but she was not among them. This fight marked the end of the Apache trouble in west Texas.

Years passed and Joe Peacock was getting on in age. He retired to his ranch and at intervals he would take up the search in the nearby Eagle Mountains for the elusive cave. With the passing of the years he had forgotten most of the landmarks described by Juanita.

In 1895 Joe Peacock met Race Compton. Compton was passing through Van Horn on his way to the Eagle Mountains with the intention of doing some prospecting. The two struck up an instant friendship and learned they shared an interest in gold. Peacock told Compton the story about Victorio's treasure and for the next several years the two men worked together to try to locate the cave. They remained partners for fifteen years.

In 1910 Joe Peacock died from a lingering case of pneumonia. Compton stayed on at the Peacock Ranch and continued his search for Victorio's cave. From time to time Compton would hitchhike throughout west Texas in search of work in order to earn money to purchase supplies; then he would return to the mountains until his food ran out. It was during one of his trips to El Paso to look for work and buy some dynamite that Compton was picked up for vagrancy by the sheriff and eventually introduced to Myrtle Love.

He confided to Miss Love that, as soon as they let him out of the county jail, he was going to return to the Eagle Mountains with the dynamite. He said he had finally located the cave and that it was approximately five miles west of Eagle Springs and on the south side of the old Indian trail, a full day's horseback ride south from Sierra Blanca and a half-day's ride west out of Indian Hot Springs. Compton told Miss Love that a recent heavy rain in the area had washed away a lot of the debris the Apaches had used to conceal the entrance to the cave and all that remained was to blast away the large rocks blocking the entrance.

The next morning Compton was released from the El Paso County Jail and given a ride to the city limits. He was last seen hitchhiking toward Sierra Blanca with a canvas sack of dynamite.

Miss Love never heard from Race Compton again. Was he successful in opening Victorio's long hidden cave? And did he in fact find the gold that was reputed to be hidden there? Perhaps not. It has been suggested that Compton never made it back to the Eagle Mountains. One old-timer in Sierra Blanca said that Compton died of a heart attack on his trip back to the mountains from El Paso. His body was found on the side of the road early one morning, his head lying atop the sack of dynamite that was to open the cave of riches he had searched for so many years. Compton was given a pauper's burial in Sierra Blanca.

There is now a historical marker at Eagle Springs where the old stage station used to be located. Aside from deer hunters, few people ever enter the harsh and forbidding realm of the Eagle Mountains. The area is far from well-traveled roads and is by and large inaccessible.

Most of those who are familiar with the story of Chief Victorio's lost gold claim that it is still there, in the lost cave in the Eagle Mountains.

Riches in the Franklin Mountains

Fortunato Salas was like many young Mexican boys growing up in the Rio Grande valley downriver from El Paso, Texas. He came from a large family, all of whom worked in the rich cotton fields along the river. He was reasonably content with his life; he had many relatives on both sides of the river and never lacked for companionship. Though poor, he was never deprived. Yet like so many others, Fortunato tired of the backbreaking labor in the fields and yearned to do something else, yearned to see what lay beyond the mountains to the west. To his way of thinking his world was too small. He felt he needed to grow, to explore and experience what lay over the next ridge.

One day he heard that the Southern Pacific Railroad was going to build a bridge across the Rio Grande between Texas and New Mexico and was hiring laborers. Seeing an opportunity to try something different, Fortunato wrapped his belongings in a tattered sheet of canvas and walked the twenty miles upriver to the bridge site. He was hired immediately and put to work breaking and hauling rocks. Fortunato did not mind the hard work so much but the fourteen-hour day drained him completely and he sought sleep immediately after his evening meal. By the time he stretched out on his bedroll at the worker encampment near Smeltertown, he was in a deep slumber.

But his rest was short-lived. In a little while Fortunato discovered that his companions were not inclined to go to sleep as early as he did, preferring instead to stay awake most of the night drinking and gambling. In order to keep from being disturbed, Fortunato carried his bedroll and other belongings far up the hillside and away from the boisterous chatter of his workmates. Such carryings-on were new to him, and at times like this Fortunato missed his family very much. Not having any experience at drinking and gambling, he found that he did not have much in common with his fellow workers. Therefore, he contented himself with his solitude on the hillside.

The workers were given weekends off. As it was too far to walk to visit his family and he did not care to accompany the other workers to the cantinas, Fortunato contented himself with quiet walks along the slopes and crags of the adjacent Franklin Mountains. He would sometimes sit for hours on a certain slope watching the river below and the activities of the inhabitants of the small Mexican communities on the other side. Sometimes he would watch the plume from the great smokestack at the copper refinery in Smeltertown drift off into the distance and out of sight.

One Sunday morning as he was following a narrow path in the mountains he came upon a small dwelling. The low simple adobe hut did not appear to be occupied and, feeling a need to get out of the hot desert sun, Fortunato pushed open the sagging door and stepped inside. As he related the story years later, he was surprised and embarrassed to discover he had entered the home of an old man who was sitting quietly at a small table in the middle of the hut. The old man's mane of long white hair and beard framed a dark leathery face cut by numerous wrinkles caused by too many years in the sun. He stared at Fortunato for a moment, waved him inside, and told him he was welcome. Fortunato shyly apologized for his brazen intrusion as he seated himself in the chair opposite the old man. The two began to converse about the hot weather and the work of the railroad crew. Both seemed to enjoy passing the time of day with each other. Fortunato had not succeeded in making friends with his fellow workers on the railroad gang and took great pleasure in the visit with this old man. For his part, the old man seemed to truly enjoy the company of young Fortunato.

The day passed quickly for the two men. Soon Fortunato bid the old one farewell as he had to return to his sleeping place before it became too dark to walk the mountain trail. The old man told Fortunato good night and invited him to visit again the next weekend.

Next Saturday morning Fortunato made his way once again up the mountainside to the old man's dwelling. The old man had prepared a simple meal which the two shared while they visited. Fortunato listened intently as the old man told stories of his youth in Mexico. Most exciting were his experiences working in the silver mines deep in the Sierra Madres in Chihuahua and Sonora.

Fortunato continued to look forward to his weekend visits with the old man. With his first paycheck he walked to the little store in Smeltertown and purchased some flour, beans, and coffee which he carried to the little house. Months passed and the two continued to share meals and conversation. They became close friends.

One Saturday morning as Fortunato approached the hut, the old man was standing outside waiting for him. He told the youth that they were going to take a hike up to Mount Franklin, the highest peak in the range. He had packed some tortillas and beans and a gourd of water for lunch. Leaning against the hut were two shovels; the old man took one and motioned for Fortunato to carry the other. When the youth inquired about the shovels the old man just smiled and started walking at a brisk pace up the mountainside. The hike was long and Fortunato was surprised at the ability of the old man to maintain his rapid pace along the difficult trail. Presently they arrived at a wide flat area in the shade of Mount Franklin. Here the old man motioned for Fortunato to sit down and enjoy the view. From where they sat Fortunato recalled in later years how they could see the railroad camp off toward the west and the site near the river where the bridge would soon connect Texas and New Mexico. As they ate lunch the old man pointed out old trails that came up from Mexico on which he had led pack trains loaded with silver many years earlier. He talked for a long time about the silver mines in Mexico, about digging the ore out by hand and smelting it into ingots so it could be loaded onto the mules and carried away. As the old man told his stories Fortunato wondered how this hermit came to be so involved with mining operations in Mexico.

After their meal, the old man rose and motioned for Fortunato to follow him. He told the youth that he wanted to give him something that he could put to good use in the future after he acquired a family.

The two climbed higher toward Mount Franklin and eventually came to a clump of the scrawny oak trees that grow on hillsides in this area. Here they paused to take the shade and catch their breath. From the clump of trees they continued just a little farther until they came out onto another flat area, smaller than the first. The old man walked deliberately over to a large flat rock near the center of the flat clearing, knelt down, and began scraping away the thin layer of soil that had gathered on top. This done, the old man used his shovel to dig under one edge of the rock. Within a few minutes his shovel broke through into an empty space that apparently existed just under the rock. He told Fortunato to wedge his shovel handle under the rock at this point so they could lever it up. Fortunato did as he was instructed and together the two men were able to lift the heavy rock nearly a foot off the ground, exposing a small cavern underneath.

Fortunato peered into the shadowy hole and his heart jumped in his chest. There, no more than four or five feet down in the hole, he could discern several stacks of silver ingots. There must have been two hundred of the bars.

The two men held the rock up for nearly thirty seconds when the handle of the shovel held by Fortunato snapped under the weight. It slammed back down atop the small cavern with a loud hollow thump.

After they caught their breath the old man told Fortunato how much he treasured their friendship and said he wanted to do something for him. He also said he had more silver bars hidden in other places throughout the mountains. He wanted him to know of this storehouse of wealth in order to share it with someone after he was gone. Fortunato, embarrassed, fumbled several expressions of gratitude and told the old man that he didn't believe he was worthy of such a gift.

By now the sun was low in the west and the old man suggested they return to the house before it got too dark to travel. Fortunato looked once more at the huge slab of rock, turned, and descended the trail.

Fortunato continued to visit the old man every weekend, but nothing more was said of the great wealth that lay in the hole up near Mount Franklin. After several more months passed the work crew was disbanded, and Fortunato knew he would have to look for work elsewhere. The old man invited him to move into the hut and remain there, but Fortunato said he would feel guilty if he were not working and earning a living on his own. He learned from some of the other workers that the orange groves in California were needing laborers so he joined the migration to the west coast.

At every opportunity Fortunato would correspond with his friend. He told the old man about his job in California and got letters from him about the weather in west Texas.

After a year in California, Fortunato met and married a girl who was the daughter of a fellow worker. He could not wait to inform his old friend of his plans to settle down and have a big family so he wrote him a long letter describing his wife and their modest home. Several weeks passed and his letter was returned with DECEASED stamped across the envelope.

Feeling a great loss, Fortunato tearfully pondered his next move. As his letter had been several weeks in the mail, it was apparent that the old man was already buried. Furthermore, he did not have enough money to make the trip back to El Paso. He decided he would save a little money and at the first opportunity would return to the Franklin Mountains to retrieve some of the silver bars lying in the small cavern. As time passed, Fortunato's family grew and it became harder and harder to put away the money for the trip.

One day out of frustration Fortunato wrote a long letter to a priest he knew living in the river valley southeast of El Paso and told him the entire story of the old man and the buried treasure on the mountain. He placed great trust in the priest and asked him if he would make the trip up the west side of the Franklin Mountains, past the old adobe hut, and on up to the clearing near the top where the silver bars lay concealed.

Several weeks later Fortunato received a letter from the priest, which he tore open with great anticipation. The priest had followed Fortunato's directions as best he could. He started out at the point of the railroad bridge and, using the landmarks provided, began to ascend the hillside. He did not get far before he encountered a large subdivision that had sprung up on this side of the mountain since Fortunato left for California. Doing his best, the priest continued searching for relevant landmarks and trails leading to the mountaintop. The subdivision had obliterated all traces of the adobe hut, and the entire lower slope of the mountain had been turned into streets and neighborhood. Still the priest persevered. He finally climbed to the ridge above the subdivision and searched for the cluster of scrub oaks and the flat area on which a large rock could be found, but he had no luck.

Though disheartened, Fortunato still clung to his dream of retrieving the silver bars. Several more years passed, and he was finally able to take his wife and four children to El Paso for a vacation. They spent several days with relatives in the small community where Fortunato had lived as a boy. One day when he was able to excuse himself from the family activities he drove his car over to the west side of the Franklin Mountains. The sight shocked him. Where years before there had been only sand hills and creosote bush, there were now hundreds of residences and businesses that had sprung up as the border city of El Paso grew and expanded. Eventually he located the railroad bridge and from that point he intended to retrace the old trail to the mountaintop, but as he scanned the area he realized that would now be impossible. Sadly, Fortunato reentered his automobile and drove back to his family, casting one last look at the mountains that still held the gift of buried treasure from the old hermit.

The Lost Padre Mine

The year 1659 saw the establishment of the mission Nuestra Señora de Guadalupe in El Paso del Norte, now Ciudad Juarez, Mexico. As the padres supervised the construction of the church, a group of seven mission priests crossed the Rio Grande each morning and proceeded to the nearby Franklin Mountains where they labored in a rich gold mine. The ore from this mine was transported down the mountain to the riverbank, where it was smelted into ingots and shipped to church headquarters in Spain.

The Franklin Mountains are a north-south oriented range with the southern foothills accommodating the spreading population of the border city of El Paso, Texas. While not as impressive as many other segments of the Rocky Mountain chain, the Franklins offer welcome relief from the otherwise flat topography of this part of the Chihuahuan Desert. They may also conceal the oldest lost Spanish gold mine in the history of the west.

Several months after the mission was chartered the structure was finished, complete with a thirty-five-foot bell tower. Each morning one of the friars would enter the tower and toll the bell, calling the priests to morning prayer. As he rang the huge bell, the friar could look across the river toward the Franklin Mountains and see the dark opening of the mine in which his compatriots worked.

For several years the mission operations proceeded smoothly. Many of the local Indians were converted to Catholicism, and the mine in the Franklin Mountains continued to produce several mule loads of gold ore each month for the mother church in Spain. Things could not have been better for the padres.

Then one day in 1680 word was received that the Pueblo Indians in New Mexico had risen up against their Spanish leaders, killing many and driving the remainder out of the province. Several priests who had escaped fled south toward Mexico and along the way alerted their fellows that Pueblo Chief Cheetwah was gathering an army of Indians and was intent on eliminating Spanish rule in the region.

The priests at the Juarez mission loaded up the golden vessels, chalices, candlesticks, platters, and a large store of gold ingots they had accumulated and carried it all across the river and up to the mine to hide it. Legend tells that it took 250 mule loads to transport all of the mission wealth. Once the church valuables were placed in the mine shaft, the padres transported river silt up from the banks of the Rio Grande and filled the entire shaft with it. Then they took great pains to disguise the entrance by covering it with rocks so that the area looked like any other part of the mountainside. This task completed, they returned to the mission to defend it against the attacking Pueblos.

It was not until 1692 that the Spanish finally subdued the Pueblos and recaptured New Mexico. The Rio Grande valley near El Paso del Norte was peaceful again, but when the padres returned to the Franklin Mountains to rework the mine they could not find it! Some of the original padres who had worked in the mine had been transferred to other provinces and the rest were no longer living. For several weeks the mission priests searched for the mine, but the entrance had been hidden so well they were unable to relocate it. Eventually the gold mine in the Franklin Mountains faded from the friars' memories, and they turned their attention to other activities.

In 1881 a group of men from El Paso reportedly discovered some documents in the archives of the old mission in Juarez that told of a rich gold mine located in the Franklin Mountains. The men also claimed that they obtained substantiating documents of the existence of the mine from church records in Spain. The group financed several highly organized and well-manned expeditions into the mountains in search of the mine but consistently met with failure.

In 1888 a man named Robinson claimed to have located the mine shaft by standing in the old bell tower of the mission and looking for evidence of old trails leading up into the canyons of the Franklin Mountains. He selected a point in a canyon that could be seen from the tower, and when he arrived there he discovered that a lot of rock debris had been moved to cover a part of the rock face of the canyon. With considerable effort, Robinson removed tons of rock and discovered the entrance to an ancient mine. Receiving some small financial backing and using it to hire some laborers, he proceeded to remove what was described as reddish river silt clogging the shaft. Robinson and his workers labored for several days excavating the soil from the shaft when the financial support was pulled back. In a fit of anger, Robinson had his men refill the shaft with the dirt and cover the opening once again with rocks.

In 1901, a man named L.C. Criss announced he had located the Lost Padre Mine in the Franklin Mountains, which he had been seeking for fourteen years with the aid of an old manuscript he had located in Juarez. Criss stated one could climb the nearest ridge adjacent to the mine and look down upon the city of El Paso.

Criss had indeed located an entrance into the mountain which had been concealed by piles of rocks. Once they were removed, Criss found that red river silt plugged the shaft. With the help of several men, Criss spent a great deal of time and effort cleaning the silt out of the shaft and eventually opened up 125 feet of the tunnel. During the excavation he found several Spanish artifacts, including a Spanish spur and an ancient anvil. For a while these artifacts were placed on display at the W.G. Walz Company in El Paso.

At the end of the shaft Criss encountered two more tunnels going in opposite directions, each walled up by adobe bricks. He tore through one of them and removed more fill dirt for about twenty feet. During this part of the excavation Criss observed that the old shaft was not well-supported and appeared very dangerous. He told his foreman he was going to El Paso to buy some timbers with which to shore up the tunnel and left instructions for everyone to stay out of the shaft until he returned. One of the workers, apparently sensing he was very close to the hidden treasure of the padres, resumed digging as soon as Criss was out of sight. In just a few moments after he started digging, the shaft caved in, burying the man alive and filling most of the tunnel with collapsed rock. Unable to proceed and out of funds, Criss abandoned the digging and left El Paso, never to be heard from again.

In 1968 a Spiritualist minister named Martin, his wife, and an assistant named McKinney arrived in El Paso from California. They announced they knew the location of the Lost Padre Mine and would commence digging within a few days. Reverend Martin claimed he had obtained some ancient Spanish documents that revealed the location of the mine as well as an inventory of the valuables concealed therein by the padres over three centuries earlier.

Martin contracted for some heavy machinery and, amidst a large crowd of onlookers and two local television crews, started excavating a long trench down into the rock at a point on the mountain not far from a well-traveled road. Tons of rock were removed until the trench was finally about fifteen feet deep. At this point, Reverend Martin climbed down into the trench and proceeded to dig with his hands into an accumulation of loose soil. After a few moments of scraping away at the soil the outline of a shaft could be seen. McKinney joined the Reverend, the two men applied shovels to the task, and within two hours they had excavated about ten yards of fill, revealing what appeared to be a shaft that led into the mountain. Excited by this discovery, several onlookers jumped into the trench to help with the digging, which went on for another three hours. At one point during the afternoon, however, an official arrived at the scene and pronounced the excavation hazardous as well as illegal. Despite considerable arguing and pleading by Reverend Martin, the excavation was ordered halted and the trench covered up. Dejected, Martin and his followers returned to California.

Over three centuries have passed since the Spanish padres mined the Franklin Mountains. Hundreds have searched for the mine since then but apparently with no success. No one doubts that there is gold in the mountain. Residents of the foothills of the Franklins have been known to pan for and retrieve fine nuggets of gold that are washed into their back yards by the infrequent rains.

There is also some evidence that silver may have been discovered in the Franklin Mountains. The June 22, 1873, edition of the Galveston, Texas, *Daily News* reported the discovery of two old shafts on the mountain and said that tons of fill dirt had been excavated by a mining company. After the dirt was removed, according to the article, a three-feet thick vein of silver was discovered! One of the shafts was reported to be one hundred feet deep and the other was estimated at ninety feet. The newspaper noted that the shafts were located within two and a half miles from the old mission in Juarez.

Some investigators claim that when the priests buried the wealth of the church in the shaft they also buried alive three of the padres and placed a curse on the area, dooming all nonbelievers who dare enter the mine. Although the store of golden artifacts and ingots has not been retrieved, at least two ancient shafts have been found in the Franklin Mountains, and the legend of the Lost Padre Mine continues.

The Curse of the Bill Kelley Mine

The Big Bend country of west Texas is one of the harshest landscapes in all of America. This great expanse of semi-explored land is famous for its extreme aridity, rugged mountains, deep and mysterious canyons, and a variety of wildlife, much of which is poisonous or clawed. Lying within the Chihuahuan desert, the Big Bend stretches many miles into Mexico, where if anything it becomes wilder and more dangerous. It has been the home or hiding place of Apaches, Comanches, bandits, and Mexican raiders. Early ranchers in the Big Bend were impressed by its beauty and frustrated by its severity.

In 1884 the four Reagan brothers (John, Jim, Frank, and Lee) established a cattle ranch near the mouth of what is now known as Reagan Canyon in southern Brewster County. They settled in sight of the Rio Grande, which at this point is a relatively slow-flowing stream after a rapid and tortuous journey through several twisting canyons. The Reagans herded cattle up from Mexico and grazed them on the lush grasses that grew near their quiet settlement.

On occasion, the Reagans would drive a bunch of cattle to the railroad loading pens at Dryden. This seventy-five-mile journey to the northeast was followed by loading the animals onto cattle cars provided by the Southern Pacific Railroad. During one of these loading operations, the Reagans met Bill Kelley, a half-Seminole, half-Negro who had walked from the old Seminole Indian settlement in northern Coahuila, Mexico. He was only nineteen years old, unable to read or write, and dressed in rags, and was looking for work. He told the Reagans he was a good man with horses and, as they needed help on the ranch, they hired him on the spot.

Kelly proved to be every bit as good a wrangler as he claimed, and the Reagans soon allowed him to go out and work the riding stock on his own. One evening Kelley arrived late for supper after rounding up several horses that had strayed to the Mexican side of the river. He told those already gathered at the table that he had found a gold mine during his search for the animals. The men, assuming that Kelley wouldn't know the slightest thing about gold, laughed at him.

The next day Kelley and Lee Reagan rode out to the same area where the wrangler claimed he had found the gold mine. Once more they were searching for stray horses. Near the end of the day, when they found themselves on a low ridge south of the Rio Grande, Kelley told Lee that the mine was no more than a half-mile from where they stood and that he would show it to Lee if he wished. Reagan said it was getting late and he was tired and thought they ought to get back to the ranch. Kelley pulled a fist-sized chunk of gold-laden quartz from his saddlebag and showed it to Lee, saying he had dug it out of the mine. Lee, not believing that it was gold, threw the rock to the ground and told Kelley that he was being paid to look for horses, not gold mines.

A few weeks later the brothers drove another bunch of cattle to the loading pens at Dryden. Here Kelley hopped a freight bound for San Antonio, telling the brothers he would return in two weeks. He entered into a conversation with the conductor, a man named Locke Campbell. He told Campbell about the mine and gave him general information about the location. When he arrived at San Antonio, he gave Campbell a small piece of the gold-laden quartz as proof. Campbell said he would have it evaluated and then try to get in touch with him. Kelley left another piece of the gold with an assayer in San Antonio named Fisher.

As promised, Kelley returned to the Reagan ranch within two weeks and went back to working the livestock. A few weeks passed and Kelley received a letter at the ranch from Fisher. Because Kelley was expected to be out on the range for a few more days, the brothers opened the letter and read that the gold was proclaimed to be very rich, worth perhaps $80,000 a ton. Two days later when Kelley rode into the ranch he was told by the cook that the brothers had opened and read his letter. Kelley suspected that the men wanted him to lead them to the mine and then kill him. Before anyone but the cook knew he had returned, he stole a horse from the corral and rode away.

The Reagans trailed Kelley for two days, but gave up the search where his tracks crossed the Rio Grande into Coahuila.

After entering Coahuila, Kelley rode to the Piedra Blanca Ranch, owned by George Chessman. He asked for work and was assigned to the foreman, John Stillwell. After getting to know and trust Stillwell, Kelley described the lost mine and his escape from the Reagan brothers. He told Stillwell he was afraid for his life and was thinking about returning to his relatives at the Seminole settlement. Kelley also showed Stillwell a saddlebag full of gold nuggets he claimed had come from the mine. A short time later Kelley, along with a dozen other cowhands, was sent to drive a large herd of cattle to Mexico City. He arrived there and dropped out of sight.

The only solid lead on Bill Kelley surfaced several decades later in the summer of 1946. Monroe Payne, a Seminole-Negro like Kelley, eighty-four years old at the time, claimed to be a relative of Kelley. He told a researcher, Virginia Madison, that Kelley returned to the Seminole settlement in Coahuila after his trip to Mexico City. From there he fled to Oklahoma, got involved in a bootlegging operation, and went to prison. Upon his release from jail he moved to San Antonio, where he resided until he died.

Eventually Locke Campbell initiated a search for the lost mine based on directions provided by Kelley. When he learned of Kelley's disappearance from the Reagan ranch, he also started looking for him. Once, during a cattleman's convention in San Antonio, Campbell met Jim Reagan and they discussed Bill Kelley's supposed mine. Reagan told Campbell that he believed his brother could lead them to the exact spot where Kelley had told Lee about the mine.

Five years had elapsed since Kelley's disappearance when the Reagan brothers and Campbell undertook a systematic search for the lost mine. Returning to the site where Lee and Kelley had hunted horses, they spread out and searched for several miles in each direction but were unable to find anything. The men decided they could do no more until they found Kelley.

They eventually located his mother at the Seminole settlement. She told them that her son had returned one day with a saddlebag full of gold, remained for several weeks, and then left. The old woman did not know where he went. The Reagan brothers resumed the search and over the next few years invested thousands of dollars and hundreds of hours hunting the gold mine they had once scoffed.

Campbell continued to believe the key to rediscovering the lost mine was to locate Bill Kelley, and to this end he placed advertisements in newspapers around the country and made numerous inquiries during his travels. Around this time a black man appeared at a store in Eagle Pass, Texas, and dumped a small bag of gold nuggets on the counter. He told the proprietor of the store that he would show him the location of a rich gold mine across the river in the Ladrones Mountains if the man would pay him one thousand dollars. The storekeeper refused but learned several months later that the man was Bill Kelley.

In response to Campbell's newspaper advertisements, reports came in from several people who either claimed to be Kelley or knew of his whereabouts. Several rumors also surfaced that Kelley had died.

On July 19, 1899, Campbell, Jim Reagan, Big Bend ranchers D.C. Bourland and O.L. Mueller, and a prospector named John Finky entered into an agreement to look for the mine. Finky was to conduct the actual search while the others provided financing. Any gold they found was to be shared equally by the five men.

For weeks Finky hunted in the Ladrones Mountains on the Mexican side of the river. One day he arrived at Bourland's ranch and announced he had located the mine! He told Bourland he had come across the long-dead body of a Negro in a remote canyon in the range. Three hundred yards up the canyon and just out onto a low ridge Finky discovered the gold mine. He showed Bourland several large pieces of nearly pure gold he had dug out of it. Finky wanted Bourland to assemble the others and go directly there, but Bourland said it would have to wait. At that time west Texas was in the middle of a severe drought and ranchers were working night and day trying to save their livestock. Bourland promised Finky that when the situation was under control they would all ride to the mine.

That night as Finky settled onto the cot Bourland had provided, he was stung on the face and neck by a scorpion. The next day his face had swollen so badly that he had to be taken to a doctor in Sanderson. While Finky was recovering in the hospital he was visited by Bourland and Reagan, who tried to get him to reveal the location of the mine. Not trusting the two men, Finky refused. Instead he told them that it was against Mexican law for Americans to operate a mine in that country without special permission from the Mexican government. He told the men that when he recovered he would travel to Mexico City to obtain the necessary permission and then return to lead them to the mine. Two weeks later Finky recovered and undertook his journey to Mexico City. He traveled by train to El Paso, where he was to make a connection to the Mexican capital. He had a two-day layover in El Paso and spent most of it drinking at a local bar. He made friends with the bartender and told him about his discovery of the Lost Bill Kelley Mine and asked him to accompany him to Mexico City. The bartender agreed and provided Finky with a free room and all the liquor he could drink while they waited for the train. Two days later Finky was found dead.

Bourland and Mueller gradually lost interest in the mine. Jim Reagan died, and his brothers moved to Arizona to ranch. Campbell continued to search for Bill Kelley and for information on the mine until his death in 1926.

One day in 1909, a man named Wattenburg arrived in the Big Bend area with a map reputedly showing the location of a gold mine in the Ladrones Mountains and spent several weeks asking area residents about certain landmarks. Wattenburg claimed that a nephew, condemned to death in an Oklahoma prison, had provided the directions from which the map was made. The nephew had gone to Mexico with four other men to steal horses and herd them into the United States for sale. While passing through the Ladrones Mountains, the bandits encountered an old man carrying two large leather sacks of gold-laden quartz. They took the gold and told the old man they would kill him if he did not reveal its source. As it was only a short distance away, the old man took them directly to a mine on top of a nearby ridge. There they found a large pile of rock debris next to a narrow shaft that led straight down. Not far into the shaft, the bandits could see the gleam of a thick and rich vein of gold ore. Because a Mexican posse was not far behind them, the bandits made mental notes of the surrounding landmarks and fled across the border, but not before they had shot the old man and thrown his body into a canyon.

Wattenburg soon became acquainted with a man named John Young who was familiar with the environment around the Ladrones Mountains and Reagan Canyon, and who assured him that the map's features were all correctly placed. Young, Wattenburg, and another man named Felix Lowe entered into a partnership to search for the mine. Young went to Mexico City and got the necessary permission from the government to operate a mine in the Ladrones Mountains.

In 1910 the three men crossed the river. Optimism ran high, but once into the range they realized the immensity of their undertaking. So vast were the mountains that the spot on the map indicating the mine's location was extremely difficult to detect.

While the landmarks appeared to be accurate, the scale of measurement was not clear. The three men searched the range for three months but had no success. Still hopeful, they were preparing supplies for yet another expedition into the Ladrones Mountains when the Mexican Revolution broke out. Now the border area was swarming with Villistas, Carranzistas, and bandits, and it would have been foolhardy to journey into the mountains. The men waited several months, but no end to the revolution was in sight. Thoroughly discouraged, they abandoned the search.

Several months later, in an interview in a San Antonio newspaper, Young told the entire story of the Lost Bill Kelley Mine. Jack Haggard, a rancher in Coahuila, read the story and immediately wrote a letter to Young. He said that Bill Kelley had worked on his ranch for several years and had told him about the gold mine. One of Haggard's foremen, using directions provided by Kelley, had made a trip to the Ladrones Mountains and apparently located the mine. He brought back several ore samples that were assayed and identified as "rich as the gold in a twenty-dollar gold piece." Haggard's foreman also worked as a contractor at a nearby mine, and as he was rushing to finish up his job in order to spend time digging gold in the Ladrones Mountains, he was killed in an accidental gas explosion. Haggard also told Young that he searched for the mine himself. He sincerely believed he had located it when he was chased out of the mountains by a band of Villistas. Years later, Haggard was preparing for another expedition to the range to relocate the mine when he drowned in a fishing accident.

In 1915 Will Stillwell, son of the foreman of the Piedra Blanca Ranch, told his brother Roy, who lived in Marathon, Texas, that he had found Bill Kelley's lost mine. He said that on returning from a cattle-buying trip to Mexico he and a companion had happened upon an aged Indian woman who had been left out in the desert to die. Will and his partner gave her food and water and carried her to the nearest settlement, where she recovered. In gratitude she told them about a very rich gold mine and gave them directions from which they sketched a map. She told them to go to a certain canyon where they would find the stumps of several petrified trees. They were to pass beyond the stumps and proceed up the canyon until they reached a very large boulder. On the left side of the boulder they would find a buried hatchet and on the opposite side they could dig up two saddlebags filled with gold. The mine from which the gold was obtained was just a few hundred yards up the canyon and was filled with rocks and dirt.

Stillwell and his partner found the canyon with the petrified trees. On one side of the boulder they dug up an Indian tomahawk but were unable to locate the saddlebags filled with gold. Continuing up the canyon they entered out onto a low ridge. They located the mine almost immediately. It appeared to go straight down into the ground and was partially filled with rock and debris. The outlaws were out of water and decided to return to a spring at the bottom of the canyon before digging into the mine. On returning to the spring they spied a gang of Mexican bandits entering the canyon from the lower end. The Mexicans spotted Stillwell and his companion and chased after them. The two men fled into the maze of canyons and ridges that are the Ladrones Mountains. After two days of running from the Mexicans they recrossed the Rio Grande and decided to wait for the revolution to die down before making another attempt at locating the mine.

A few weeks later, Stillwell joined the Texas Rangers and was assigned to a post in the Big Bend area. His company was supposed to protect area ranchers from bandits crossing over from Mexico. While stopped at the small settlement of Castolon, Stillwell was shot in the back by a Mexican outlaw and died instantly.

Roy Stillwell, Will's younger brother, came into possession of the directions to the Lost Bill Kelley Mine. Several men approached Roy to get him to lead an expedition into the Ladrones Mountains to dig for the gold, but he steadfastly refused to become involved. Roy told everyone he believed there was a curse on the mine and that all who located it were destined to die. He pointed out all the violent deaths associated with those who claimed to have found the gold. Roy had had several skirmishes with bandits in Mexico and had been shot several times. He had no wish to tempt fate any further.

A group of men approached Roy with an offer to purchase the directions to the lost mine. Roy said he would like to think about it but two days later he was killed when a truck overturned on him. The directions to the lost mine were never located.

During the late 1940s two men who identified themselves as mining engineers arrived in the area of the old Reagan Ranch. For a month they explored in the Ladrones Mountains on the Mexican side of the river. They left for Colorado, only to return to Big Bend several months later. They employed one Ed Shirley of Marathon as a guide into the Ladrones but never told him what they were looking for. Because they carried mining tools, Shirley assumed they were either prospecting or searching for the Lost Bill Kelley Mine. One day the two men appeared very excited about something they had discovered and told Shirley he would have to leave. They paid him off and sent him away.

Ed Shirley remains convinced that the two engineers discovered the Lost Bill Kelley Mine. He also wonders if they lived to spend their wealth or if they, like so many others, fell victim to the fatal curse.

References

Allsopp, Fred W. *Folklore of Romantic Arkansas: Volume I.* The Grolier Society, 1931.

Anderson, Eugene. Interview. Pine Springs and Nickel Creek, Texas, 15 and 16 July 1985.

———. "Ben Sublett's Lost Mine: Did It Ever Exist?" *True West* (September-October 1970): 23–27.

———. "Ben Sublett's Lost Mine: Did It Ever Exist?" *True West* (September-October 1970): 23–27.

———. "Hidden Gold of the Guadalupes." *True Treasure* (January-February 1972): 28–31.

Bailey, Tom. "Oklahoma's Buried Gold Mystery." *True Western Adventures* (August 1959): 10–13, 60–62.

Barker, Ballard M., and Jameson, W.C. *Platt National Park: Environment and Ecology.* Norman: The University of Oklahoma Press, 1975.

Braddy, Haldeen. *Mexico and the Old Southwest.* Port Washington, New York: Kennikat Press, 1971.

Bryan, Howard. "Off the Beaten Path." *Albuquerque Tribune,* 7 April 1953.

———. Untitled commentary. *Albuquerque Tribune,* 6 June 1957; 15 December 1960; 13 September 1962; 9 September 1965; 14 September 1965; 5 April 1966; 19 April 1966.

———. "The White Sands' Doc Noss Treasure Story May Not Be Myth After All." *El Paso Herald Post,* 20 October 1973.

———. "Mrs. Noss Tells Her Story of Discovery." *El Paso Herald Post,* 21 October 1973.

Campa, Arthur L. *Treasure of the Sangre de Cristos.* Norman: The University of Oklahoma Press, 1963.

Carson, Kit. "Lost Ben Sublett Mine." *True Treasure* 4.1 (January-February 1970): 30–36.

Carson, Xanthus. "The Incredible Victorio Peak Treasure." *True Treasure* 2.7 (November-December 1968): 11–21.

Chandler, David. "The Mysterious Treasure of Victorio Peak." *Rolling Stone* (18 December 1975).

Cremony, John C. *Life Among The Apaches*. Lincoln: The University of Nebraska Press, 1983.

Curlee, Mabel. "Hidden Treasure." *Baxter County History* 3.3: 44–46.

Dickason, Doris. "Gold Diggin's at Golden City." *Wagon Wheels* 2.4: 18–19.

Dobie, J. Frank. *Legends of Texas*. Dallas: Southern Methodist University Press, 1924.

——. *Apache Gold and Yaqui Silver*. Albuquerque: The University of New Mexico Press, 1928.

——. *Tales of Ol' Time Texas*. Boston: Little, Brown, and Company, 1928.

——. "The Treasure is Always There," *True West* (September 1954): 35.

——. *Coronado's Children*. Austin: The University of Texas Press, 1978.

Driftwood, Jimmy. Interview. Timbo, Arkansas, 7 March 1983.

Glover, Bertha. Interviews. Pine Springs, Texas, 6 June 1961, 13 June 1965, 25 July 1971.

Glover, Walter. Interviews. Pine Springs, Texas, 6 June 1961, 13 June 1965.

Hunter, J. Marvin. "Mysterious Gold Mine of the Guadalupe Mountains." *Hunter's Frontier Magazine* 1.6 (October 1916): 177–79.

——. "The Lost Gold Mine." *Frontier Times* 1.6 (March 1924).

Jameson, W.C. "Found: Old Ben Sublett's Mine." *Gold* (Winter 1975).

——. "Inn at Happy Bend." *True West* 31.6 (January 1984): 29–30.

——. "Lost Treasure of the Cossatot." *True West* 31.10 (January 1985): 47–49.

——. "The Lost Juniper Springs Treasure." *Treasure* (March 1985).

——. "The Legend of the Lost Soldier's Bluff." *The Arkansawyer* 1.4 (March-April 1985): 22–23.

——. "The Sad Saga of Rolth Sublett, Treasure Hunter." *True West* (August 1985).

——. "Tobe Inmon's Silver Bullets." *True West* 33.3 (March 1986): 60–61.

——. "The Legend of Golden City." *True West* 35.4 (1988): 26–29.

——. "The Lost Cossatot Gold Mine." *Arkansas Times* 14.10 (June 1988): 23–26.

——. "The Gold Rush of '86, Then and Now." *Treasure Search* 16.4 (July-August 1988): 30–32, 66.

Jameson, William S. Numerous conversations from 1963 to 1972.

Kelley, J.C. "Aged Settler Recalls Rush to Golden City." *Booneville Democrat*, date unknown, 1929.

Lambrecht, Gordon. "Gold." *Baxter County History* 1.4: 51.

Leet, L. Don, and Judson, Sheldon. *Physical Geology.* Englewood Cliffs, New Jersey: Prentice-Hall, Inc., 1954.

"The Lost Adams Diggings." *Colorado.* March-April 1972, pp. 24–32.

Madison, Virginia. *The Big Bend Country of Texas.* Albuquerque: The University of New Mexico Press, 1955.

McKenna, James A. *Black Range Tales.* Chicago: The Rio Grande Press, Inc., 1965.

McCartney, Scott. "Treasure Tales Prove Puzzling." *Arkansas Democrat* (26 April 1987).

Morgan, Buford. "Treasures of the Wichitas." *Chronicles of Comanche County* 3 (1957): 93–96.

"Mystery and Romance in Old Diggings, Devil's Canyon, Wichita Mountains, Bears Old Legends of Spaniards." *Daily Oklahoman*, 23 April 1939.

"Nugget at Lawton." *Mangum Star*, 10 April 1902.

Page, Tate C. *The Voices of Moccasin Creek.* Point Lookout, Missouri: School of the Ozarks Press, 1972.

The Pinery Station. Carlsbad, New Mexico: Carlsbad Caverns Natural History Association, 1979.

Rascoe, Jesse Ed. *The Golden Crescent.* Toyahvale, Texas: Frontier Book Company, 1962.

———. *Oklahoma Treasures.* Fort Davis, Texas: Frontier Book Company, 1974.

Roberts, Jim. "Golden City, Arkansas." *Booneville Democrat,* April 1946.

"Search For Treasure Ended, But Legends Expected To Live." *Arkansas Gazette,* 9 April 1977.

Stillwell, Hallie. Interview. Stillwell Ranch, Brewster County, Texas, 7 July 1988.

"Treasure Hunters May Seek Fabled Gold." *Arkansas Gazette,* 18 September 1976.

"The Tres Piedras Legend." *Daily Oklahoman,* 27 September 1903.

Tuton, J.O. "Under Fourteen Flags." *Mangum Daily Star,* 13 October 1937.

Wattson, Ben. Interview. Pine Springs, Texas, 13 August 1961.

Wattson, Mrs. Ben. *Hidden Gold of the Guadalupes.* El Paso, Texas: Tumbleweed Press, 1966.

White, Lester. Interview. White City, New Mexico, 23 July 1961, 17 July 1962.

Whitmer, Deana Kirk. Letters to author, 6 August 1985 and 2 October 1985.

"Wichita Mountains: Their Mining History Told Briefly." *Purcell Register,* 16 February 1893.

Wilson, Steve. *Oklahoma Treasures and Treasure Tales.* Norman: The University of Oklahoma Press, 1984.